Sister Emily's Lightship

AND OTHER STORIES

Tor Books by Jane Yolen

Briar Rose
The One-Armed Queen
The Books of Great Alta

Sister Emily's Lightship

AND OTHER STORIES

*

JANE YOLEN

A Tom Doherty Associates Book
New York

SISTER EMILY'S LIGHTSHIP AND OTHER STORIES

Edited by Beth Meacham

A Tor Book
Published by Tom Doherty Associates, LLC
175 Fifth Avenue
New York, NY 10010

www.tor.com

Tor® is a registered trademark of Tom Doherty Associates, LLC.

Book design by Lisa Pifher

Library of Congress Cataloging-in-Publication Data

Yolen, Jane.
     Sister Emily's lightship and other stories / Jane Yolen.
          p.   cm.
     "A Tom Doherty Associates book."
     ISBN 0-312-87378-6 (hc)
     ISBN 0-312-87523-1 (pbk)
     1. Fantasy fiction, American. I. Title.
     PS3575.043 S56 2000
     813'.54—dc21   00-029908
                                                                        CIP

First Hardcover Edition: August 2000
First Trade Paperback Edition: August 2001

Printed in the United States of America

0 9 8 7 6 5 4 3 2 1

For David and Marilyn,
more than thirty years
of love and thanks

Acknowledgments

"The Traveler and the Tale," copyright © 1995, first published in *Ruby Slippers, Golden Tears,* edited by Terri Windling and Ellen Datlow, Avon Books.

"Snow in Summer," copyright © 2000, first published in *Black Heart, Ivory Bones,* edited by Terri Windling and Ellen Datlow, Avon Books.

"Speaking to the Wind," copyright © 2000, first published herewith.

"The Thirteenth Fey," copyright © 1985, first published in *Faery,* edited by Terri Windling, Ace Books.

"Granny Rumple," copyright © 1994, first published in *Black Thorn, White Rose,* edited by Terri Windling and Ellen Datlow, William Morrow & Co.

"Blood Sister," copyright © 1994, first published in *Am I Blue?,* edited by Marian Dane Bauer, HarperCollins.

"Journey into the Dark," copyright © 1995, first published in *The Book of Kings,* edited by Richard Gilliam and Martin Greenberg, Roc/Penguin.

"The Sleep of Trees," copyright © 1980, first published in *Fantasy and Science Fiction Magazine.*

"The Uncorking of Uncle Finn," copyright © 1986, first published in *Fantasy and Science Fiction Magazine.*

"Dusty Loves," copyright © 1988, first published in *Fantasy and Science Fiction Magazine.*

"The Gift of the Magicians, with Apologies to You Know Who," copyright © 1992, first published in *Fantasy and Science Fiction Magazine.*

"Sister Death," copyright © 1995, first published in *Sisters of the Night,* edited by Barbara Hambly and Martin Greenberg, Warner/Aspect.

Contents

The Traveler and the Tale

Traveling south from Ambert you must pass the old stoney abbey of La Chaise-Dieu. It was near that abbey in 1536 that a young woman fell asleep on a dolmen and dreamed of the virgin.

There are some who said such dreams come as a consequence of lying out in the night air. Others that it was the cold stone beneath her that prompted such haverings. A few bitter souls said that she was, alas, no better than she should have been and women like that cannot dream of the Queen of Heaven and it was perforce a lie.

But the dreamer was a simple peasant woman caught out between Ambert and Le Puy, having turned her ankle on the rough road. She did not realize how close she was to the abbey or she would have gone there for the night. The dolmen, raised up as it was, kept her free of the damp and safe from vipers. Such safety was the extent of her imagination. She did not dream of the virgin; she was waking and she saw me.

I was caught in the Aura of a time change, when the centuries lie side by side for the moment of Pass-Through. The woman saw what she thought was a crown of stars on my head, which was nothing more than the Helmet. Aura and Helmet and an untutored sixteenth century mind. What else could she believe than that I was either an angel or the Mother of God?

When I saw her and realized that I had been caught out, I swore under my breath. "Merde!"

If the expletive startled her, she did not show it. I believe she must have mistaken it for a name.

"Marie," she whispered, crossing herself three or four times in rapid succession before passing out in an excess of ecstasy and oxygen.

I knew enough to leave her alone and hurry along my way. My destination was a small town in Auvergne where a cottage awaited me. I was well versed in the local dialect—Occitan. It sat comfortably on my tongue. The stories in Henri Pourrat's vast collection of regional tales I had memorized, my memory only sightly enhanced by Oxipol. I was always a good and quick study. As my teaching machine chose to jest with me in the same dialect: "Qu'aucu t'aye liceno." ("Someone has been teaching you a lesson!" No one has ever said machines have good senses of humor. It has to do with a lack of the funny bone.)

It was my duty to infiltrate the community and interpolate several stories artfully prepared by our Revolutionary Council some three thousand years in France's future. Odd, isn't it, that with all the time traveling we have done since the invention of the Module, it has become abundantly clear that no shot fired, no knife thrown, no spear in the gut has the power to change the world of the future. Le Bon Dieu knows we have tried. Hitler blown up. The Khan poisoned. Marie Antoinette throttled in her cradle. And all to no avail. History, like a scab, calcifies over each wound and beneath it the skin of human atrocity heals. Only through stories, it seems can we really influence the history that is to come. Told to a ready ear, repeated by a willing mouth, by that process of mouth-to-ear resuscitation we change the world.

Stories are not just recordings. They are prophecies. They are dreams. And—so it seems—we humans build the future on such dreams.

If I am successful in my storytelling, the Auvergne of the future will be a garden of earthly splendor. Gone will be the long lines of the impoverished children walking dull-eyed toward Paris under the lash of the Alien Horde. Gone will be the ravaged fields, the razed houses, the villages' streets strewn with bones.

But when I stepped into the past, ready to play my part for the future, wrapped in the ocreous glow of transfer, a peasant woman lying uneasily on a dolmen with a bad ankle added a new story, one we had not planned: how the Mother of God visited Ambert that spring. The peasant circles would soon be abuzz with it and it would in its own way change the future of the Auvergne. Would it bring a resurgence of piety to the land whose practical approach to religion had led to an easy accommodation with the socialism of the twentieth century, the apostacy of the twenty-first, the capitulation to Alien rites of the twenty-second? Without the Council's Modular Computes I could not know.

"Merde!" I cursed, stepping back.

She crossed herself and fainted.

Smoothing my skirts down, I glanced toward the road. I had planned to add two stories to Pourrat's collection. One was a Beast fabliau, about two mice and a cricket who throw off the yoke of slavery put on them by a race of cats, the other a tale we call Dinner-in-an-Eggshell which is about discovering the alien that lives in your house. We hope that one or the other or both will have the effect of warning our people. The odds have been calculated carefully but I will never know if they will succeed.

The traveler cannot return from the trip. I expect to live my thirty years as a weaver in the cottage hard by the mill, telling my stories that will pass from my mouth to my neighbors' ears at night when we work at our several tasks, one perhaps scutching hemp, another spinning, the servants tidying their threshing flails. Oh, we will have a lovely time of it, for what else is there to do on a cold harvest eve but tell stories before the fire before bundling off to our straw beds.

Dinner-in-an-Eggshell

A woman was nursing her baby and it was the sweetest child you can imagine, with bright blue eyes and a mouth like a primrose.

One March day, the mother took her child and put him in his crib by the fire and went out to get water for the stone sink. When she returned, she heard a strange, horrible snuffling sound from the baby's crib.

She almost dropped the jug in alarm, and ran over to see what was wrong. And what did she see? Instead of her sweet baby lying in his crib, there was a *something* on the pillow as ugly and misshappen as a toad. It had bulging eyes and a green tongue and when it breathed, it made an awful snuffling sound.

The mother screamed, but then she knew what she had to do because this was a fairy's changeling child. She would have to compel him to speak and it would be no easy task, because she would have to surprise him.

So for three days she pretended to the changeling that she thought it her own child. She petted it and praised it though its very looks made her ill.

On the third day, she said to herself aloud, "I have ten strong laborers coming over for dinner." And she rushed about the house getting ready for them, filling six milk pails with milk and four basins with cream carving away a side of lard and taking down an entire rope of onions.

"Oh me, oh my," she sighed, "what a job to cook dinner for ten in an eggshell."

The changeling sat up in its crib, a startled look on its ugly toad face.

> *Three hundred years I have lived well,*
> *But never seen dinner in a white eggshell.*

At that, the mother took out a whip and she whipped and whipped the baby, crying:

> *Ugly toad in baby's cot,*
> *My sweet baby you are not.*
> *Who are you?*

And because the ugly changeling had already spoken, it had to speak again. It cried out because the whip hurt it. "I am a fairy child. Ow. Ow. Ow."

At that the fairies had to come and take their ugly baby home, bringing the mother's own child in exchange.

She picked him up and hugged him to her and she never let him out of her sight again.

To The Armies of the Revolution:
  We greet you.
  The enemy is gone. No more do we suffer under their whip. No more do we offer them our sons and daughters as slaves.

Now we must rebuild our nation, our world. Now we must tell the story of our travails and recall our heroes home.

—The Marian Council

My good Robin is as fine a husband as a woman could want. And a fine storyteller, too. His stories are of the land—when Fox stole fish from the fishmongers, when Crow lost his cheese. He expects me to tell only women's stories, the stork tales, the tales of *ma mère l'Oye.* This I know. This I do. I tell the tales my Maman told me. But—oh—I wish in this one thing Robin could know my heart. When Maman was dying, she often rambled about a world ruled by frogs and toads. A world in which humans were able to travel along the great river of time, but backward, only backward.

"I am a traveler," she would cry out, and weep. And Papa could not help her then, nor Jouanne or me. We would hold her hands and only when we said, "Maman, tell us a story," would she be comforted.

"A story," she would say, the mist going from her eyes. "I can tell you many stories. I *must* tell you many stories." She called them *pourrats,* these tales, and they were such strange stories. Hard to understand. Hard to forget.

I tell them to my own children, as Jouanne does, I am sure, to hers. But stories do not feed a mouth, they do not salve a wound, they do not fill the soul. Only God does that. And the Mother of God. We know that surely here in our village, for did not two women just thirty years past see Mary, Mother of God, on a dolmen? Her head was crowned with stars and she named herself.

"I am Marie," she said. "Believe in me and you will be saved."

One of the women who saw her was Maman.

Snow in Summer

They call that white flower that covers the lawn like a poplin carpet Snow in Summer. And because I was born in July with a white caul on my head, they called me that, too. Mama wanted me to answer to Summer, which is a warm, pretty name. But my Stepmama, who took me in hand just six months after Mama passed away, only spoke the single syllable of my name, and she didn't say it nicely.

"Snow!" It was a curse in her mouth. It was a cold, unfeeling thing. "Snow, where are you, girl? Snow, what have you done now?"

I didn't love her. I couldn't love her, though I tried. For Papa's sake I tried. She was a beautiful woman, everyone said. But as Miss Nancy down at the postal store opined, "Looks ain't nothing without a good heart." And she was staring right at my Stepmama when she said it. But then Miss Nancy had been Mama's closest friend ever since they'd been little ones, and it nigh killed her, too, when Mama was took by death.

Papa was besot with my Stepmama. He thought she couldn't

do no wrong. The day she moved into Cumberland he said she was the queen of love and beauty. That she was prettier than a summer night. He praised her so often, she took it ill any day he left off complimenting, even after they was hitched. She would have rather heard those soft nothings said about her than to talk of any of the things a husband needs to tell his wife: like when is dinner going to be ready or what bills are still to be paid.

I lived twelve years under that woman's hard hand, with only Miss Nancy to give me a kind word, sweep pop, and a magic story when I was blue. Was it any wonder I always went to town with a happier countenance than when I had to stay at home.

And then one day Papa said something at the dinner table, his mouth greasy with the chicken I had cooked and his plate full with the taters I had boiled. And not a thing on that table that my Stepmama had made. Papa said, as if surprised by it, "Why Rosemarie . . ." which was my Stepmama's Christian name . . . "why Rosemarie do look at what a beauty that child has become."

And for the first time my Stepmama looked—really looked—at me.

I do not think she liked what she saw.

Her green eyes got hard, like gems. A row of small lines raised up on her forehead. Her lips twisted around. "Beauty," she said. "Snow," she said. She did not say the two words together. They did not fit that way in her mouth.

I didn't think much of it at the time. If I thought of myself at all those days, it was as a lanky, gawky, coltish child. Beauty was for horses or grown women, Miss Nancy always said. So I just laughed.

"Papa, you are just fooling," I told him. "A daddy *has* to say such things about his girl." Though in the thirteen years I had been alive he had never said any such over much. None in fact that I could remember.

But then he added something that made things worse, though I wasn't to know it that night. "She looks like her Mama. Just like her dear Mama."

My Stepmama only said, "Snow, clear the dishes."

So I did.

But the very next day my Stepmama went and joined the Holy Roller Mt. Hosea Church which did snake handling on the fourth Sunday of each month and twice on Easter. Because of the Bible saying "Those who love the Lord can take up vipers and they will not be killed," the Mt. Hosea folk proved the power of their faith by dragging out rattlers and copperheads from a box and carrying them about their shoulders like a slippery shawl. Kissing them, too, and letting the pizzen drip down on their checks.

Stepmama came home from church, her face all flushed and her eyes all bright and said to me, "Snow, you will come with me next Sunday."

"But I love Webster Baptist," I cried. "And Reverend Bester. And the hymns." I didn't add that I loved sitting next to Miss Nancy and hearing the stories out of the Bible the way she told them to the children's class during the Reverend's long sermon. "Please Papa, don't make me go."

For once my Papa listened. And I was glad he said no. I am feared of snakes, though I love the Lord mightily. But I wasn't sure any old Mt. Hosea rattler would know the depth of that love. Still, it wasn't the snakes Papa was worried about. It was, he said, those Mt. Hosea boys.

My Stepmama went to Mt. Hosea alone all that winter, coming home later and later in the afternoon from church, often escorted by young men who had scars on their cheeks where they'd been snakebit. One of them, a tall blonde fellow who was almost handsome except for the meanness around his eyes, had a tattoo of a rattler on his bicep with the legend "Love Jesus Or Else" right under it.

My Papa was not amused.

"Rosemarie," he said, "you are displaying yourself. That is not a reason to go to church."

"I have not been doing this for myself," she replied. "I thought Snow should meet some young men now she's becoming a woman. A *beautiful* woman." It was not a compliment in her mouth. And it was not the truth, either, for she had never even introduced me to the young men nor told them my true name.

Still Papa was satisfied with her answer, though Miss Nancy, when I told her about it later, said, "No sow I know ever turned a boar over to her litter without a fight."

However, the blonde with the tattoo came calling one day and he didn't ask for my Stepmama. He asked for me. For Snow. My Stepmama smiled at his words, but it was a snake's smile, all teeth and no lips. She sent me out to walk with him, though I did not really want to go. It was the mean eyes and the scars and the rattler on his arm, some. But more than that, it was a feeling I had that my Stepmama wanted me to be with him. And that plum frightened me.

When we were in the deep woods, he pulled me to him and tried to kiss me with an open mouth and I kicked him in the place Miss Nancy had told me about, and while he was screaming, I ran away. Instead of chasing me, he called after me in a voice filled with pain. "That's not even what your Stepmama wanted me to do to you." But I kept running, not wanting to hear any more.

I ran and ran even deeper into the woods, long past the places where the rhododendron grew wild. Into the dark places, the boggy places, where night came upon me and would not let me go. I was so tired from all that running, I fell asleep right on a tussock of grass. When I woke there was a passel of strangers staring down at me. They were small, humpbacked men, their skin blackened by coal dust, their eyes curious. They were ugly as an unspoken sin.

"Who are you?" I whispered, for a moment afraid they might be more of my Stepmama's crew.

They spoke together, as if their tongues had been tied in a knot at the back end. "Miners," they said. "On Keeperwood Mountain."

"I'm Snow in Summer," I said. "Like the flower."

"Summer," they said as one. But they said it with softness and a kind of dark grace. And they were somehow not so ugly anymore. "Summer."

So I followed them home.

And there I lived for seven years, one year for each of them. They were as good to me and as kind as if I was their own little sister. Each year, almost as if by magic, they got better to look at. Or maybe I just got used to their outsides and saw within. They taught me how to carve out jewels from the black cave stone. They showed me the secret paths around their mountain. They warned me about strangers finding their way to our little house.

I cooked for them and cleaned for them and told them Miss Nancy's magic stories at night. And we were happy as can be. Oh, I missed my Papa now and then, but my Stepmama not at all. At night I sometimes dreamed of the tall blonde man with the rattler tattoo, but when I cried out one of the miners would always comfort me and sing me back to sleep in a deep, gruff voice that sounded something like a father and something like a bear.

Each day my little men went off to their mine and I tidied and swept and made-up the dinner. Then I'd go outside to play. I had deer I knew by name, grey squirrels who came at my bidding, and the sweetest family of doves that ate cracked corn out of my hand. The garden was mine, and there I grew everything we needed. I did not mourn for what I did not have.

But one day a stranger came to the clearing in the woods. Though she strived to look like an old woman, with cross-eyes and a mouth full of black teeth, I knew her at once. It was my stepmama in disguise. I pretended I did not know who she was, but when she inquired, I told her my name straight out.

"Summer," I said.

I saw "Snow" on her lips.

I fed her a deep-dish apple pie and while she bent over the table shoveling it into her mouth, I felled her with a single blow of the fry pan. My little man helped me bury her out back.

Miss Nancy's stories had always ended happy-ever-after. But she used to add every time: "Still you must make your own happiness, Summer dear."

And so I did. My happiness—and hers.

I went to the wedding when Papa and Miss Nancy tied the knot. I danced with some handsome young men from Webster and from Elkins and from Canaan. But I went back home alone. To the clearing and the woods and the little house with the eight beds. My seven little fathers needed keeping. They needed my good stout meals. And they needed my stories of magic and mystery. To keep them alive.

To keep me alive, too.

Speaking to the Wind

I was younger than my cousin Michael by a year and a half, always content to follow where he led, but never content to stay at home like a good southern girl. Even at six, two years away from New York City where I had lived until war had brought us all back to my Grandma's old brick house, I hung on to the obstinacy that was bred, or so my grandmother always said, in the stone bones of the north.

"She's her daddy's girl, not yours, Belle," she told Mamma. "She's got that stone mind. Once made up it never moves."

But Mamma always laughed when Grandma said that. "I've got the same stone mind, then, Mom. I married him," she reminded her mother.

"And against my better judgement, too," Grandma said, though she always liked Dad, flirted with him in that way Virginia women have that promises much but means nothing at all. She'd even flirted with him as he went off on the big boat, his second lieutenant's khakis the color of dog poo. That's what Michael had said, with his hand over his mouth so he could deny having said it. Dad went off to win the Big War; he'd promised and we all pretended to believe him.

We were huddled in the house that day, marooned on the settee. Mama was reading George Macdonald to Michael and me, and we were all trying not to notice the wind. A hurricane had come through, rattling the windows for hours, moaning down the chimney like a sick woman. The sky had been black at midday, and if there had been any eye to the storm, Mama said, it never blinked over Hampton Roads.

"Why can't we just ride on its back," I asked, pointing to the book. "Like Diamond does." I half believed, half didn't believe the story.

"Because that's the North Wind in the book, stupid," Michael said. "Not a hurricane."

I was so used to accepting whatever Michael told me, I didn't question his reasoning. Or lack of same.

The time the hurricane punished us seemed like days, though it was only a single long morning, and then the thing finally passed. But there were still high winds squealing over the bay and upturned boats bobbing about like bathtub toys. Waves splashed against the sea wall as if the old storm were still making angry feints at the town. The air was electric with the tail end of the storm and we all felt it.

"Very dangerous still," Mamma said and coming from New York City we understood danger.

As soon as the storm subsided, we piled into the car and Mamma drove us to back to Michael's house. There the grownups made endless lists of storm damage, arguing over what had to be attended to first.

Michael was the first to leave that boring parley, going outside onto the ruined lawn and calling me to follow.

I let myself out while Mamma and Grandma continued to quarrel good-naturedly, Aunt Cecily helping first one side, then the other with her sharp answers. No one even noticed when I was gone.

Michael didn't greet me. It wasn't necessary. He just turned and ran and I ran after him.

If I had given thought to it, I would have said that I would follow Michael forever. He was my knight, my champion, closer to me than any brother.

We galloped along the crumbling sidewalk, split by years of grass intrusions, like young colts let out of the barn. Then we cut across Miz Marshall's lawn, and slipped through the back yard of the Parson house where we could hear Joshua Parson, the one whose head was too big for his body, calling out in his high genderless voice—"Mama-papa-baby-o," the only sentence he knew.

The sycamores' heavy sighing covered any noise we made and the Parson's dog, used to our daily incursions, did not bark but whined as if he would go with us.

And then we were entirely free, spitting ourselves out onto the road that led to the sea wall. When we were close enough to see the spray and the gray misty bay beyond, we stopped, considering.

"Let's walk on the wall," I said, the wind tearing the words from my mouth and forcing my lips into a kind of grimace. I suddenly loved the hardness of that wind against my face, enjoyed the way it molded my little print dress to my body and tore the red ribbons out of my hair.

Michael hesitated.

It was only a moment, really. But in that moment I suddenly understood how different we were. His hesitation wasn't a lack of courage but rather an older child's calculation of odds. He knew we'd be punished if we did what I wanted and he was figuring out whether it was worth the spanking. Michael understood many things I did not. He'd already guessed that my father would not come home whole. But I still had a young child's faith in the persistence of youth, in the promise of magic, in the inconceivability of change.

And yet it was a moment of change nontheless.

"Come on," I said.

But still he stood, hesitating, as if it was not my place to make suggestions, only his.

I gave him a disgusted look and ran head down into the wall of wind till I managed to get on to the stone wall overlooking the bay.

As I climbed onto the gray rock, my red sandals gave me little purchase. My right knee scraped painfully on the stone. And once I was standing up, I was almost swept backward into the street by the force of the wind. If it had not been coming off the bay, but rather blowing toward it, I would probably have fallen in and drowned, for the tide was full and great gray-white waves beat time after time against the wall. They drenched me, as if a monstrous animal was spitting in my face.

I licked my lips. My tongue tasted salt from the spray. Laughing, I turned to look behind me.

Michael was still across the road his face puckered with anger and something else. Perhaps it was concern. Perhaps it was fear. I couldn't read his expression. All I knew was that he suddenly looked like a little old man. He didn't move.

For the first time ever, I turned my back to him, and opened my arms wide to the wind. I spoke to it as one talks to a cat— softly but with authority, yet ever mindful of the claws. I made it some promises, promises that were couched in the grammar of the day, in the vocabic lapses of a six year old.

In that instant the wind beast grabbed me up, its claws momentarily sheathed, and blew me out over the ocean. I was not guiled by its gentleness. At any minute it could change.

Below I could see boats straining at their anchors, and waves like catspaws making runnels along the green water.

"Higher," I crowed with delight. "Higher!"

The wind beast laughed at me and whipped me higher, till we were way up amongst the clouds.

The closer clouds were white and strung out like pearls along a grey strand. I opened my mouth and drank them in, but they melted away, like cotton candy at the fair, only not nearly so sweet.

Ahead the clouds were banked one atop another, cumbersome castles with rooms that constantly shifted.

"There!" I cried, "take me there." And the wind beast carried me where I willed: up to the cloud castles, across a growing thunderhead, over a flock of dark birds that moved as a single entity.

In thanks I patted the wind's great head down on the forehead, while its mane flew out in every direction, great streamers of white-gold hair.

We flew high and low; we skimmed the bright caps of water and we busted through the clouds. We spun ships around in the bay and we toyed with lost kites and a red balloon. We were not always kind.

But I was only six and—somewhere over the water—I grew tired of playing. I might have even yawned. I certainly felt heavy-lidded.

The wind, too, seemed to have tired. It sagged a bit and flew more slowly now, back across the bay till we were a small shadow over the land. Cars and buses crawled like cumbersome ants beneath us as the wind bore me on toward the town.

I knew that town, with its cozy bus lanes, the familiar white clapboard library and its brass-handled door, the rows of red brick workers' houses in double lines back-to-back. So small, like a game board spread below me.

The wind was softer now, and almost out of breath. It puffed and huffed, an old, tired cat.

"It's all right," I whispered, stroking the back of its whitened head. "We can go home, now."

And then it set me down, in the sand beyond the seawall, the landscape exposed by the ebbing tide.

"Janie! Janie!" Michael screamed, racing over to where I sat with my feet in a small tidepool. "Are you alright? What happened? Where have you been?"

What could I tell him? What would he believe?

Shrugging, I looked down into the depths of the tidepool. I watched as a wisp of wind, hardly more than a kitten's claw, made a line across the water.

A warning?

Or a promise?

"You disappeared," Michael accused, guessing he'd be blamed if I got hurt.

"I fell," I said. "I'm fine." Then I looked up at him and smiled. It was the wind's smile, all wildness and air. He could not bear to look at it and turned away. Away from fairy stories and phantastes, into the world of mathematics and retorts and facts.

But what did I care, who had sat astride the wind, who had flown above the earth and eaten the clouds. What did I care, then—or now—a grandmother whose own grandchildren have made friends of the wind beast, riding behind me over the miles of dark sea and brown sand.

Sometimes bargains with wildness are better than any pledges to the polite and tame world.

Better made.

And better kept.

The Thirteenth Fey

I n the middle of a stand of white birch on a slight rise is a de-caying pavilion, inferior Palladian in style. The white pi-lasters have been pocked by generations of peashooters, and several kite strings, quite stained by the local birds, still twine around the capitols. The wind whistles through the thin walls, especially in late spring, and the rains—quite heavy in November and April—have made runnels in the paper. It is very old paper anyway. As a child I used to see different pictures there, an ever-changing march of fates. My parents once thought I had the sight until they realized it was only a vivid imagina-tion supplemented by earaches and low grade fevers. I was quite frequently ill.

I was born in that pavilion, on the marble and velvet couch my parents used for the lying-in for each of my twelve brothers and sisters and me. And I was hung on my baby board in the lower branches of the trees, watched over by butterflies; the mourning doves to sing me to sleep, a chorus of crows to wake me. It was not until I reached my thirteenth year that I understood what my dear mother and her mother before her knew and grieved for but could do nothing about. It was then that I discovered that we are tied to that small piece of land circling the pavilion, tied with bonds of magic as old and secure as common law. We owe our fortunes, our existence, and the lives of our children to come to the owners of that land. We are bounden to do them duty, we women of the fey. And during all the time of our habitation, the local lords have been a dynasty of idiots, fornicators, louts, greedyguts and fools.

As the last of thirteen children I was not expected to be of any special merit. It is the first and seventh whose cranial bones are read, whose palms are searched, whose first baby babblings are recorded. Yet I had been marked with a caul, had been early to walk, early to talk, early to fly. And then there were my vivid dreams, my visions brought on by ague and earache and the peculiar swirling patterns of moldy walls. I was, in my father's words, "ever a surprise."

My father was a gentle soul. His elven ancestry showed only in his ears, which he was careful to hide beneath a fringe of greying hair, so as not to insult his wife's innumerable relatives who dwelt nearby in their own decaying whimseys, reposes, and belvederes. They already believed my mother had married beneath her. But my father, though somewhat shy on magic, lived for his library, stocked with books of the past, present, and future. He was well read in Gramarye, but also in Astrology, Philosophy, and Computer Science, an art whose time was yet to come.

My mother was never so gentle. She came from the Shouting Fey, those who could cause death and consternation by the timber of their voices. She had a sister who, on command, could bring down milk from dried-up cows with one voice, or gum it up with another. There was a great-aunt, about whom little else was said except that she could scream in six registers at once and had broken windows in all of the Western Counties as a child when bidden to do so by a silly prince one vivid day in spring.

My sisters and brothers and I were a mix, of course, both gentle and loud. But I, the thirteenth fey, was supposedly the gentlest and loudest of all.

The events I am about to relate really began nine months before the princess was born. Her birth had been long awaited. The queen, a wart-ridden harridan, was thought barren. Years of royal marriage had produced nothing but promises. Yet one steaming hot day, so the queen said, she had gone bathing in a mountain stream with her young women. More for the sake of cooling than cleanliness, I imagine. Humans are, for the most part, a disgustingly filthy lot. And a frog had climbed upon her knee and prophesied a child.

Now I have known many frogs in my time and though the peepers especially are a solipsistic tribe, believing they alone bring spring up from the edge of the world, frogs have no magical talents and they do not have the gift of prophecy. The queen was entirely wrong. It was not a frog at all. It might have been a Muryan. Tiny, dressed in green, one might be mistaken for a frog by a distraught, hot, and desperate queen. But Muryans are a mischievous lot and their natterings are never to be taken seriously.

The queen had rushed home, trailed by her still dripping handmaidens, and told the king. He was well past believing her promises. But much to everyone's surprise (except my father, who expressed the gentle judgment that, according to a law to be enacted years hence called Probability or Murphy's—I forget just which—occasionally a Muryan prophecy might be accurate) the queen gave birth some nine months later to a girl.

They named her Talia and invited—or rather insisted—all

the local feys come and bring a gift. We who were so poor as to be forced to live on moonbeams, the free fare of the faery world, had to expend our small remaining store of magicks on that squawling, bawling human infant whose father owned a quarter million acres of land, six rivers, five mountains, and the tithing of all the farms from the Western Sea to the East. It was appalling and unfair and Mother cried about it for days. But Father cautioned her to keep her voice low and, as she knew he was right, she did.

The family gathered to discuss the possibilities but I was sick again with a fever and so had no part in the family council. Who would have believed that a bout of ague brought on by dancing one starry night in a wet field should become so important to the fate of us all.

Father portioned out the magicks at that meeting, one to each child and something for Mother and himself. But he forgot me, sick abed, and so left nothing but an old linden spindle, knotted about with the thread of long life, in the family trunk. The instruction sheet to it was in tatters, mouse nibbled, shredded for nests. Besides, the spindle lay on the very bottom of the trunk and was covered with a tatty Cloth of Invisibility that worked only occasionally and, as it happened to be one of those occasions, Father hadn't even noticed it. Besides, having decided on gifts of beauty, riches, and wit—all appropriate and necessary gifts for that particular human princess—he wasn't likely to think of giving a newborn the end of life spun out on a wooden distaff.

So the family went to the christening without me, though Mother laid a cool cloth on my head, left a tisane in our best cup by my bed, and kissed both my cheeks before leaving.

"Sleep well, little one," she whispered. It was always special when she was careful to modulate her voice and I knew then how much she loved me. "Sleep well and long."

I expect her admonition forced itself into my fever dreams. I woke about an hour later, feeling surprisingly cool but parched. I had drunk up the tisane already and so cried out for some weak tea. When no one but the doves answered me with their soft *coo-coo-co-rros* from the rafters, I remembered where the family had gone.

Rising from my sickbed, I slipped a silvery party dress on over my shift. The dress was well patched with spider webbing, but the stitches scarcely showed, especially in moonlight.

I looked in the glass. My hair seemed startled into place and I combed it down with my fingers, not feeling up to searching for my brush. Then I pinched my cheeks to bring a blush to them.

The doves *coo-coo-co-rooed* again, nannylike in their warnings. Their message was clear.

"A gift!" I reminded myself out loud, beginning to shiver, not from fever but from fear. What if I had arrived *without* a gift? The king, a fat slug who was so obese he had to ride his charger sidesaddle, would have had my father exorcised by his priests if I forgot to gift his child. Exorcism on a male fey is very painful for the essence is slowly drawn out and then captured in a bottle. Imagine my dear, gentle father corked up for as long as the king or his kin liked. It was too horrible to contemplate. One of Father's brothers had been exorcised by a Kilkenny abbot and was still locked up in a dusty carafe on the back shelf of the monastery wine cellar and labeled *Bordeaux, 79.* As that was a terrible year for wines, Father does not expect anyone will ever uncork him. Father visits once a year and they shout at one another through the glass. Then Father returns whey-faced and desperate-looking. But only a human can free Uncle Finn. Father, alas, cannot.

Is it any wonder that I turned right around and ran back into the pavilion to the storeroom in which the trunk stood?

The oaken trunk was locked with a fine-grained pinewood key but the key was only for show. The trunk was bolted with a family spell. I spoke it quickly:

> *Come thou, cap and lid.*
> *Lift above what has been hid,*
>
> *All out!*

The last two words were done in the shouting voice and the whole, as with all magic, made my head hurt. But as the final note ended, the top of the trunk snapped open.

I peered in and at first thought the trunk was empty for the tatty Cloth was working again. Then, as I looked more closely, the Cloth suddenly failed around the edges and I saw the tip of the spindle.

"Blessed Loireg," I said with a sigh, praising my great-great-aunt, a patroness of Hebrides spinners. I reached down and the spindle leaped to my hand.

Clutching the spindle to my breast, I ran out the door and along the winding forest paths towards the castle. Since it was morning, and I being still weak with fever, I could not fly. So of course I was very late. The christening, begun promptly at cock's crow—how humans love the daylight hours—was almost done.

I had wrapped the Cloth about my shoulders for warmth and so, on and off, I had been invisible throughout the trip. A cacaphony of crows had noticed me; a family of squirrels had not. A grazing deer, warned by my scent, had seemed puzzled when I did not appear; a bear, pawing honey from a tree, was startled when I popped into view. But by the time I reached the castle the Cloth was working again and so the guards did not question my late entrance for they did not know I had come in.

I stopped for a moment at the throne room door and peered

around. The king and queen were sitting upon their high gilded chairs. He was—as I have noted before—fat, but Father said he had not always been so. Self-indulgence had thickened his neck and waist and the strong chin that had marked generations of his family repeated itself twice more, the third chin resting on his chest. On the other hand his wife, unsoftened by childbirth, had grown leaner over the years, vulpine, the skin stretched tightly over her cheekbones and marked with lines like a plotter's map.

Before them was a canopied cradle, its silken draperies drawn back to reveal the child who was, at present, screaming in a high-pitched voice that demonstrated considerable staying power. My father and brothers and sisters were encircling the cradle where Father, having just conferred his gift, was still bending down to kiss the squawling babe.

I stepped into the room and had passed several bored courtiers, when the Cloth suddenly failed, revealing me before I had time to recomb my hair or straighten my bent wings or paste a smile across my mouth. I had two bright spots of fever back on my cheeks and my eyes were wild. I looked, my eldest sister later told me, "a rage." But at least I did not shout. In fact, it was all I could do to get out a word, what with all that running. Stumbling forward, the spindle thrust out before me, I almost fell into the cradle. I accidentally stepped on one of the rockers and the cradle tilted back and forth. The infant, its attention caught by the movement, stopped crying.

Into the sudden silence, I croaked, "For Talia—a present of Life." And I pulled on the black thread that was wrapped around the spindle. But I must have pulled too hard on the old knotted thread. It broke after scarcely an inch.

Everyone in the court gasped and the queen cried out, "Not Life but Death."

The king stood up and roared, "Seize her," but of course at that moment the Cloth worked again and I disappeared. In my horror at what I had done, I took several steps back, dropping the spindle and the snippet of thread. Both became visible the moment they left my hand, but no one could find me.

Father bent down, picked up the thread, and shook his head.

"What damage?" whispered Mother. Or at least she tried to whisper. It came out, as did everything her family said in haste, in a shout.

"Indeed," the king cried, "what damage?"

Father took out his spectacles, a measuring tape, and a slide rule. After a moment, he shook his head. "By my calculations," he said, "fifteen years, give or take a month."

The king knew this to be true because Father's family had a geasa laid upon them to always tell the truth.

The queen burst into furious sobbing and the king clutched his hands to his heart and fell back into his chair. Baby Talia started crying again, but my eldest sister surreptitiously rocked the cradle with her foot which quieted the babe at once.

"Do something!" said the king and as it was a royal command, my mother had to obey.

"Luckily I have not yet given *my* gift, Sire," Mother began, modulating her voice, though she could still be heard all the way out to the courtyard.

Father cleared his throat. He did not believe in that kind of luck.

But Mother, ignoring him, continued. "My gift was to have been a happy marriage, but this must take precedence."

"Of course, of course," murmured the king. "If she is dead at fifteen, what use would a happy marriage be?"

At that the queen's sobs increased.

Father nodded and his eyes caught the king's and some spark of creature recognition passed between them.

Mother bent down and retrieved the spindle. Father handed her the bit of thread. Then she held up the thread in her right hand, the spindle in her left. With a quick movement of her fingers, she tied the thread back, knotting it securely, mumbled a spell which was really just a recipe for bread, then slowly unwound a much longer piece of thread. She measured it with a calculating eye and then bit it through with a loud, satisfying *snick.*

"There," she said. "Talia shall have a long, long life now. But . . ."

"But what?" the queen asked between sobs.

"But there is still this rather large knot at her fifteenth year of course," Mother explained.

"Get on with it. Get on with it," shouted the king. "You fey are really the most exasperating lot. Say it plainly. None of your fairy riddles."

Mother was about to shout back when Father elbowed her. She swallowed hastily and said, "It means she shall fall asleep on her fifteenth birthday . . ."

"Give or take a month," my father inserted.

". . . and she shall sleep for as long as it takes for the knot to be unraveled."

The queen smiled, smoothing out many of her worst wrinkles but adding several new ones around the mouth. "Oh, that should be no time at all."

Mother smiled back and said nothing, but the smile never reached her *eyes.* She had had no geasa laid on *her* tongue.

Father, ever honest, opened his mouth to speak and Mother elbowed him back. He swallowed hastily and shut his mouth. Lies take spoken words, at least according to the restriction of his fate.

Just then I became visible again, but at that point no one really cared.

.   .   .

Fifteen years can be a long or a short time, depending upon whether one is immortal or not. Princess Talia spent her fifteen as though she had an eternity to enjoy, learning little but how far the bad temper she had inherited from her father could take her. She had the gifts of beauty and wit that we had conferred upon her and they stood her in good stead with the company she kept. But she was rather short on gratitude, kindness, and love, which take rather longer to bestow than a morning's christening.

I spent the fifteen years reading through the L section in Father's library. I discovered I had an aptitude for Logic, which surprised everyone but Father. I also studied Liturgy, Lepidoptery, and Linguistics; I could do spells in seventeen tongues.

My eldest sister seriously questioned this fast accomplishment. "If you can never leave this land, why do you need more than one language?" she asked.

I could not explain the simple love of learning to her, but Father hushed her. "After all," he said, "when fifteen years are up . . ."

"Give or take a month," I added.

". . . Things may be very different around here." He smiled but would say no more.

On her fifteenth birthday, Talia summoned all the local fey to her party except for me. I had been left off of every guest list since her christening. My sisters and brothers were jealous of the fact, but there was nothing they could do about it. Even fairies cannot change the past.

Talia called her party a "Sleep-Over Ball" and announced that everyone was to come in nightclothes. Talia herself ordered a new gown for the occasion that resembled a *peignoir*, with peek-a-boo Aleçon lace and little pink ribbons sewn in strategic places. She was much ahead of her peers and had a positive genius for seduction. There was not a male member of the peerage who had escaped her spell and several fowlers and a stable boy were languishing for love of her. Even my oldest brother Dusty, who had rather common tastes, was smitten and planned to go to the party with a handful of crushed pennyroyal in each pocket, to keep the magic—as he put it—"close to the seat of his affection."

"Affliction," I said.

Dusty smiled and tousled my hair. He was smitten, but not without a sense of humor about it all.

Father and Mother were allowed to beg off since this was to be a party for young folk.

We three watched from the pavilion steps as the twelve flew into the moonlight, the wind feathering their wings. As they passed across the moon, like dust motes through light, I had a sudden fit of shivers. Father put his arm around me and Mother fetched me a shawl. They thought it was the cold, you see.

But it was more than that. "The fifteenth year," I whispered, "give or take a month." My voice was thinned out by the night air.

Father looked at Mother and they both looked at me. Whatever I had felt, whatever had made me shiver, suddenly communicated to them as well. Mother said not a word but went into the pavilion and emerged moments later with a hat and a long wool scarf for me, an Aran Island sweater for Father, and a muff for herself. She had bad circulation and flying always leaves her with cold hands.

We closed our eyes and spoke the spell.

> *Far frae earth and far frae barrows,*
> *Up to where the blue sky narrows,*
> *Wind and wildness, wings and weather,*
> *Allie-up together.*

Now!

As I lifted into the air I could feel the beginnings of a magic headache coming on, and my shoulders started to hurt as well. I have always had weak wings, but they are adequate for simple travel. We landed at the palace only minutes behind my brothers and sisters, but we were already too late. The sleeping spell had begun.

There was a cook asleep with her hand raised to strike the scullery and she, poor little wench, had been struck by sleep instead. It had happened at the moment of her only retaliation against the cook, which she got by kicking the cook's cat. The cat, unaware of the approaching kick, was snoring with one paw wrapped around a half-dead sleeping mouse.

Along the hall guards slept at their posts: one had been caught in the act of picking his teeth with his knife, one was peeling an orange with his sword, one was scraping his boot with his javelin tip, and one was picking his nose.

The guests, dressed in nightgowns and nightshirts, snored and shivered and twitched but did not wake. And in the midst of them all, lying in state, was Talia, presents piled at her feet. She blew delicate little bubbles between her partially opened lips, and under her closed eyelids I could see the rapid scuttling of dreams.

My brothers and sisters, immune to the spell, hovered above the scene nervously, except for Dusty who darted down to the bed every now and then to steal a kiss from the sleeping Talia. But, as he later admitted, she was so unresponsive, he soon wearied of the game.

"I am not a necrophile, after all," he said petulantly, which was a funny thing for him to say since right before Talia, he had been in love with the ghost of a suicide who haunted the road at Miller's Cross.

Mother put her fingers to her mouth and whistled them down.

Father announced, "Time for a family conference."

We looked in every room in the castle, including the garde-robe, but there were sleepers in every one. So we met on the castle stairs.

"Well, what now?" asked Mother.

"It's Gorse's spell," Dusty said, his mouth still wet from Talia's bubbly kisses. He hovered, pouting, over the steps.

"Of course it is Gorse's spell," said Father, "but that does not mean it is Gorse's *fault.* Don't be angry, Dusty. Just shake out your pockets and sit down."

Dusty did as he was told as Father's voice was very firm and not to be argued with. As soon as the grains of pennyroyal had touched the ground, his mood lightened and he even sat next to me and held my hand.

In fact, we all held hands, that being the best way to augment a family conference. It aids the thinking, it generates energy, and it keeps one's hands warm as well.

Mother looked up. "The knot," she said. "We must remember the knot in the thread."

Father nodded. "The Laws of Correspondence and Balance . . ." he mused.

And then I knew what to do, my reading in Logic having added texture to my spells. "There must be a similar knot about the palace," I said. I let go of Dusty's hand and stood, waving my hand widdershins. A great wind began to blow from the North. It picked up the pennyroyal, plucked seeds from the thorn, gathered wild rose pips and acorns and flung them into the air. Faster and faster the whirlwind blew, a great black tunnel of air.

> *Blow and sow*
> *This fertile ground*
> *Until the knot*
> *Be all unwound,*

I sang. One by one everyone joined me, Dusty immediately, then my other brothers and sisters, and at the last Father and finally Mother. We spoke the spell a hundred times for the hundred years and, in the end, only Mother and I had the voice for it. My voice was husky and rasping but Mother's was low and there was a longing in it compounded of equal parts of wind and sea, for the Shouting Fey came originally from the Cornish coast, great-great-great-grandfather being a sea sprite with a roving sailor's eye.

And then I dropped out of the spell with the worst headache imaginable and Mother ended it with a shout, the loudest I had ever heard her utter. It was so loud, the earth itself was shocked and opened up hundreds of tiny mouths in surprise. Into every one of those tiny mouths a seed or pip or nut popped and, in moments, they had begun to grow. We watched as years were compressed into seconds and green shoots leaped upward towards the sky. By the time the last echo of Mother's shout had died away, a great forest of mammoth oak and thorny vines surrounded the palace. Only one small passage overhead remained open where the moon beamed down a narrow light. Inside the rest of the knotted wood it was as dark as a dream, as deep as sleep.

"Come, children," said Father.

We rode the moonbeam up and out and, as the last of us passed through the hole, the thorns sewed themselves shut behind us over the deathly quiet. We neither spoke nor sang all the way home.

Having read through the Ls in Father's library, I turned my attention to the H's, my choice dictated by the fact that the wall with those books has a window that overlooks the orchard. The gnarled old trees that manage to bring forth their sweet red gifts every year fill me with wonder. It is a magic no fey could ever duplicate. And so now I have a grounding in Hagiography, Harmonics, Hormones, and History. It has been a lucky choice.

One of the books I read spoke about the rise of a religion called Democracy which believes in neither monarchs nor magic. It encourages the common man. When, in a hundred years, some young princeling manages to unravel the knot of wood about Talia's domain, I plan to be by his side, whispering the rote of Revolution in his ear. If my luck holds—and the Cloth of Invisibility works just long enough—Talia will seem to him only a musty relic of a bygone era whose bedclothes speak of decadence and whose bubbly breath of decay. He will wed the scullery out of compassion, and learn Computer Science. Then the spell of the land will be broken. No royal wedding—no royal babes. No babes—no inheritance. And though we fey will still be tied to the land, our wishes will belong to us alone.

Father, Mother, my sisters, my brothers, sometimes freedom is won by a long patience, something that works far better than any magical spell.

Granny Rumple

She was known as Granny Rumple because her dress and face were masses of wrinkles, or at least that's what my father's father's mother used to say. Of course, the Yolens being notorious liars, it might not have been so. It might simply have been a bad translation from the Yiddish. Or jealousy, Granny Rumple having been a great beauty in her day.

Like my great-grandmother, Granny Rumple was a moneylender, one of the few jobs a Jew could have in the Ukraine that brought them into daily contact with the *goyim*. She could have had one of the many traditional women's roles—a matchmaker, perhaps or an *opshprekherin* giving advice and remedies, or an herb vendor. But she was a moneylender because her husband had been one, and they had no children to take over his business. My great-grandmother, on the other hand, had learned her trade from her father and when he died and she was a widow with a single son to raise, she followed in her father's footsteps. *A sakh melokhes un vynik brokhes:* Many trades and little profit. It was a good choice for both of them.

If Granny Rumple's story sounds a bit like another you have heard, I am not surprised. My father's father used to entertain customers at his wife's inn with a rendition of Romeo and Juliet in Yiddish, passing it off as a story of his own invention. And what is folklore, after all, but the recounting of old tales. We Yolens have always borrowed from the best.

Great-grandmother's story of Granny Rumple was always told in an odd mixture of English and Yiddish, but I am of the generation of Jew who never learned the old tongue. Our parents were ashamed of it, the language of the ghetto. They used it sparingly, for punchlines of off-color jokes or to commiserate with one another at funerals. So my telling of Granny Rumple's odd history is necessarily my own. If I have left anything out, it is due neither to the censorship of commerce nor art, but the inability to get the whole thing straight from my aging relatives. As a Yolen ages, he or she remembers less and invents more. It is lucky none of us is an historian.

As a girl, Granny Rumple's name was Shana and she had been pursued by all the local boys. Even a Cossack or two had knocked loudly at her door of an evening. Such was her beauty, she managed to turn even them away with a smile. When she was finally led under the wedding canopy, the entire village was surprised, for she married neither the chief rabbi's son, a dark-eyed scholar named Lev, nor the local butcher, who was a fat, ribald widower, nor the half dozen others who had asked her. Instead she chose Shmuel Zvi Bar Michael, the money-changer. No one was more surprised than he, for he was small, skinny and extremely ugly, with his father's large nose spread liberally across his face. Like many ugly people, though, he was also gentle, kind, and intensely interested in the happiness of others.

"Why did you marry him?" my great-grandmother had wondered.

"Because he proposed to me without stuttering," Shana had replied, stuttering being the one common thread in the other suits. It was all the answer she was ever to give.

By all accounts, it was a love match and the expected children would have followed apace—with Shana's looks, her mother had prayed—but Shmuel was murdered within a year of the wedding.

It is the telling of that murder, ornamented by time, that my great-grandmother liked to tell. Distance lends a fascination to blood tales. It runs in our family. I read murder mysteries; my daughter is a detective.

There was, you see, a walled Jewish ghetto in the town of Ykaterinislav and beyond it, past the trenches where the soldiers practiced every spring, the larger Christian settlement. The separate Jewish quarters are no longer there, of course. It is a family joke: What the Cossacks and Hitler only began, Chernobyl finished.

Every day Shmuel Zvi Bar Michael would say his prayers in his little stone house, donning *tefillin* and giving thanks he was not a woman—but secretly giving thanks as well that he had a woman like Shana in his bed each night. He was not a man unmindful of his blessings and he only stuttered when addressing the Lord G-d.

Then he would make his way past the gates of the ghetto, past the trenches, and onto the twisting cobbled streets of Ykaterinislav proper. He secreted gold in various pockets of his black coat, and sewed extra coins and jewels into the linings of his vest. But of course everyone knew he had such monies on him. He was a changer, after all.

Now one Friday he was going along the High Street where the shops of the merchants leaned despondently on one another.

Even in Christian Ykaterinislav recessions could not be ignored and the czar's coinage did not flow as freely there as it did in the great cities. As he turned one particular corner, he heard rather loud weeping coming from beside the mill house. When he stopped in—his profession and his extreme ugliness allowing him entrée other Jews did not have—he saw the miller's daughter sobbing messily into her apron. It was white apron embroidered with gillyflowers on the hem; of such details legends are made real. Shmuel knew the girl, having met her once or twice when doing business with her father, for the miller was always buying on margin and needing extra gold. As a miller's wares are always in demand, Shmuel had no fear that he would not be repaid. *Gelt halt zikh nor in a grobn zak:* Money stays only in a thick sack. The miller's sack, Shmuel knew, was the thickest.

The girl's name was Tasha—Tana to her family—and as pretty as her blond head was, it was empty. If she thought something, she said it, true or not. And she agreed with her father in everything. She would have been beaten otherwise. She was not smart—but she was not *that* stupid.

"Na—na, Tana," Shmuel said, using her familiar name to comfort her. "What goes?"

In between the loud snuffles and rather muffled sobs, she offered up the explanation. Her father had boasted to the mayor of Ykaterinislav that Tana could spin miracles of flax and weave cloth as beautiful as the gold coats of the Burgundian seamstresses.

"And where is Burgundian anyway?" Tana asked, sniffling.

"A long way from here," replied Shmuel. It was little comfort.

"I am a poor spinner at best," Tana confessed. She whispered it for it was nothing to boast of. "And I cannot weave at all. But I *can* cook."

"Na—na, Tana," Shmuel said, "but what is the *real* problem?"

"The real problem?"

"Why are you *really* crying?"

"Oh!" She took a deep breath. "Unless I can spin and sew such a cloth, my father's boast will lose us both our heads."

"This sounds like a fairy tale to me," said Shmuel, though of course he did not use the word *fairy,* that being a French invention. He said "It sounds like a story of the *leshy.*" But if I had said that, you would not have understood. And indeed, I did not either, until it was explained to me by an aunt.

"But it is *true!*" she wailed and would be neither comforted nor moved from her version of the facts.

"Then I shall lend you the money—and at no interest—to buy such a cloth and you can give that to your father, who can offer it to the mayor in place of your own poor work."

"*At no interest!*" Tana exclaimed, that in itself such a miraculous event as to seem a fairy story.

"In honor of a woman as dark as you are fair, but equally beautiful," Shmuel said.

"Who is that?" asked Tana, immediately suspecting sorcery.

"My new bride," Shmuel reported proudly.

At which point she knew it to be devil's work indeed, for where would such an ugly little man get a beautiful bride except through sorcery. But so great was her own perceived need, she crossed herself surreptitiously and accepted his loan.

Shmuel found her a gold coin in the right pocket of his coat and made a great show of its presentation. Then he had her sign her X on a paper, and left certain he had done the right thing.

Tana went right out to the market of a neighboring town, where she bought a piece of gold-embroidered cloth from a tinker. It was more intricate than anything either she or her father could have imagined, with the initials T and L cunningly intertwined beneath the body of a dancing bear.

The mayor of Ykaterinislav was suitably impressed, and he immediately introduced his son Leon to Tana. The twined initials were not lost upon them. The son, while not as smart as his father, was handsome, and he was heir to his father's fortune as well. Dreaming of another fortune to add to the family's wealth, he proposed.

Good husband that he was, Shmuel reported all his dealings to Shana. He was extremely uxorious; nothing pleased him more than to relate the day's business to her.

"They would not have killed her for a story," she said. "Probably her father had wagered on it."

"Who knows what the *goyim* will do," he replied. "Trust me, Shana, I deal with them every day. They do not know story from history. It is all the same to them."

Shana shrugged and went back to her own work; but as she said the prayers over the Sabbath candles that evening, she added an extra prayer to keep her beloved husband safe.

Who says the Lord G-d has no sense of humor? Just a week went by and Shmuel once again passed along the High Street and heard the miller's daughter sobbing.

"Na—na, Tana," he said. "What goes this time?"

"I am to be married," she said.

"That is not an institution to be despised. I myself have a beautiful bride. Happiness is in the marriage bed."

This time she did not bother to hide her genuflection, but Shmuel was used to the ways of the *goy*.

"My father-in-law-to-be, the mayor, insists that I produce the wedding costume, and the costumes of my attending maidens besides."

"But of course," Shmuel agreed. "Even beyond the gates . . ."—and he gestured toward the ghetto walls—"even there the bride's family supplies . . ."

"Myself!" she cried. "I am to make each myself. And embroider them with my own hands. *And I cannot sew!*" She proceeded to weep again into her apron, this time so prodigiously, the gillyflowers would surely have grown from the watering had the Lord G-d been paying attention as in the days of old.

"A-ha!" Shmuel said, reaching into his pockets and jangling several coins together. "I understand. But my dear, I have the means to help you, only . . ."

"Only?" She looked up from the soggy apron.

"Only this time, as you have prospects of a rich marriage . . ."—for gossip travels through stone walls where people themselves cannot pass; it is one of the nine metaphysical wonders of the world—number three actually.

"Only?" To say the girl was two platters and a bottle short of a banquet is to do her honor.

"Only this time you must pay interest on the loan," Shmuel said. He was a businessman after all, not just a Samaritan. And Samaria—like Burgundy, was a long way from there.

Tana agreed at once and put her X to a paper she could not read, then gratefully pocketed three gold pieces. It would buy the services of many fine seamstresses with—she reckoned quickly—enough left over for a chain for her neck and a net for her hair. She could not read but, like most of the girls of Ykaterinislav, she *could* count.

"I do not like such dealings," Shana remarked that evening. "The men at least are honorable in their own way. But the women of the *goyim* . . ."

"I am a respected moneylender," Shmuel said, his voice sharp.

Then afraid he might have been *too* sharp, he added, "Their women are nothing like ours; and *you* are a queen of the ghetto."

If she was appeased, she did not show it, but that night her prayers were even longer over the candles, as if she were having a stern talking to with the Lord G-d.

Ah—you think you know the tale now. And perhaps you are right. But, as Shmuel noted, some do not know story from history. Perhaps you are one of those. Story tells us that the little devil, the child stealer, the black imp was thwarted. Of such blood libels good rousing pogroms are made.

Still, history has two sides, not one. Here is the other.

Tana and her Leon were married, of course. Even without the cloth it was a good match. The miller's business was a thriving one; the mayor was rich on graft. It was a merger as well as a marriage. Properties were exchanged along with the wedding pledges. Within the first month Tana was with child. So she was cloistered there, in the lord mayor's fine house, while her own new house was being built, so she did not see Shmuel again.

And then the interest on the loan came due.

A week after Tana's child was delivered, she had a visitor.

It was not Shmuel, of course. He would never have been allowed into the woman's section of a Christian house, never allowed near the new infant.

It was Shana.

"Who are you?" asked Tana, afraid that in her long and difficult pregnancy her husband had taken a Jewish concubine, for such was not unheard of. The woman before her was extraordinarily beautiful.

"I am the wife of Shmuel Zvi Bar Michael."

"Who is that?" asked Tana. For her, one Jewish name was as unpronounceable as another.

"Shmuel Zvi Bar Michael," Shana explained patiently, as to a child. "The moneylender. Who lent you money for your wedding."

"My father paid for my wedding," Tana said, making the sign of the cross as protection for herself and the child in her arms.

Shana did not even flinch. This puzzled Tana a great deal and frightened her as well. "What do you want?"

"Repayment of the loan," Shana said, adding under her breath in Yiddish: *"Vi men brokt zikh ayn di farfl, azoy est men zey oyf"* which means "The way your farfl is cut, that's how you'll eat it." In other words, *You made your bed, now you'll lie in it. Trust me,* you don't want to ask about *farfl.*

"I borrowed nothing from you," Tana said.

Talking as if to an idiot or to one who does not understand the language, Shana said, "You borrowed it from my husband." She took a paper from her bosom and shoved it under Tana's nose.

Tana shrank from the paper and covered the child's face with a cloth as if the paper would contaminate it, poor thing. Then she began to scream: "Demon! Witch! Child stealer!" Her screams would have brought in the household if they had not all been about the business of the day.

But a Jew—any Jew—knows better than to stay where the charge of blood libel has been laid. Shana left at once, the paper still fluttering in her hand.

She went home but said nothing to her husband. When necessary, Shana could keep her own counsel.

Still, the damage had been done. Terrified she would have to admit her failures, Tana told her husband a fairy tale indeed, complete with a little, ugly black imp with an unpronounceable name who had sworn to take her child for unspeakable rites. And as it was springtime, and behind the ghetto walls the Jewish community of Ykaterinislav was preparing for Passover, Tana's accusations of blood libel were believed, though it took her a full night of complaining to convince Leon.

Who but a Jew, after all, was little and dark—never mind that half of the population both in front of and behind the walls were tall and blonde thanks to the Vikings who had settled their trade center in Kiev generations before. Who but a Jew had an unpronounceable name—never mind that the local goyish names did not have a sufficiency of vowels. Who but a Jew would steal a Christian child, slitting its throat and using the innocent blood in the making of matzoh—never mind that it was the Jews, not the gentiles, who had been on the blade end of the killing knife all along.

Besides, it had been years since the last pogrom. Blood calls for blood, even if it is just a story. Leon went to his friends, elaborating on Tana's tale.

What happened next was simple. Just as the *shammes* was going around the ghetto, rapping with his special hammer on the shutters of the houses and calling out "Arise, Jews, and serve the Lord! Arise and recite the psalms!" the local bullyboys were massing outside the ghetto walls.

In house after house, Jewish men rose and donned their *tefillin* and began their prayers; the women lit the fires in the stoves.

Then the wife of Gdalye the butcher—his new wife—went out to pull water from the well and saw the angry men outside the gate. She raised the alarm, but by then it was too late. As they hammered down the gate, the cries went from the streets to Heaven, but if the Lord G-d was home and listening, there was no sign of it.

The rabble broke through the gates and roamed freely along the streets. They pulled Jews out of their houses and measured them against a piece of lumber with a blood red line drawn halfway up. Any man found below the line was beaten, no matter his age. And all the while the rabble chanted "Little black imp!" and "Stealer of children!"

By morning's end the count was this: two concussions, three broken arms, many bruises and blackened eyes, a dislocated jaw, the butcher's and baker's shops set afire, and one woman raped. She was an old woman. The only one they could find. By pogrom standards it was minor stuff and the Jews of Ykaterinislav were relieved. They knew, even if the *goyim* did not, that this sort of thing is easier done in the disguise of night.

One man only was missing—Shmuel Zvi Bar Michael, the moneylender. He was the shortest and the ugliest and the blackest little man the crowd of sinners could find.

Of course the rest of the Jews were too busy to look for him. The men were trying to save what they could of Gdalye the butcher's shop and Avreml the baker's house. The women were too busy binding up the heads of Reb Jakob and his son Lev, and the arms of the three men, one a ten-year-old boy, and the jaw of Moyshe the cobbler, and tending to the old woman. Besides Shana had been too guilt-ridden to press them into the search.

It was not until the next day that she found his body—or the half of it that remained—in the soldiers' trenches.

At the funeral she tore her face with her fingernails and wept until her eyes were permanently reddened. Her hair turned white during the week she sat *shiva.* And it was thus that Granny Rumple was born of sorrow, shame, and guilt. At least that was my great-grandmother's story. And while details in the middle of the tale had a tendency to change with each telling, the ending was always tragic.

But the story, you say, is too familiar for belief? *Belief!* Is it less difficult to believe that a man distributed food to thousands using only a few loaves and fishes? Is it less difficult to believe the Red Sea opened in the middle to let a tribe of wandering desert dwellers through? Is it less difficult to believe that Elvis is alive and well and shopping at Safeway?

Look at the story you know. Who is the moral center of it? Is it the miller who lies and his daughter who is complicitous in the lie? Is it the king who wants her for commercial purposes only? Or is it the dark, ugly little man with the unpronounceable name who promises to change flax into gold—and does exactly what he promises?

Stories are told one way, history another. But for the Jews—despite their long association with the Lord G-d—the endings have always been the same.

Blood Sister

The Myth:

Then Great Alta reached into the crevice of night and pulled up two light sisters with her left hand. She reached in again and pulled up two dark sisters with her right. The one pair, light and dark, she set facing one another, belly to belly and breast to breast. The other pair she set back against back so that their hairs intertwined but they knew one another not.

"Ye are all my daughters," quoth Great Alta, "whether you look toward or away, whether you look far or near. You will not lose any love wherever your gaze should fall."

She touched their eyes with her right forefinger, their mouths with her left forefinger, and their hearts with her open palm, and thus were they made fully awake.

The Parable:

As told by Mother Anda, great-great-grandaughter of Magna, last of the Sisters Arundale:

Once there was a garden in which our mothers and fathers

lived. It was a comfortable place where fruit grew without cultivation and water ran over twenty-one stones to become pure.

But one of the fathers turned to his companions and said, "I want to see the world outside the garden. Who would go with me?"

Some of the fathers said yes. Some of the mothers, too.

But there were two mothers who did not go. "We are happy here," they said. "Where the sun shines on us and the wind cools us and the fruit grows without cultivation." And so they stayed in the garden and raised their children.

Only once in a lifetime, some of the children followed the others into the outside world we call the Dales.

The Story:

Selna had never wanted a child to care for. Not a baby sister nor a little cousin. And so she had paid little heed to the Hame's infirmarer during lessons about how children were got and how they were not. Of course she paid as little attention to the kitchener's explanations about food. All Selna had ever wanted, even before she had to choose in the great ceremony before Mother, was to be in the woods with Marda.

Her voice had never wavered when she and her seven-year sisters had been asked "Do you, my children, choose your own way?" Marda's voice had been quiet, and Zenna's quieter still. Lolla and Senja had replied in their high, light way. But Selna's answer came strong and pure.

And when she had marched up the stairs to touch the Book of Light, her knees had not wobbled. Not even when the priestess's sour breath had touched her. Not even then.

"I am a child of seven springs," she had said. "I choose and I am chosen. The path I choose is a warrior. A huntress. A keeper of the wood."

No one, especially not Mother Alta, had been surprised.

But now things were different, had been different for months. And Selna could not exactly say what was wrong, only that things were different. And Marda was gone. Marda, her best friend, who had trained all those years with her and who was her companion and blood sister—the last sworn with knives at the wrist where the blood makes a blue branching beneath the fragile shield of skin, a poultice of aloe leaves applied afterward. Marda had gone missioning.

Selna's mother had found her sobbing in the night. "She will return," her mother reminded her, kneeling by the bed. "A mission year is but one world's turning."

"Or she will not," Selna had said, too miserable to hide her tears as a warrior should. "Some stay at their mission Hame. Or go to another."

Her mother nodded. "Or she will not. After her mission year in her new Hame, she may have other, newer dreams. But her decision will be between Marda and her dark sister. It is not between Marda and you."

"But . . ." The cry was out before Selna could stop it.

"But what?"

Selna's traitor mouth would not contain the words. "But *I* was her sister. Her blood sister. There was no one closer."

Her mother's dark sister kneeling at the bedside chuckled. "Soon you will understand, child."

"I will never understand. Never. I will be a solitary. I will call no one to take Marda's place."

Selna's mother stood and her dark sister with her. "Come," the dark sister said. "She will know soon enough."

Selna looked up from her pillow. *"The heart is not a knee that can bend,"* she said. "Or did you not tell me that often enough?"

Then deliberately she reached over and snuffed out the candle by her bed.

Her mother's footsteps were the only ones to go out of the room. Her mother's dark sister, without a candle's flame to guide her, was no longer there.

The Song:

Dark Sister

Come by moonshine,
Come by night,
Come by flickering
Candlelight,

Come by star rise,
Come by shine,
Come by hearthlight,
Come be mine.

In the darkness
Be my spark,
In the nighttime
Be my mark.

Come by star rise,
Come by shine,
Come by hearthlight,
Come be mine.

Come by full moon,
Come by half,

Come with tears,
Come with a laugh.

Come by star rise,
Come by shine,
Come by hearthlight,
Come be mine.

The Story:

Zenna called her own dark sister the next moon. Lolla and Senja, twins in everything, called theirs together.

"It is a wonder they did not call up just one," their mother said. But she said it laughing.

Everyone joined in the laugher but Selna. Selna laughed very little these days. No—Selna did not laugh at all. She left the table where the conversation continued and went out into the courtyard of the Hame. She got her throwing knife from the cupboard and fitted it into her belt, then took down her bow from its slot against the wall. The quiver she filled with seven arrows and slung over her shoulder. Then she went out the gate.

She ran down the path easily, her mocs making little sound against the pebbles. She used wolf breath to give her the ability to run many miles. It was not that far till she would reach the woods. As she ran, she thought about how she and Marda had raced almost every day along this same path, the one keeping breath with the other. How they ran left foot with left, right foot with right. How they matched in everything—the color of their hair the same wheat gold, their eyes both the slate blue of the rocks by the little river. Only she was tall and Marda was a hand's breadth shorter.

"I love you, Marda," she had said the day they had opened their wrists and sealed their lives together.

"I love you, Selna," Marda had answered, as she smoothed the aloe onto the leaf and bound it with the vine.

They had been children of nine summers then. Now they were fourteen.

"I still love you, Marda," Selna said. But she said it to the white tree standing sentinel at the woods's first path. She said it to the three tall rocks that they had played on so often as children. And she said it to the river that rippled by uncaring. *Twenty-one stones,* the saying went, *and water is pure.*

The History:

The women of the mountain warrior clans lived in walled villages called Hames. As far as we can tell, there were five main buildings in each Hame: the central house, in which were the sleeping and eating and cooking quarters, was the largest building. It opened onto a great courtyard where the training of warriors took place. What animals they kept—goats, fowl, possibly cows—were in one small barn. A second, even smaller barn housed the stores, part of which were kept down in a cellar, where stoneware bottles were put by with fermented drinks—berry wines and even, in a few of the Hames, a kind of ginger beer. A small round building housed a bathing pool heated by a series of pipes to a central wood heater. There were two smaller, shallower pools. From the Lowentrout essay "The Dig Arundale: Pooling Resources," *Nature and History,* Vol. 57, comes the interesting theory that one of the small pools was for the children while the other, with a separate series of exit pipes, was for women during their menses. The other building, some scholars feel, was a training center or school. Others hypothesized that this fifth building was a place of worship.

The Story:

Selna found the deer tracks by the river's edge. They were incautious tracks, scumbled tracks, for the deer was still young and looking for any kind of footing. In the imprint of one was the imposition of a large cat's track.

"Ho, my beauty," Selna said. Whether she meant the deer or the cat was not clear.

Both deer and cat had crossed the river at the shallow turning. Selna followed them carefully, the bow already strung. She knew she might be too late. The deer might have made a dash for safety and the cat, in its frustration, got its fill of rabbit or mice. Or the cat might even now be feasting on raw venison. Or tracking behind Selna . . . but she did not believe the last. The cat's prints showed it clearly and steadily behind the deer.

She went back and forth across the river three times after those tracks and, at last, lost them both when night closed in. She was neither angry nor frustrated; only suddenly Marda's treason gnawed anew. Once Selna had nothing left to do but make a hide in a tree for sleeping, her unhappiness came over her again, wave after wave of it, like a river in flood.

Sleep would not come. Each time she closed her eyes, she saw Marda leaving.

"We will think of you," Marda had said, kissing her on both cheeks. *We.* Once, Selna knew, that would have meant Marda and Selna. Now it meant Marda and her dark sister, that black-haired, black-eyed echo, that moon child.

"I hate her!" Selna said aloud.

Below her in the woods a cat coughed in answer. Selna

reached for her knife and, holding it in two hands, waited a long time for the dawn.

The History:

Here in the Museum of the Lower Dales is the only Daleite mirror archeologists have recovered, though mirrors play such an important part in Hame histories and legends. The ornate wood frame has been reliably dated at two thousand years, of a laburnum that has not been found in those parts for centuries. It was found in the dig at Arundale, wrapped separately and buried some hundred meters distant from the buildings.

Many scholars have ventured informed guesses about the mirror. They include Cowan's thesis that the mirror was the property of the Hame's ruling priestess and that only she was allowed to own such a priceless treasure; Temple's more conventional opinion that the Hame, being a place of women, would naturally be filled with mirrors; and Magon's bizarre and discredited idea that the mirror was part of a ritual in which the young girls called up their twin or dark sisters from some unnamed and unknown alternate universe.

Note that all the carvings on the mirror frame are mirror images of one another, a symmetry that has been much commented upon. We do not *really* know what they stand for.

—FROM *AT HAME IN THE DALES*, MUSEUM BOOKLET
PRODUCED BY MUSEUM OF THE LOWER DALES, INC.

The Story:

Dawn came before the cat. Or instead of it. Selna had finally napped a bit, just enough to take the edge off her exhaustion.

The imprint of the knife handle seemed etched into her palms. Her hands ached, and her back and legs. As she climbed down the tree, her stomach rumbled as well. Spending all night in a tree was never comfortable, but as her teacher always reminded them, *Better the cat at your heel than at your throat.* And there *had* been a cat.

She shoved the knife back into the belt and went to find something to eat. There would be berries down near the river. She had long since learned which mushrooms could be safely eaten, which could not. A good hunter never went hungry in the woods. She could always fish. When she and Marda went fishing . . .

And there it was again, the ache when she thought of Marda. It was as if she had been halved with a great sword, cleaved in two. Everything she had done before had been done *with* Marda. And now nothing ever again would be. Always and always Marda's dark sister, Callo, would be between them, whether or not there was moon or candle flame to call her out.

The ache was so real, she clutched her stomach with it, turned off the path, and thought she would vomit. Only nothing came up. Nothing.

"I am a warrior," she reminded herself. "I am a hunter." It did not stop the tears. It did not stop the pain.

The Song:

Beloved

Oh, my beloved,
My sister, my friend,
I do not know where you begin,
Where I end.

My hand is your hand,
My breast your breast,
The soft pillow
Where I take my rest.

Oh, my beloved,
My sister, my wife,
If you are severed from me,
So is my life,

So is the earth gone,
So is the sky,
So the life from me,
And so I die.

Oh, my beloved,
My sister, my friend,
You are the beginning of me
And the end.

The Story:

She fished anyway. Wanting to die and dying, she found, were two separate things. The pain in her heart could not be fixed. The pain in her gut could. She caught a splendid silvery trout with a rainbow of scales. The act of fishing made her forget Marda for a while. The act of gutting it did, too. But as the fish cooked on the fire, the ache came back again, worse than before. It was so bad, she thought she might bring the fish back up again as well. But her body was stronger than that. It had taken her a day and a night and another whole day to understand that.

The body has its own logic, her mother often told her. *The heart has none.*

She buried the fish bones, scattered the remains of the fire. She had been taught well.

When she went into the woods to relieve herself, she found her pants spattered with blood and for the first time understood. The ache in her belly, the pain that spread like fire from her heart, had nothing to do with Marda after all. She was come into womanhood for the first time, here in the wood, here in her deserted state.

The body has its own logic. She laughed and said it aloud. "The body has its own logic." She covered the hole carefully with dirt, packed it down. She would have to go back to the Hame. A menstruating woman did not belong alone in a place of big cats. Especially with night coming on. She would wash in the river, and then she would go back to the Hame.

The History:

As in all warrior societies, the Amazonian women of the Dales did not concern themselves about gender. Homosexual couplings were common in the all-female society within the Hames. But in order for that society to continue, there *had* to be children. They were got in two ways. Either the women who were not exclusively female-to-female oriented went outside the community and mated with males, bringing any female offspring back to the Hame with them, or they took care of cast-off female children belonging to the outside world.

Such outside mating when done within the armies was known as Blanket Companions. A woman of the Hames who went into the nearby towns for the express purpose of conceiving a child was known as a Year Wife. One who stayed longer, but eventually returned to the Hame with her girl children, was called a Green Widow. We do not know why.

The Story:

The river was cold, especially with night closing in around her, so Selna built a fire as close to the water as she could. Then she stripped off her leathers and, without giving herself time to think, plunged into the pool.

The water scrubbed at her and she shivered at first, but soon the act of bathing made her almost warm. She looked up at the sky. The moon—full and round—was creeping over the tops of the trees.

Selna stood still and the pool waters stopped rippling. The surface was like glass. When she looked down into the water, the moon was reflected back, as clear as in Mother Alta's mirror. Selna was reflected too, as if there were two of her. Selna—and her other. Marda.

The body has its own logic, she thought, slowly raising her hands and speaking the words of the Night of Sisterhood.

She meant the words to call Marda back. If they had power—and she knew they did, everyone in the Hame knew it—then maybe here in the woods, where she and Marda had sealed their love in blood, she would come. Marda would come.

> *Dark to light,*
> *Day to night,*
> *Here my plea,*
> *Thee to me.*

She turned her palms toward her breast and made a slow, beckoning motion, reciting the chant over and over.

It got dark, except for the moon overhead, except for the fire crackling on the shore. A slight mist rose from the pool's mirror surface, a mist that at first Selna could see through. And then she could not.

Thee to me,
Thee to me,
Thee to me.

Her hands kept up the beckoning. *The body has its own logic.* Her mouth kept up the chant. The girls had trained so long with Mother Alta in that chant that once started, Selna could not stop. Her body was cold, almost immobilized by the cold. But the chant kept rolling from her mouth, and the mist kept rising, as if carrying away the last of her body's heat with it.

And then the mist seemed to turn and shape itself, head and hair and long neck and broad shoulders and arms that beckoned back to her and a face that was as familiar as Marda's and yet not familiar at all. And the mouth echoing her own:

Thee to me,
Thee to me,
Thee to me.

"Alta's hairs! It's cold. Do we have to stand here till dawn?"

"We?" Selna wondered if she were dreaming.

"You, Selna. Me, Marjo. Your dark sister. You *did* call me out, you know. Blood to blood. Dark to light. Only it's hideously cold. And I can't move out of this stream until you do."

"Do?" Selna echoed. And then in an instant it came clear to her. Out here, in the woods, not in the cozy warmth of Mother Alta's chambers before the mirror with the other mothers there for support, here she had called her dark sister. Marjo, not Marda. "I don't want you," she said.

"Doesn't matter," Marjo answered. "You've got me. At least for the night. Now can we go get dry. And warm?"

"Dry," Selna echoed. "Warm."

"Right," Marjo said.

It seemed so sensible, and she suddenly was shivering so uncontrollably, that Selna turned, plowed through the pool on stiffened legs, and stumbled up the embankment to the fire, which was all but out. She fed logs into it and more sticks and leaves, Marjo exactly following her movements. With two working, the fire was quickly renewed, though it took much longer for the warmth to seep through and make them both stop shaking.

The Legend:

Near the town of Selsberry is a small pond, fed by an underground stream. It is called Sisters' Pond or Sels Pond. It is said that once a year, at the Spring Solstice, when the moon is at its highest point overhead, the mist rising up looks just like a beautiful young woman. The mist woman will call you with her mist arms beckoning. "Come to me, come to me," she calls over and over. But you'd better not go. If you do, she'll drown you, just as she was, herself, drowned some hundreds of years ago when that underground stream was a great, roaring river.

At least that's what the folks in Selsberry say.

The Story:

Selna got dressed quickly and Marjo matched her, leather pants, linen shirt, leather jerkin, mocs. It was like a dance, really, the way they kept time to one another. Selna had known what to expect, of course. She had been around other women's dark sisters all her life. But expecting and *knowing,* it seems, were two very different things.

In the end Selna strapped on the belt and knife and grabbed up her bow. Marjo did the same.

"Are you really very like me?" Selna asked at last. She thought Marjo looked older, guanter. It might have been the black hair, the darker features. It might have been the moonlight.

"Very like," Marjo said. "And not like at all."

Selna put out the fire with her moc. Together they buried the coals. There was still enough moon to keep Marjo quick and eager.

"I need to get out of the woods. I'm —"

"*We* need to get out of the woods. One moon time is bad enough. Two is an open invitation," Marjo said.

Selna hadn't thought of that. "What if a cat gets me?"

"It gets me, too." Marjo laughed, though her face hardly changed with the humor. "I guess it is true as the Book says: *Sisters can be blind.*"

"I . . . am . . . not . . . blind to this," Selna said. She found no humor in the situation.

"You do not know how to laugh. In this way we are different. And in other ways. I am you, and I am also what you will not let yourself be."

Selna turned away. "I have no wish to be what you are."

"*If your mouth turns into a knife, it will cut off your lips,* or so it is said where I come from." Marjo had turned away, too, and her voice got very quiet. "You may not wish to be what I am, but we are together. Forever."

"Forever?" Selna turned back.

"At least as long as you live."

Selna was thinking so hard about that, she did not hear the sound. The first she knew there was a cat nearby was when he had launched himself, hitting her square in the back. Without hesitating, even as she was falling, she drew her knife.

The Ballad:

Ballad of the Cat's Bride

Do not go to the woods, my girl,
Red ribbands in your hair,
Do not go to the woods at night,
For Lord Catmun is there.

He'll spring upon you silently,
He'll leave you there for dead,
He'll take away your virtue
And leave you a babe instead.

He'll take away your virtue,
And he'll take away your name,
And leave you but a weanling child
To carry to your shame.

Do not go to the woods, my girl,
If you a maid would stay,
Do not go to the woods at night,
Go only in the day.

The Story:

As Selna turned, knife in her hand, she thrust upward. The cat thew back his head at the same time as if trying to fight something behind him. Then he screamed—an awful sound—and collapsed on top of Selna.

She pushed him off and stood up shakily. "What . . . ?" she began. Then she saw the knife in the cat's back and Marjo looking at her oddly.

"Lucky you drew your knife so I could draw mine," Marjo said.

"I don't know what to say."

"That's a good start," Marjo said. "Let's skin this cat down quickly and go. It's spring. There might be a mate."

"There's sure to be one," Selna said. "But she's probably laired up with kits."

That was the last they spoke, working side by side as easily and as silently as old friends. Or new enemies.

When they were finished, another night was all but gone. They started on the path together, but the moon could find them only intermittently. Each time it disappeared, so did Marjo.

When they reached the road at last, the moon was slowly setting behind the hills. It was long gone by the time Selna got to the gates of her Hame alone.

Her mother was sleeping on Selna's bed, her cheeks still wet with tears. Selna got in beside her and put her head against her mother's back. "I am a woman now," she whispered, loud enough to be heard, quiet enough not to waken anyone.

Her mother stirred, turned in her sleep. A stray strand of white-gold hair fell across her mouth. Selna carefully picked it off and smoothed it back. "But that doesn't mean I have to forget, does it?"

Her mother woke briefly. "Forget what, dear?" she mumbled.

"I will *never* forget her," Selna whispered. She stood and took the guttered candle from the bedside, walked out to the hearth to light it. As she bent over the fire, a voice whispered in her ear.

"I will never forget her, either."

Selna turned. And looking into her other, darker eyes, at last she smiled.

The Myth:

Then Great Alta drew aside the curtain of her hair and showed them her other face, her hidden face. It was dark where she was light. She was two and she was one. "And so ye shall be," quoth the two Atlas. "So shall all my daughters be. Forever."

Journey into the Dark

Translation from the altar stone at the great temple at Chichén Itzá, excavated May 14, 2030

L et me tell you a story my children.

When the young prince Ho ch'ok lay dying on his small bed, he had around him the four that he loved best.

Kneeling by his head was his lady mother, the queen, who had pulled out all the pins from her hair in mourning and likewise the pin from her lip.

His brother, the king-that-was-to-be, Qich Mam, sat by his feet; tears kept in check by the slow breathing he had been taught since a child.

His sister, who was to have been the young prince's bride, sat closer to his heart, by the left side, the tears like rivers running down her unpainted cheeks.

And standing at the bedfoot was his old nurse, weeping loudly and beating upon her bosom with a closed fist.

The young prince Ho ch'ok opened his mouth to speak and all four about him fell silent, for his voice was but a whisper. He reached out his hand and his sister took it loosely in hers.

"I am afraid," Ho ch'ok said, for though he was a prince he

was, still, a small boy. "I am afraid of the journey. I am afraid of the dark."

"Then," his mother said softly, "I shall give you something to light the way." She plucked her heart from her breast and held it out to him. And when he took it, it shone with a light that was even and white.

"And I will give you that which can tell dark from light," said his sister, plucking out her third eye and putting it on his forehead. "It can tell the hard places from the soft."

"And I will give you a weapon that you shall not be afraid," said his brother, breaking off a little finger, the last one on the left. He placed it on his brother's chest.

"But still I am cold," said Ho ch'ok. "So cold."

At that the nurse took a great leather wallet which was hanging from a thong on her belt. She opened it and there was the young prince's foreskin. Since he had not yet wed his sister, the foreskin was as soft and supple as the day it had been cut from him. The old nurse took it from the wallet and shook it out, and it became as great and as wide and as warm as a cloak, and she wrapped him in it.

And the young prince smiled, closed his eyes, and rose up out of his body for his journey, leaving but a roughened hulk behind.

The first step he took went to the East where the sun hit him full in the face, leaving a bright red scar on his cheek. The next step he took went to the South where a branch of the world tree slapped him across the chest, and a sliver of wood slipped in under his nipple into the meat of his breast. The third step took him to the West where the wind whirled his cape up over his head and burnished his buttocks with hot sand.

But the fourth step took him to the North and the Cavern of Night, where all those who die have to go.

The way into the cavern was dark and winding, like the

stomach of a serpent. Ho ch'ok held aloft his mother's heart. The light it cast crept into all the pockets of the dark and sent the shadows screaming silently from its rays. At that Ho ch'ok smiled.

But as he went deeper into the cavern, even his mother's heart light grew dim.

"Oh, my mother," cried the young prince, "what am I to do?" And receiving no answer, he reached into his own breast through the opening made by the sliver of the world tree. But his heart would not leave his body, for he was not a woman. Still, there was just enough light from the opening of his chest with which to see, and so he went on.

After a while, he came to a cavern flooded with water that seemed to be both red and black. Ho ch'ok stopped, and bent close to the water but he could not tell if it was possible to cross.

He opened his sister's third eye and saw that that which was black was, indeed, water; but that which was red was a bridge of smooth stones. So being careful to step only on the stones, he started to the other side.

He was halfway across when his sister's eye, being tired, closed. And as he was a man he had no third eye of his own.

"Oh, my sister," cried Ho ch'ok, "what am I to do?"

He would have thrown himself down and wept except that a man does not do such a thing, except that he did not know how to tell the wet places from the dry. But as the first tear touched his cheek, it touched also the red scar. And where it touched the scar, the tear turned aside.

The young prince felt the turning of the tear, and so he bent down and, gathering up a handful of black water in his hand, he splashed it against his face. Where it touched the scar, the water turned roughly aside. So then Ho ch'ok did throw himself down, but not to weep. And when his face touched the water, the water rushed away from his sun scar and in this way he was able to walk upon dry land.

Soon he came to the farthest side and there he stopped, for ahead, in the feeble light, he could see three diverging paths. Guarding the paths was a giant vulture, the curved knife of its beak snapping at the shadows. At its feet were the bones of false princes who had gone before.

"Oh, my brother, Qich Mam," said the young prince, "may I use the weapon you have given me well." He took out the finger which had been kept in a pouch around his neck and held it in his right hand. There it grew and grew until it was a great spear as strong as muscle, as sharp as bone.

When the vulture saw the spear, it laughed, a sound like death itself, and the bones at its feet rose up and assembled themselves into a cage whose door gaped wide. Then the vulture sucked in a great breath which pulled Ho ch'ok forward until he was all but in the cage.

But the young prince took his spear and flung it at the vulture. It pierced the great bird's breast, but not very deep. With a snap of its curved knife of a beak, the vulture snapped the spear in two.

"Oh, my brother," Ho ch'ok cried, "what am I to do?"

The vulture leaned down and picked up the young prince by the back of his cape and shook him from side to side. But Ho ch'ok, like his brother, knew the trick of the little finger. Still, he did not break that one off, but instead broke the second finger, the one with which a man points to his eye to show that he understands. The finger grew into a spear even greater and sharper than the one Ho ch'ok had had before. With one mighty thrust, he pierced the vulture's breast exactly where the first had gone, thus sending the piece of Qich Mam's spear straight into the monster's heart.

Then Ho ch'ok gathered up the vulture's bones and locked tight the bone cage. Next he looked at the three paths, hoping to find a sign pointing the way.

The left path was rocky and narrow and there was barely room for a man to pass. The right path was smooth and wide, and an army could walk between. But the path in the middle was as dark and hidden as a secret.

Wrapping his cloak tightly around him, and trusting to the light of his heart, the young prince Ho ch'ok chose the secret path because the unknown way always holds the deepest rewards. And it was this path that led him safely to the garden of delights where all true princes live forever.

And if you, my children, can unriddle this tale, at the end of your days you may live in that garden as well.

The Sleep of Trees

*"Never invoke the gods unless
you really want them to appear.
It annoys them very much."*
—CHESTERTON

I t had been a long winter. Arrhiza had counted every line and
blister on the inside of the bark. Even the terrible binding
power of the heartwood rings could not contain her longings.
She desperately wanted spring to come so she could dance
free, once again, of her tree. At night she looked up and through
the spiky winter branches counted the shadows of early birds
crossing the moon. She listened to the mewling of buds making
their slow, painful passage to the light. She felt the sap veins
pulse sluggishly around her. All the signs were there, spring was
coming, spring was near, yet still there was no spring.

She knew that one morning, without warning, the rings
would loosen and she would burst through the bark into her
glade. It had happened every year of her life. But the painful
wait, as winter slouched towards its dismal close, was becoming
harder and harder to bear.

When Arrhiza had been younger, she had always slept the
peaceful, uncaring sleep of trees. She would tumble, half-awake,
through the bark and onto the soft, fuzzy green earth with the

other young dryads, their arms and legs tangling in that first sleepy release. She had wondered then that the older trees released their burdens with such stately grace, the dryads and the meliade sending slow green praises into the air before the real Dance began. But she wondered no longer. Younglings simply slept the whole winter dreaming of what they knew best: roots and bark and the untroubling dark. But aging conferred knowledge, dreams change. Arrhiza now slept little and her waking, as her sleep, was filled with sky.

She even found herself dreaming of birds. Knowing trees were the honored daughters of the All Mother, allowed to root themselves deep into her flesh, knowing trees were the treasured sisters of the Huntress, allowed to unburden themselves into her sacred groves, Arrhiza envied birds. She wondered what it would be like to live apart from the land, to travel at will beyond the confines of the glade. Silly creatures though birds were, going from egg to earth without a thought, singing the same messages to one another throughout their short lives, Arrhiza longed to fly with one, passengered within its breast. A bird lived but a moment, but what a moment that must be.

Suddenly realizing her heresy, Arrhiza closed down her mind lest she share thoughts with her tree. She concentrated on the blessings to the All Mother and Huntress, turning her mind from sky to soil, from flight to the solidity of roots.

And in the middle of her prayer, Arrhiza fell out into spring, as surprised as if she were still young. She tumbled against one of the birch, her nearest neighbor, Phyla of the white face. Their legs touched, their hands brushing one another's thighs.

Arrhiza turned toward Phyla. "Spring comes late," she sighed, her breath caressing Phyla's budlike ear.

Phyla rolled away from her, pouting. "You make Spring Greeting sound like a complaint. It is the same every year." She sat up with her back to Arrhiza and stretched her arms. Her hands were outlined against the evening sky, the second and third fingers slotted together like a leaf. Then she turned slowly towards Arrhiza, her woodsgreen eyes unfocused. In the soft, filtered light her body gleamed whitely and the darker patches were mottled beauty marks on her breasts and sides. She was up to her feet in a single fluid movement and into the Dance.

Arrhiza watched, still full length on the ground, as one after another the dryads and meliades rose and stepped into position, circling, touching, embracing, moving apart. The cleft of their legs flashed pale signals around the glade.

Rooted to their trees, the hamadryads could only lean out into the Dance. They swayed to the lascivious pipings of spring. Their silver-green hair, thick as vines, eddied around their bodies like water.

Arrhiza watched it all but still did not move. How long she had waited for this moment, the whole of the deep winter, and yet she did not move. What she wanted was more than this, this entering into the Dance on command. She wanted to touch, to walk, to run, even to dance when she alone desired it. But then her blood was singing, her body pulsating; her limbs stretched upward answering the call. She was drawn towards the others and, even without willing it, Arrhiza was into the Dance.

Silver and green, green and gold, the grove was a smear of color and wind as she whirled around and around with her sisters. Who was touched and who the toucher; whose arm, whose thigh was pressed in the Dance, it did not matter. The Dance was all. Drops of perspiration, sticky as sap, bedewed their backs and ran slow rivulets to the ground. The Dance *was* the glade, *was* the grove. There was no stopping, no starting, for a circle has no beginning or end.

Then suddenly a hunter's horn knifed across the meadow. It was both discordant and sweet, sharp and caressing at once. The

Dance did not stop but it dissolved. The Huntress was coming, the Huntress was here.

And then She was in the middle of them all, straddling a moon-beam, the red hem of Her saffron hunting tunic pulled up to expose muscled thighs. Seven hounds lay growling at Her feet. She reached up to Her hair and in one swift, savage movement, pulled at the golden cords that bound it up. Her hair cascaded like silver and gold leaves onto Her shoulders and crept in tendrils across Her small, perfect breasts. Her heart-shaped face, with its crescent smile, was both innocent and corrupt; Her eyes as dark blue as a storm-coming sky. She dismounted the moon shaft and turned around slowly, as if displaying Herself to them all, but She was the Huntress, and She was doing the hunting. She looked into their faces one at a time, and the younger ones looked back, both eager and afraid.

Arrhiza was neither eager nor afraid. Twice already she had been the chosen one, torn laughing and screaming from the glade, brought for a night to the moon's dark side. The pattern of the Huntress' mouth was burned into her throat's hollow, Her mark, just as Her words were still in Arrhiza's ears. "You are mine. Forever. If you leave me, I will kill you, so fierce is my love." It had been spoken each time with a kind of passion, in between kisses, but the words, like the kisses, were as cold and distant and pitiless as the moon.

The Huntress walked around the circle once again, pausing longest before a young meliáde, Pyrena of the appleblossoms. Under that gaze Pyrena seemed both to wither and to bloom. But the Huntress shook Her head and Her mouth formed the slightest moue of disdain. Her tongue flicked out and was caught momentarily between flawless teeth. Then She clicked to the hounds who sprang up. Mounting the moonbeam again, She squeezed it with Her thighs and was gone, riding to another grove.

The moment She disappeared, the glade was filled with breathy gossip.

"Did you see . . ." began Dryope. Trembling with projected pleasure, she turned to Pyrena, "The Huntress looked at you. Truly looked. Next time it *will* be you. I *know* it will."

Pyrena wound her fingers through her hair, letting fall a cascade of blossoms that perfumed the air. She shrugged but smiled a secret, satisfied smile.

Arrhiza turned abruptly and left the circle. She went back to her tree. Sluggishly the softened heartwood rings admitted her and she leaned into them, closed her eyes, and tried to sleep though she knew that in spring no true sleep would come.

She half-dreamed of clouds and birds, forcing them into her mind, but really she was hearing a buzzing. Sky, she murmured to herself, remember sky.

> *"Oh trees, fair and flourishing, on the high hills*
> *They stand, lofty.*
> *The Deathless sacred grove . . ."*

Jeansen practiced his Homeric supplication, intoning carefully through his nose. The words as they buzzed through his nasal passages tickled. He sneezed several times rapidly, a light punctuation to the verses. Then he continued:

> *". . . The Deathless sacred grove Men call them,*
> *And with iron never cut."*

He could say the words perfectly now, his sounds rounded and full. The newly learned Greek rolled off his tongue. He had always been a fast study. Greek was his fifth language, if he counted Esperanto. He could even, on occasion, feel the meanings that hid behind the ancient poetry, but as often the meanings slid away, slippery little fish and he the incompetent angler.

He had come to Greece because he wanted to be known as the American Olivier, the greatest classical actor the States had ever produced. He told interviewers he planned to learn Greek—classic Greek, not the Greek of the streets—to show them Oedipus from the amphitheaters where it had first been played. He would stand in the groves of Artemis, he had said, and call the Goddess to him in her own tongue. One columnist even suggested that with his looks and voice and reputation she would be crazy not to come. If she did, Jeansen thought to himself, smiling, I wouldn't treat her with any great distance. The goddesses like to play at shopgirls; the shopgirls, goddesses. And they all, he knew only too well, liked grand gestures.

And so he had traveled to Greece, not the storied isles of Homer but the fume-clogged port of Pyreus, where a teacher with a mouthful of broken teeth and a breath only a harpy could love had taught him. But mouth and breath aside, he was a fine teacher and Jeansen a fine learner. Now he was ready. Artemis first, a special for PBS, and then the big movie: Oedipus starring *the* Jeansen Forbes.

Only right now all he could feel was the buzz of air, diaphragm against lungs, lungs to larynx, larynx to vocal chords, a mechanical vibration. Buzz, buzz, buzz.

He shook his head as if to clear it, and the well-cut blonde hair fell perfectly back in place. He reached a hand up to check it, then looked around the grove slowly, admiringly. The grass was long, uncut, but trampled down. The trees—he had not noticed it at first—were a strange mixture: birch and poplar, apple and oak. He was not a botanist, but it seemed highly unlikely that such a mix would have simply sprung up. Perhaps they had been planted years and years ago. *Note to himself, check on that.*

This particular grove was far up on Mount Cynthus, away from any roads and paths. He had stumbled on it by accident. Happy accident. But it was perfect, open enough for re-enacting some of the supplicatory dances and songs, yet the trees thick enough to add mystery. The guide book said that Cynthus had once been sacred to the Huntress, virgin Artemis, Diana of the moon. He liked that touch of authenticity. Perhaps her ancient worshippers had first seeded the glade. Even if he could not find the documentation, he could suggest it in such a way as to make it sound true enough.

Jeansen walked over to one birch, a young tree, slim and gracefully bending. He ran his hands down its white trunk. He rubbed a leaf between his fingers and considered the camera focusing on the action. He slowed the movement to a sensuous stroking. *Close up of hand and leaf, full frame.*

Next to the birch was an apple, so full of blossoms there was a small fall of petals puddling the ground. He pushed them about tentatively with his boot. Even without wind, more petals drifted from the tree to the ground. *Long tracking shot as narrator kicks through the pile of white flowers, lap dissolve to a single blossom.*

Standing back from the birch and the apple tree, tall and unbending, was a mature oak. It looked as if it were trying to keep the others from getting close. Its reluctance to enter the circle of trees made Jeansen move over to it. Then he smiled at his own fancies. He was often, he knew, too fanciful, yet such invention was also one of his great strengths as an actor. He took off his knapsack and set it down at the foot of the oak like an offering. Then he turned and leaned against the tree, scratching between his shoulder blades with the rough bark. *Long shot of man in grove, move in slowly for tight close-up. Voice over.*

"But when the fate of death is drawing near,
First wither on the earth the beauteous trees,
The bark around them wastes, the branches fall,
And the Nymph's soul, at the same moment, leaves
The sun's fair light."

He let two tears funnel down his cheeks. Crying was easy. He could call upon tears whenever he wanted to, even before a word was spoken in a scene. They meant nothing anymore. *Extremely tight shot on tear, then slow dissolve to . . .*

A hand touched his face, reaching around him from behind. Startled, Jeansen grabbed at the arm, held, and turned.

"Why do you water your face?"

He stared. It was a girl, scarcely in her teens, with the clearest complexion he had ever seen and flawless features, except for a crescent scar at her throat which somehow made the rest more perfect. His experienced eyes traveled quickly down her body. She was naked under a light green chiffon shift. He wondered where they had gotten her, what she wanted. A part in the special?

"Why do you water your face?" she asked again. Then this time she added, "You are a man." It was almost a question. She moved around before him and knelt unself-consciously.

Jeansen suddenly realized she was speaking ancient Greek. He had thought her English with that skin. But the hair was black with blue-green highlights. Perhaps she *was* Greek.

He held her face in his hands and tilted it up so that she met him eye to eye. The green of her eyes was unbelievable. He thought they might be lenses, but saw no telltale double impression.

Jeansen chose his words with care, but first he smiled, the famous slow smile printed on posters and magazine covers.

"You," he said, pronouncing the Greek with gentle precision, his voice carefully low and tremulous, "you are a goddess."

She leaped up and drew back, holding her hands before her. "No, no," she cried, her voice and body registering such fear that Jeansen rejected it at once. This was to be a classic play, not a horror flick.

But even if she couldn't act, she was damned beautiful. He closed his eyes for a moment, imprinting her face on his memory. And he thought for a moment of her pose, the hands held up. There had been something strange about them. She had too many—or too few—fingers. He opened his eyes to check them, and she was gone.

"Damned bit players," he muttered at last, angry to have wasted so much time on her. He took the light tent from his pack and set it up. Then he went to gather sticks for a fire. It could get pretty cold in the mountains in early spring, or so he had been warned.

From the shelter of the tree, Arrhiza watched the man. He moved gracefully, turning, gesturing, stooping. His voice was low and full of music and he spoke the prayers with great force. Why had she been warned that men were coarse, unfeeling creatures? He was far more beautiful than any of the worshippers who came cautiously at dawn in their black-beetle dresses, creeping down the paths like great nicophorus from the hidden chambers of earth, to lift their year-scarred faces to the sky. They brought only jars of milk, honey, and oil, but he came bringing a kind of springy joy. And had he not wept when speaking of the death of trees, the streams from his eyes as crystal as any that ran near the grove? Clearly this man was neither coarse nor unfeeling.

A small breeze stirred the top branches, and Arrhiza glanced up for a moment, but even the sky could not hold her interest today. She looked back at the stranger, who was pulling oddments from his pack. He pounded small nails into the earth, wounding it with every blow, yet did not fear its cries.

Arrhiza was shocked. What could he be doing? Then she realized he was erecting a dwelling of some kind. It was unthinkable—yet this stranger had thought it. No votary would dare stay in a sacred grove past sunfall, dare carve up the soil on which the trees of the Huntress grew. To even think of being near when the Dance began was a desecration. And to see the Huntress, should She visit this glade at moonrise was to invite death. Arrhiza shivered. She was well-schooled in the history of Acteon, torn by his own dogs for the crime of spying upon Her.

Yet this man was unafraid. As he worked, he raised his voice—speaking, laughing, weeping, singing. He touched the trees with bold, unshaking hands. It was the trees, not the man, who trembled at his touch. Arrhiza shivered again, remembering the feel of him against the bark, the muscles hard under the fabric of his shirt. Not even the Huntress had such a back.

Then perhaps, she considered, this fearless votary was not a man at all. Perhaps he was a god come down to tease her, test her, take her by guile or by force. Suddenly, she longed to be wooed.

"You are a goddess," he had said. And it had frightened her. Yet only a god would dare such a statement. Only a god, such as Eros, might take time to woo. She would wait and let the night reveal him. If he remained untouched by the Huntress and unafraid, she would know.

Jeansen stood in front of the tent and watched the sun go down. It seemed to drown itself in blood, the sky bathed in an elemental red that was only slowly leeched out. Evening, however, was an uninteresting entire-act. He stirred the coals on his campfire and climbed into the tent. *Lap dissolve . . .*

Lying in the dark, an hour later, still sleepless, he thought about the night. He often went camping by himself in the California mountains, away from the telephone and his fans. *Intercut other campsites.* He knew enough to carry a weapon against marauding mountain lions or curious bears. But the silence of this Greek night was more disturbing than all the snufflings and howlings in the American dark. He had never heard anything so complete—no crickets, no wind, no creaking of trees.

He turned restlessly and was surprised to see that the tent side facing the grove was backlit by some kind of diffused lighting. Perhaps the moon. The tent had become a screen, and shadow women seemed to dance across it in patterned friezes. That had to be a trick of his imagination, trees casting silhouettes. Yet without wind, how did they move?

As he watched, the figures came more and more into focus, clearly women. This was no trick of imagination, but of human proposing. If it was one of the columnists or some of his erstwhile friends . . . Try to frighten him, would they? He would give them a good scare instead.

He slipped into his khaki shorts and found the pistol in his pack. Moving stealthily, he stuck his head out of the tent. And froze.

Instead of the expected projector, he saw real women dancing, silently beating out a strange exotic rhythm. They touched, stepped, circled. There was no music that he could hear, yet not one of them misstepped. And each was as lovely as the girl he had met in the grove.

Jeansen wondered briefly if they were local girls hired for an evening's work. But they were each so incredibly beautiful, it seemed unlikely they could all be from any one area. Then suddenly realizing it didn't matter, that he could simply watch and enjoy it, Jeansen chuckled to himself. It was the only sound in the clearing. He settled back on his haunches and smiled.

The moon rose slowly as if reluctant to gain the sky. Arrhiza watched it silver the landscape. Tied to its rising, she was pulled into the Dance.

Yet as she danced a part of her rested still within the tree, watching. And she wondered. Always before, without willing it, she was wholly a part of the Dance. Whirling, stepping along with the other dryads, their arms, her arms; their legs, her legs. But now she felt as cleft as a tree struck by a bolt. The watching part of her trembled in anticipation.

Would the man emerge from his hasty dwelling? Would he prove himself a god? She watched and yet she dared not watch, each turn begun and ended with the thought, the fear.

And then his head appeared between the two curtains of his house, his bare shoulders, his bronzed and muscled chest. His face registered first a kind of surprise, then a kind of wonder, and at last delight. There was no fear. He laughed and his laugh was more powerful than the moon. It drew her to him and she danced slowly before her god.

Setting: moon-lit glade. 30–35 girls dancing. No Bushy Berkley kick-lines, please. Try for a frenzied yet sensuous native dance. Robbins? Sharp? Ailey? Absolutely no dirndles. Light makeup. No spots. Diffused light. Music: an insistent pounding, feet on grass. Maybe a wild piping. Wide shot of entire dance then lap dissolve to single dancer. She begins to slow down, dizzy with anticipation, dread. Her god has chosen her . . .

Jeansen stood up as one girl turned slowly around in front of him and held out her arms. He leaned forward and caught her up, drew her to him.

A god is different, thought Arrhiza, as she fell into his arms. They tumbled onto the fragrant grass.

He was soft where the Huntress was hard, hard where She was soft. His smell was sharp, of earth and mold; Hers was musk and air.

"Don't leave," he whispered, though Arrhiza had made no movement to go. "I swear I'll kill myself if you leave." He pulled her gently into the canvas dwelling.

She went willingly though she knew that a god would say no such thing. Yet knowing he was but a man, she stayed and opened herself under him, drew him in, felt him shudder above her, then heavily fall. There was thunder outside the dwelling and the sound of dogs growling. Arrhiza heard it all, hearing, did not care. The Dance outside had ended abruptly. She breathed gently in his ear, "It is done."

He grunted his acceptance and rolled over onto his side, staring at nothing but a hero's smile playing across his face. Arrhiza put her hand over his mouth to silence him and he brought up his hand to hers. He counted the fingers with his own and sighed. It was then that the lightning struck, breaking her tree, her home, her heart, her life.

She was easy, Jeansen thought. Beautiful and silent and easy, the best sort of woman. He smiled into the dark. He was still smiling when the tree fell across the tent, bringing the canvas down around them and crushing three of his ribs. A spiky branch pierced his neck, ripping the larynx. He pulled it out frantically and tried to scream, tried to breathe. A ragged hissing of air through the hole was all that came out. He reached for the girl and fainted.

Three old women in black dresses found him in the morning. They pushed the tree off the tent, off Jeansen, and half carried, half dragged him down the mountainside. They found no girl.

He would live, the doctor said through gold and plaster teeth, smiling proudly.

Live. Jeansen turned the word over in his mind, bitterer than any tears. In Greek or in English, the word meant little to him now. *Live.* His handsome face unmarred by the fallen tree seemed to crack apart with the effort to keep from crying. He shaped the word with his lips but no sound passed them. Those beautiful, melodious words would never come again. His voice had leaked out of his neck with his blood.

Camera moves in silently for a tight close-up. Only sounds are routine hospital noises; and mounting over them to an overpowering cacophony is a steady, harsh, rasping breathing, as credits roll.

The Uncorking of Uncle Finn

ncle Finn had angered the Abbott. It had something to do with blasphemy—the Abbot's, not Uncle Finn's. Uncle had been converted several centuries before by the Irish saint, Patrick, and was deeply religious still, given to falling on his knees in the unlikeliest of places: rookeries, backstairs, tidal pools, butter churns. The Abbott, on the other hand, was a pagan and a drunk besides. It was inevitable that the two should clash over matters of faith.

Now I grant you that it is unnerving for the locals to have a fanatically Christianized elf forever exhorting them to eschew evil and seek the good, popping up unexpectedly in their most secret places of vice. He knew where every still was working, every mistress kept, every bit of falsified paper stored. He had a nose for venialness. But as he had been proselytizing for more than three centuries in his own curious way, one would have thought the humans would have grown used to it. And indeed, those who could stand it the least had long since left, moving to Killarney or Glocamorra or catching a ride with itin-

erant saints, sailing westward over the treacherous seas in cora-
cles made of glass. There were some just that desperate to escape
Uncle Finn's exhortations.

The Abbott, however, was newly appointed, being a sinner
of great reknown on the Continent. It was thought by the
bishop that a year or two in Kilkenny under the watchful eye of
Uncle Finn would wear him down. It was the bishop's own version of a finishing school, and he was prepared to finish the Abbot or kill him in the process.

The war had begun as soon as the Abbot had set foot in the
cellar, that being Uncle Finn's province. He was partial to dark
places; his maternal great-grandmother had once lived with a
troll, and Finn took after that side.

The Abbot's first trip to the cellar was without warning. He
had disconnected the bell that rang over the cellarer's head, a
precaution even his most fervid detractors had applauded. That
way, of course, no one could count the number of times he visited belowstairs. Kilkenny Abbey was well known not only for
its wines and a surprisingly good claret, but also for its hardier
brews: Kümmel made with an imported caraway seed, a plum
drink concocted with the help of a recipe lent by the Slovakian
saint Slivos, and a wild blackthorn gin that had been said to
rock even the toughest of European soldiery.

To say that Uncle Finn was surprised by the Abbot is an un-
derstatement. He was astonished out of three Hail Marys. They
bled from his lips and lost him the conversion of three recalci-
trant mice and a reprobate rat.

One must also imagine the Abbot's astonishment, for no one
had warned him about Uncle Finn. He had come tripping down
the stairs, ready for further lubrication, and suddenly there was
this wee attenuated creature garbed in green on knobby knees
before a congregation of reluctant rodents. Is it any wonder the
Abbot cried out and held his head? Or that Uncle Finn recipro-

cated with the bloody Hail Marys and an elvish curse that shattered three bottles of the best claret that the Abbot had hoped to save for after midnight Mass?

The Abbot fired the second shot of the war, a letter to the pope requesting excommunication for all faerie folk on the grounds that everyone knew they had no souls. But the pope refused the request, for he himself had once held similar views when he was but a seminarian. And then he had pronounced that his walking stick would sooner grow blossoms than a certain nixie of the local pond might enter heaven. He had not known she was a convert, one of the magdalens brought round by a recent crusade. No sooner had the words been out of his mouth, than his staff had sprouted a feathering of ferns and spatulate leaves and begun to bud. So the pope was not about to deny the possibility of souls to any of the Good Folk. In effect, he left the matter entirely in the bishop's hands.

This so displeased the Abbot, he turned his displeasure into a monumental drunk using the sacramental wine, a drunk that ended only when he awoke in his cell the Sunday before Lent to see Uncle Finn perched on his bedfoot, hands upraised, the spirit of the Lord and all the Irish saints moving in his mouth.

"Arise," cried Uncle Finn, "and go forth."

The Abbot arose, and his sandal went forth and smacked Uncle Finn right between the eyes while all the while the Abbot praised the Lord.

Now a sandal and Uncle Finn are about the same size, so there was more damage than either the Abbot or the Good Lord intended. So the Abbot was, indeed, forced to arise and scoop up Uncle Finn's body from the stone floor. He brought Uncle Finn, wrapped in a linen handkerchief, to the infirmarer, a certain Brother Elias.

"What can you do with this thing?" asked the Abbot. However, as he was holding Uncle Finn wrapped in the handkerchief in his left hand and his right was holding his own head (and it still ringing from the three days of steady drinking), it was no wonder Brother Elias's answer was confusing.

"If you'd stop bending your elbow, my lord Abbot," said the old monk, "your head would be marvelously improved. It's a wonder of anatomy, it is, that head and elbow are so connected." The infirmarer, being a reformed tippler himself, had plenty more salvos where that one came from. He had given up drink and taken up religion with the same fervor.

"Not my elbow and not my head, you Kilkenny clodpate! This!" The Abbot held out his left hand, where, in the linen, Uncle Finn was just coming to.

"Saints in heaven, but it's Finn," cried Elias, making the sign of the cross hastily and missing a fourth of it.

"That's not fine at all," said the Abbot, who had no tolerance for any accents save his own.

"Not fine, Finn," explained the infirmarer, but since he pronounced them the same, it led to a few more moments of misunderstanding until he reached over and gently removed Uncle Finn from his winding sheet. "You had better be asking his pardon, my lord. He's a Christian now for sure, which means he will turn the other cheek as often as not. But he's still quite a hand at elvish curses when he's riled. Better not to be on his bad side."

"He's already on *my* bad side," roared the Abbot, remembering with renewed fury the three bottles of claret. "Fix him up, tidy him up, and shut him up. Then report to me. The minute he can handle a good strong talking-to, I want to know."

But Finn was already beginning to sit up, and reaching his wee hands up to his wee head. What was not clear to the two monks was that Finn, while awake, was not aware. The sandal had quite addled him. His magic was turned around and about widdershins. He began to moan and speak in tongues.

"Oh, for Our Lord's sake," cried the Abbot with great feeling, his own head twanging like a tuning fork by the tone of those tongues.

The supplication to Our Lord brought Uncle Finn's eyes wide open, and he began to sing hosannas.

"I wish he'd put a cork in it!" cried the Abbot, his hands to his ears.

At the word *wish,* Finn's eyes got a strange glow in them, and everything not human in the room began to stir about as if caught up in a twisting wind. Faster and faster anything not pinned down began to move: glasses and retorts; bunches of drying patience, pepperwort, and clary; mortars and pestles: long lines of linen bandages; copies of *Popular Errors in Physick,* Mithradates' receipt for *Venice Treacle,* and Drayton's *Hermit.* All the while, Uncle Finn kept chanting:

> *Pickles and peas, knife and fork,*
> *Find a bottle, carve a cork,*
> *Wind it up and in the wine*
> *A sailor's life is mighty fine.*

Which, of course, is a terribly mixed-up version of the old bottle spell used mostly by drunken mages to call up spirits.

Sea winds began to blow, spouts of whales were sighted, dolphin clicks heard, and with one last incredible *whoooosh,* the whole of the whirling stuff was sucked in through the neck of a nearby bottle of Bordeaux '79 that Elias used for medicinal purposes only, it being too sour and full of sediment for a tippler of taste. The displaced wine splattered all over the infirmary, and the room smelled like a pothouse for a week.

Then, with a final *thwap,* the cork replaced itself. The stirring continued inside the bottle for fully a minute more, and when the wind and mist and moisture had resolved itself, there appeared inside the light green bottle a passable imitation of a sailing ship, with a pestle for a mainmast and linen bandages for sails. Clinging to the mortar steering wheel was Uncle Finn, looking both puzzled and pleased. He gave a weak smile in the direction of the cork, put his hand on his head, and slid down in a faint onto the papier-mâché deck on which the ingredients for *Venice Treacle* could still be discerned.

"Oh, my Lord," said the infirmarer, not really sure if he meant the salutation to have a capital *L* or a small one.

But the Abbot, taking it was himself addressed, said softly, "And *that* should do it."

For a week he was right, for the abbey was quiet and filled with plain-song laced only with the Abbot's own version of an old capstan chantey sung fully a half note off-tune.

But the communications of the Fey, while sometimes slow, are sure. The rodent proselytes told their families, one of whose members were overheard by a wandering and early June bug. The June bug's connections included a will-o'-the wisp who had married into Uncle Finn's family. It was scarcely a week later that word of Uncle Finn's incarceration came to my father's ears.

By the time he had sorted through his meager store of magicks and translated himself to the far side of the island, using a map in one of his books that was sadly too many years ahead of its time, twelve boggles, banshees, nuggles, and a ghost (all relatives) had been to visit before him. The abbey had, in that short week's time, gotten itself a reputation for being haunted—as indeed it was, in a manner of speaking—and the humans had summarily deserted the abbey grounds until the proper exorcists might be found.

None of this, of course, helped poor Uncle Finn. No one but a human could pull the cork from the Bordeaux bottle, for it had been placed there by a human wish. And as long as the visits continued, no human would venture near the place.

My father sighed and stared at his brother, whom he re-membered fondly as an elf of high promise and a great sense of humor. Uncle Finn looked little like the memory, being sadly faded and a bit green, a property not only of the tinted glass but of his initial handling, seasickness, and a week corked up in a bottle that still reeked of wine.

Father shouted at him and Finn shouted back, but their voices were strained through the layers of green glass. Conversation was impossible. At last Father came home, whey-faced and desperate-looking. In fact, all the relatives had left, for there was nothing any of them could do except sigh. As the last of them departed, the priestly exorcists arrived. Humans have this marvelous ability to time their exits and entrances, which is why they—and not the Fey—hold theatrical events. They spoke their magic words and threw about a great deal of incense and believed it was their own efforts that rid the abbey of the Fey. But like a plumber who gets paid after a sink has fixed itself, they were praised for nothing. Visiting Fey never overstay their welcome nor hang about when nothing can be done. It is simply not in our nature.

The Abbot had, of course, sworn Elias to secrecy concerning Uncle Finn and the bottle, and the two of them had replaced the Bordeaux '79 on the wine cellar racks without the cellarer's knowledge. But Elias, after a week in a room smelling strongly of tipple, returned to his old ways, and after that his vow of secrecy mattered little, for no one would have believed a word he had to say. As for the Abbot, after a year of the most flagrant misrule, he was sent by the pope on a crusade against the infidels from which he did not return, though there were frequent rumors that he had become a sheikh in a distant emirate and had banned all peris and jinn from his borders.

That left Uncle Finn corked up in his bottle on a back shelf in a cellar of a once-haunted Abbey, marked as a wine so degraded and unpopular that it would never be taken by any knowledgeable person from the shelf. And we were afraid he would remain so forever.

But one day, as I sat reading in my father's library, which is well stocked with books of the past, present, and future, I came upon a volume in section A. A for Archaeology, Astronomy, Ancestry, and Aphorisms. It was a splendid piece of serendipity, for the book told about the Americas, where, in some distant year, a man rich in coins but lacking in wisdom would take Kilkenny Abbey stone by stone over the great waters, a feat even a Merlin might envy. And—as one of the Aphorists wrote in another volume in that section, since Americans would have no wine before its time, surely the magical words "Bordeaux '79" will reek of such time. Uncle Finn, oh Uncle Finn, you will have before you an entire continent to convert, and proselytes beyond counting, for a land that saves its saviors in plaster and seeds the heavens with saucers should have no trouble at all accepting a bottle saint.

Dusty Loves

There is an ash tree in the middle of our forest on which my brother Dusty has carved the runes of his loves. Like the rings of its heartwood, the tree's age can be told by the number of carvings on its bark. *Dusty loves . . .* begins the legend high up under the first branches. Then the litany runs like an old tale down to the tops of the roots. Dusty has had many many loves, for he is the romantic sort. It is only in taste that he is wanting.

If he had stuck to the fey, his own kind, at least part of the time, Mother and Father would not have been so upset. But he had a passion for princesses and milkmaids, that sort of thing. The worst, though, was the time he fell in love with the ghost of a suicide at Miller's Cross. *That* is a story indeed.

It began quite innocently, of course. All of Dusty's love affairs do. He was piping in the woods at dawn, practicing his solo for the Solstice. Mother and Father prefer that he does his scales and runs as far from our pavilion as possible, for his notes excite the local wood doves, and the place is stained quite enough as it is. Ever dutiful, Dusty packed his pipes and a cress sandwich and made for a Lonely Place. Our forest has many such: dells silvered with dew, winding streams bedecked with morning mist, paths twisting between blood-red trilliums—all the accoutrements of Faerie. And when they are not cluttered with bad poets, they are really quite nice. But Dusty preferred human highways and by-ways, saying that such busy places were, somehow, the loneliest places of all. Dusty always had a touch of the poet himself, though his rhymes were, at best, slant.

He had just reached Miller's Cross and perched himself atop a standing stone, one leg dangling across the Anglo-Saxon in-scription, when he heard the sound of human sobbing. There was no mistaking it. Though we fey are marvelous at banshee wails and the low-throbbing threnodies of ghosts, we have not the ability to give forth that half gulp, half cry that is so pecu-liar to humankind, along with the heaving bosom and the wet-ted cheek.

Straining to see through the early-morning fog, Dusty could just make out an informal procession heading down the road toward him. So he held his breath—which, of course, made him invisible, though it never works for long—and leaned forward to get a better view.

There were ten men and women in the group, six of them carrying a coffin. In front of the coffin was a priest in his somber robes, an iron cross dangling from a chain. The iron made Dusty sneeze, for he is allergic and he became visible for a moment un-til he could catch his breath again. But such was the weeping and carryings-on below him, no one even noticed.

The procession stopped just beneath his perch, and Dusty gathered up his strength and leaped down, landing to the rear of the group. At the moment his feet touched the ground, the priest had—fortuitously—intoned, "Dig!" The men had set the coffin on the ground and begun. They were fast diggers, and the ground around the stone was soft from spring rains. Six men and six spades make even a deep grave easy work, though it was hardly a pretty sight, and far from the proper angles. And all the while they were digging, a plump lady in gray worsted, who looked upholstered rather than dressed, kept trying to fling herself into the hole. Only the brawny arms of her daughters on either side and the rather rigid stays of her undergarments kept her from accomplishing her gruesome task.

At last the grave was finished, and the six men lowered the coffin in while the priest sprinkled a few unkind words over the box, words that fell on the ears with the same thudding foreboding as the clods of earth upon the box. Then they closed the grave and dragged the weeping women down the road toward the town.

Now Dusty, being the curious sort, decided to stay. He let out his breath once the mourners had turned their backs on him, and leaped up onto his perch again. Then he began to practice his scales with renewed vigor, and had even gotten a good hold on the second portion of "Puck's Sarabande" when the moon rose. Of course, the laws of the incorporeal world being what they are, the ghost of the suicide rose, too. And that was when Dusty fell in love.

She was unlike her sisters, being petite and dark where they had been large and fair. She had two dimples, one that could be seen when she frowned and one when she smiled. Her hair was plaited with white velvet ribands and tied off with white baby's breath, which, if she had not been dead and a ghost, would certainly with have been wilted by then. There was a fringe of dark hair almost obscuring the delicate arch of her eyebrows. Her winding sheet became her.

Dusty jumped down and bowed low. She was so new at being a ghost, she was startled by him. Though he is tall for an elf, he is small compared to most humans and rarely startles anyone.

It is the ears, of course, that give him away. That, and the fact that, like most male feys, he is rather well endowed. The fig leaf was invented for human vanity. The solitary broad-leafed ginko was made for the fey. She covered her eyes with her hands, which, of course, did not help, since she could see right through her palms, bones and all.

"What are you?" she whispered. And then she added plaintively, "What am I?"

"You are dead," Dusty said. "And I am in love," foreplay being a word found only in human dictionaries.

But the ghost turned from him and began to weep. "Alas," she cried, "then it was all for naught, for where is my sweet Roman?"

Dusty tried again. "I will play Roman for you. Or even Greek." He will promise anything when he is in the early throes of love.

But the ghost only wept the dry tears of the dead, crying, "Roman is the name of the man I love. Where is he?"

"Obviously alive and well and pursuing other maidens," said Dusty, his forthright nature getting in the way of his wooing. "For if he were dead, he would be here with you. But *I* am here."

He tried to enfold her in his arms, but she slipped away as easily as mist.

"Are you, then, dead?" she asked.

"I am of the fey," he said.

But if she listened, it was not apparent, for she continued as if answers were not a part of conversation. "He must be dead. I saw him die. It is why *I* died. To be with him."

That, of course, decided Dusty. He was always a fool for lost causes. And I must say, from my readings of history, that I knew we would all have to watch him carefully in the 1780s, the 1860s, and the 1930s, 1950s, 1970s, and 1990s.

"Tell me, gracious lady," he said, careful to speak the elfin equivalent of the Shouting Voice, which is to say, well modulated. At that level the voice could bring milk from a maiden's breast, cause graybeards to dance, and stir love in even the coldest heart.

But the suicide's ghost seemed immune. She wrung her hands into vapor, but did not step an inch closer to Dusty's outstretched arms. Sometimes the voice works, and sometimes it does not.

So, shrugging away his disappointment, Dusty tried again, this time in a more natural tone. "Start from the beginning. I may have missed something important, coming in the middle like this."

The ghost settled herself daintily some three feet above the ground, crossed her ankles prettily, and offered him her smiling dimple. "My name is . . . or was . . . oh, how *do* these things work in the afterlife?"

"Do not worry about niceties," Dusty said, patting her hand and the air beneath it at the same time. "Just begin already." I do believe it was this moment he began falling out of love. But he will never admit to that.

She sniffled angelically and pouted, showing him the other dimple. "My name is Julie. And I was in love . . . am in love . . . oh, dear!" She began to cry anew.

Dusty offered a webkerchief to her. She reached for it, and it fell between them, for, of course, she could no more touch it then Dusty could touch her. She wiped her nose, instead, on the winding sheet.

"Go on," Dusty said, blushing when she looked at him with gratitude. He often mistook such human emotions as gratitude, sympathy, and curiosity for love.

"My own true love is Roman. It is a family name, but I like it."

"A fine name," Dusty agreed hastily, having bitten back the response that children should be named after natural things like sunshine, dust, and rainbows, not unnatures like cities, countries, and empires.

Warming to her tale, Julie the ghost began to catalog her own true love's charms, an adolescent litany of cheeks, hair, muscles, and thews that anyone but another adolescent would have found unbearable. As it was, Dusty was as busy listing Julie's charms. They were certainly a pair.

The families, it seems, were feuding. Something about a pig and a poke. Dusty never did get it straight. But the upshot was that Roman's parents would not let him marry Julie, and Julie's parents would not let her marry Roman. Such are the judicious settlements of humankind.

So the two, instead of finding a sensible solution—like moving to Verona, changing their names, or buying both sets of parents new pigs and new pokes—decided on suicide as the answer. Answer! They had not even discovered the right question.

But of course, Dusty agreed with her. Even the fey have hormonal imbalances, which is all that measures the difference between adolescent and adult.

"What you need now," Dusty said in his sensible voice, "is to reunite with your own true love."

Julie began another cascade of tears. "But that is impossible. He is alive. And I am . . . I am . . ."

"Not alive," Dusty said, being as tactful as could be under the circumstances.

"Dead!" Julie finished unhappily, the cascade having become a torrent.

"But you thought he was dead," Dusty said.

"I found him lying in a pool of blood," she answered. "There was blood on his hands and on his face and on his coat and on his . . ." She blushed prettily and hid her face with her hands again.

Dusty admired her sly smile through the transparent bones.

"Everywhere!" she finished.

"Did you look for a wound?" Dusty asked.

"Blood makes me urpy," she admitted.

"Urpy?" If her giddiness had not already begun to change his mind, her vocabulary certainly would. *"Urpy?"*

"You know—throw-uppins."

He nodded, looking a bit throw-uppins himself. "So you did not look."

"No. I ran to my nurse and told her I had a headache. A very bad headache. And borrowed a powder. A very strong powder. And . . ."

"And lay down by Roman's side, having drunk the powder in a tisane. Folding your hands over your pretty bosom and spreading your skirts about you like a scallop shell."

She made a moue. "How did you know! Did you see us?"

He sighed. "My sister told me the story. She read it in one of our father's books. His library is vast and has tomes from the past and the future as well. Only, I'd better tell you the rest. Roman is not dead."

"Not dead?" She said it with less surprise than before. "How?"

"Who knows? Animal's blood or tomato sauce or spilled wine. Who knows?"

"Roman knows," she said vehemently. Then she stopped. "Why are you laughing?"

How could he explain it to her? Humor is difficult enough between consenting adults. It is impossible intraspecies. Dolphins do not trade laughs with wolves, nor butterflies joke with whales. Puns have a life span half the length of a pratfall. He fell out of love abruptly. But there was still enough attraction left for him to want to help her out.

"You must convince Roman to die," he said. "Only then can he join you."

"How?"

"Haunt him."

And so the haunting began.

Dusty was right, of course. Roman had already begun looking for alternatives. He had a passion for slatterns and sculleries, an interest that had apparently begun long before his dalliance with Julie. She would have been disappointed in him within the course of a normal year—that is, if she had not found him basted like a beef on a platter. Perhaps he had guessed it and had knowingly provoked her into death. If so, Dusty was right about the haunting.

But Julie forgave him, for spirits are so set in their ways. They long for what lingered last. She believed in Roman despite the evidence of her ears and eyes. It led, of course, to a spectacular single-minded haunting.

Poor Roman. He never had a chance. Whenever he was about to place his well-manicured hand upon a maidenly breast, Julie's ghost appeared. She sighed. She swooned. She wailed. She wept. What passion he had, fled. As did the maid to hand.

Dusty enjoyed it all enormously. He coached Julie in every nuance of necromancy: the hollow tones, the fetid breath, the call from beyond the grave. It turned out she had genius for spirit work, a sepulchral flair. Within the week, Roman was on his knees by her grave, begging for release.

Dusty supplied a knife.

Roman ignored it.

Dusty supplied a noose.

Roman ignored it.

Dusty supplied a vial of poison.

Roman joined a monastery, gagged on the plain food, choked on the sweet wine, and longed to talk to his neighbor.

He escaped less than a month later over the wall, his habit rucked up around his knees, his sandals in hand.

"Your poor hair," sighed Julie to him as he prostrated himself below the standing stone. The memory of her hand stirred the strand of golden fuzz over his tonsure.

"Give me a month to grow it back, and I will join you, my love," he said, smiling up at her. There was larceny in his smile, though she did not recognize it.

"A month I can wait," she said magnanimously. "Even two. But no more."

Dusty, sitting atop the standing stone, made a face. He might not be able to read a woman's heart, but men were no trouble to him at all.

Within the first month, Roman had converted his inheritance to cash and sailed off with a Portuguese upstart to find a brave new world, leaving Julie far behind. Ghosts, as Roman knew full well, cannot travel over water. Particularly not across a vast sea. But he could not outrun his promise. He died on a foreign shore, a poison dart between his eyes and eaten by cannibals directly after. A windspirit brought us the word. He had died messily, with Julie's name upon his lips. She liked that part.

Julie dictated her story, slightly changed, into the ear of a fine-looking poet some years later. He called her his muse, his dark lady, his spirit guide. That so impressed her, she left off haunting and took up musing with a vengeance.

Dusty went away in disgust and found a compliant milkmaid instead, with soft hands, warm thighs, and a taste for the exotic. But that, of course, is another story and not nearly as interesting or as repeatable.

The Gift of the Magicians,
with Apologies to You Know Who

One gold coin with the face of George II on it, whoever *he* was. Three copper pennies. And a crimped tin thing stamped with a fleur-de-lis. That was all. Beauty stared down at it. The trouble with running a large house this far out in the country, even *with* magical help, was that there was never any real spending money. Except for what might be found in the odd theatrical trunk, in the secret desk drawer, and at the bottom of the pond every spring when it was drained. Three times she had counted: one gold, three coppers, one tin. And the next day would be Christmas.

There was clearly nothing for her to do but flop down on the Victorian sofa, the hard one with the mahogany armrests, and howl. So she did. She howled as she had heard him howl, and wept and pounded the armrests for good measure. It made her feel ever so much better. Except for her hands, which now hurt abominably. But that's the trouble with Victorian sofas. Whatever *they* were.

The whole house was similarly accoutered: Federal, Empire,

Art Deco, Louis Quinze. With tags on each explaining the name and period. Names about which she knew nothing, but which the house had conjured up out of the past, present, and future. None of it was comfortable, though clearly all of it—according to the tags—was expensive. She longed for the simpler days at home with Papa and her sisters, when even a penniless Christmas after dear Papa had lost all his money meant pleasant afternoons in the kitchen baking presents for the neighbors.

Now, of course, she had no neighbors. And her housemate was used to so much better than her meager kitchen skills could offer. Even if the magical help would let her into the kitchen, which they—it or whatever—would not do.

She finished her cry, left off the howling, and went down the long hallway to her room. There she found her powder and puffs and repaired the damage to her complexion speedily. He liked her bright and simple and smelling of herself, and magical cosmetics could do *such* wonders for even the sallowest of skins.

Then she looked into the far-seeing mirror—there were no windows in the house—and saw her old gray cat Miaou walking on a gray fence in her gray backyard. It made her homesick all over again, even though dear Papa was now so poor, and she had only one gold, three coppers, one tin with which to buy Beast a present for Christmas.

She blinked and wished, and the mirror became only a mirror again, and she stared at her reflection. She thought long and hard and pulled down her red hair, letting it fall to its full length, just slightly above her knees.

Now there were two things in that great magical house far out in the country in which both she and the Beast took great pride. One was Beast's gold watch, because it was his link with the real past, not the magical, made-up past. The watch had been his father's and his grandfather's before him, though everything else had been wiped away in the spell. The other thing was Beauty's hair, for, despite her name, it was the only thing beautiful about her. Had Rapunzel lived across the way instead of in the next kingdom, with her handsome but remarkably stupid husband, Beauty would have worn her hair down at every opportunity just to depreciate Her Majesty's gifts.

So now Beauty's hair fell over her shoulders and down past her waist, almost to her knees, rippling and shining like a cascade of red waters. There was a magical hush in the room, and she smiled to herself at it, a little shyly, a little proudly. The house admired her hair almost as much as Beast did. Then she bound it all up again, sighing because she knew what she had to do.

A disguise. She needed a disguise. She would go into town— a two-day walk, a one-day ride; but with magic, only a short, if bumpy, ten minutes away—in disguise. She opened the closet and wished very hard. On went the old brown leather bomber jacket. The leather outback hat. She took a second to tear off the price tags. Tucking the silk bodice into the leather pants, she ran her hands down her legs. Boots! She would need boots. She wished again. The thigh-high leather boots were a fine touch. Checking in the mirror, she saw only her gray cat.

"Pooh!" she said to the mirror. Miaou looked up startled, saw nothing, moved on.

With a brilliant sparkle in her eyes, she went out of the bedroom, down the stairs, across the wide expanse of lawn, toward the gate.

At the gate, she twisted her ring twice. ("Once for home, twice for town, three times for return," Beast had drummed into her when she had first been his guest. Never mind the hair. The ring was her *most* precious possession.)

Ten bumpy minutes later, she landed in the main street of the town.

As her red hair was tucked up into the outback hat, no one

recognized her. Or if they did, they only bowed. No one called her by name. This was a town used to disguised gentry. She walked up and down the street for a few minutes, screwing up her courage. Then she stopped by a sign that read MADAME SUZ-ZANE: HAIR GOODS AND GONE TOMORROW.

Beauty ran up the steep flight of stairs and collected herself.

Madame Suzzane was squatting on a stool behind a large wooden counter. She was a big woman, white and round and graying at the edges, like a particularly dangerous mushroom.

"Will you buy my hair?" Beauty asked.

"Take off that silly hat first. Where'd you get it?" Her voice had a mushroomy sound to it, soft and spongy.

"In a catalog," Beauty said.

"Never heard of it."

The hat came off. Down rippled the red cascade.

"Nah—can't use red. Drug on the market. Besides, if . . . He . . . knew." If anything, Madame Suzzane turned whiter, grayer.

"But I have nothing else to sell." Beauty's eyes grew wider, weepy.

"What about that ring?" Madame Suzanne asked, pointing.

"I can't."

"You can."

"I can't."

"You can."

"How much?"

"Five hundred dollars," said Madame Suzanne, adding a bit for inflation. And for the danger.

Beauty pulled the ring off her finger, forgetting everything in her eagerness to buy a gift for Beast. "Quickly, before I change my mind."

• • •

She ran down the stairs, simultaneously binding up her hair again and shoving it back under the hat. The street seemed much longer much more filled with shops now that she had money in her hands. Real money. Not the gold coin, copper pennies, and crimped tin thing in her pocket.

The next two hours raced by as she ransacked the stores looking for a present for Beast and, not unexpectedly, finding a thing or two for herself: some nail polish in the latest color from the Isles, a faux-pearl necklace with a delicious rhinestone clasp, the most delicate china faun cavorting with three shepherdesses in rosebud-pink gowns, and a painting of a jester so cleverly limned on black velvet that would fit right over her poster bed.

And then she found Beast's present at last, a perfect tortoise-shell comb for his mane, set with little battery-driven (whatever *that* was) lights that winked on and off and on again. She had considered a fob for his grandfather's watch, but the ones she saw were all much too expensive. And besides, the old fob that came with the watch was still in good shape, for something old. And she doubted whether he'd have been willing to part with it anyway. Just like Beast, preferring the old to the new, preferring the rough to the smooth, preferring her to . . . to . . . to someone like Rapunzel.

Then, with all her goodies packed carefully in a string bag purchased with the last of her dollars, she was ready to go.

Only, of course, she hadn't the ring anymore. And no one would take the gold coin or the copper pennies or the crimped tin thing for a carriage and horse and driver to get her back. Not even with her promise made, cross her heart, to fill their pockets with jewels once they got to Beast's house. And the horse she was forced to purchase with the gold and copper and tin crimped thing began coughing at the edge of town, and broke down completely somewhere in the woods to the north. So she had to walk after all, all through the night frightened at every fluttering leaf, at every silent-winged owl, at all the beeps and cheeps and chirps and growls along the way.

Near dawn on Christmas Day, Beast found her wandering alone, smelling of sweat and fear and the leather bomber jacket and leather hat and leather boots and the polished nails. Not smelling like Beauty at all.

So of course he ate her, Christmas being a tough hunting day, since every baby animal and every plump child was tucked up at home waiting for dawn and all their presents.

And when he'd finished, he opened the string bag. The only thing he saved was the comb.

Beauty was right. It *was* perfect.

Sister Death

You have to understand, it is not the blood. It was never the blood. I swear that on my own child's heart, though I came at last to bear the taste of it, sweetly salted, as warm as milk from the breast.

The first blood I had was from a young man named Abel, but I did not kill him. His own brother had already done that, striking him down in the middle of a quarrel over sheep and me. The brother preferred the sheep. How like a man.

Then the brother called me a whore. His vocabulary was remarkably basic, though it might have been the shock of his own brutality. The name itself did not offend me. It was my profession, after all. He threw me down on my face in the bloody dirt and treated me like one of his beloved ewes. I thought it was the dirt I was eating.

It was blood.

Then he beat me on the head and back with the same stick he had used on his brother, till I knew only night. *Belilah.* Like my name.

How long I lay there, unmoving, I was never to know. But when I came to, the bastard was standing over me with the authorities, descrying my crime, and I was taken as a murderess. The only witnesses to my innocence—though how can one call a whore innocent—were a murderer and a flock of sheep. Was it any wonder I was condemned to die?

Oh how I ranted in that prison. I cursed the name of G-d, saying: "Let the day be darkness wherein I was born and let G-d not inquire about it for little does He care. A woman is nothing in His sight and a man is all, be he a murderer or a thief." Then I vowed not to die at all but to live to destroy the man who would destroy me. I cried and I vowed and then I called on the demonkin to save me. I remembered the taste of blood in my mouth and offered that up to any who would have me.

One must be careful of such prayers.

The night before I was to be executed, Lord Beelzebub himself entered my prison. How did I know him? He insinuated himself through the keyhole as mist, reforming at the foot of my pallet. There were two stubby black horns on his forehead. His feet were like pigs' trotters. He carried around a tail as sinuous as a serpent. His tongue, like an adder's, was black and forked.

"You do not want a man, Lillake," he said, using the pretty pet name my mother called me. "A demon can satisfy you in ways even you cannot imagine."

"I am done with lovemaking," I answered, wondering that he could think me desirable. After a month in the prison I was covered with sores. "Except for giving one a moment's pleasure, it brings nothing but grief."

The mist shaped itself grandly. "This," he said pointing, "is more than a moment's worth. You will be well repaid."

"You can put that," I gestured back, "into another keyhole. Mine is locked forever."

One does not lightly ignore a great lord's proposal, nor

make light of his offerings. It was one of the first things I had learned. But I was already expecting to die in the morning. And horribly. So, where would I spend his coin?

"Lillake, hear me," Lord Beelzebub said, his voice no longer cozening but black as a burnt cauldron. *Shema* was the word he used. I had not known that demons could speak the Lord G-d's holy tongue.

I looked up, then, amazed, and saw through the disguise. This was no demon at all but the Lord G-d Himself testing me, though why He should desire a woman—and a whore at that— I could not guess.

"I know you, *Adonai,*" I said. "But God or demon, my answer is the same. Women and children are nothing in your sight. You are a bringer of death, a maker of carrion."

His black aspect melted then, the trotters disappeared, the horns became tendrils of white hair. He looked chastened and sad and held out His hand.

I disdained it, turning over on my straw bed and putting my face to the wall.

"It is no easy thing being at the Beginning and at the End," He said. "And so you shall see, my daughter. I shall let you live, and forever. You will see the man, Cain, die. Not once but often. It will bring you no pleasure. You will be Death's sister, chaste till the finish of all time, your mouth filled with the blood of the living."

So saying, He was gone, fading like the last star of night fading into dawn.

Of course I was still in prison. So much for the promises of G-d.

At length I rose from the mattress. I could not sleep. Believing I had but hours before dying, I did not wish to waste a moment of the time left, though each moment was painful. I walked to the single window where only a sliver of moon was visible. I put my hands between the bars and clutched at the air as though I could hold it in my hands. And then, as if the air itself had fallen in love with me, it gathered me up through the bars, lifted me through the prison wall, and deposited me onto the bosom of the dawn and I was somehow, inexplicably, free.

Free.

As I have been these five thousand years.

Oh, the years have been kind to me. I have not aged. I have neither gained nor lost weight nor grayed nor felt the pain of advancing years. The blood has been kind to me, the blood I nightly take from the dying children, the true innocents, the Lord G-d's own. Yet for all the children I have sucked rather than suckled, there has been only one I have taken for mine.

I go to them all, you understand. There is no distinction. I take the ones who breathe haltingly, the ones who are misused, the ones whose bodies are ill shaped in the womb, the ones whom fire or famine or war cut down. I take them and suck them dry and send them, dessicated little souls, to the Lord G-d's realm. But as clear-eyed as I had been when I cast out *Adonai* in my prison, so clear-eyed would a child need to be to accept me as I am and thus become my own. So for these five thousand years there has been no one for me in my lonely occupation but my mute companion, the Angel of Death.

If I could still love, he is the one I would desire. His wings are the color of sun and air as mine are fog and fire. Each of the vanes in those wings are hymnals of ivory. He carries the keys to Heaven in his pocket of light. Yet he is neither man nor woman, neither demon nor god. I call the Angel "he" for as I am Sister Death, he is surely my brother.

We travel far on our daily hunt.
We are not always kind.

But the child, my child, I will tell you of her now. It is not a pretty tale.

As always we travel, the Angel and I, wingtips apart over a landscape of doom. War is our backyard, famine our feast. Most fear the wind of our wings and even, in their hurt, pray for life. Only a few, a very few, truly pray for death. But we answer all their prayers with the same coin.

This particular time we were tracking across the landscape of the Pale, where grass grew green and strong right up to the iron railings that bore the boxcars along. In the fields along the way, the peasants swung their silver scythes in rhythm to the trains. They did not hear the counterpoint of cries from the cars or, if they did, they showed their contempt by stopping and waving gaily as the death trains rolled past.

They did not see my brother Death and me riding the screams but inches overhead. But they would see us in their own time.

In the cars below, jammed together like cattle, the people vomited and pissed on themselves, on their neighbors, and prayed. Their prayers were like vomit, too, being raw and stinking and unstoppable.

My companion looked at me, tears in his eyes. I loved him for his pity. Still crying, he plucked the dead to him like faded flowers, looking like a bridegroom waiting at the feast.

And I, no bride, flew through the slats, to suck dry a child held overhead for air. He needed none. A girl crushed by the door. I took her as well. A teenager, his head split open by a soldier's gun, died unnoticed against a wall. He was on the cusp of change but would never now be a man. His blood was bitter in my mouth but I drank it all.

What are Jews that nations swat them like flies? That the Angel of Death picks their faded blooms? That I drink the blood, now bitter, now sweet, of their children?

The train came at last to a railway yard that was ringed about with barbs. BIRKENAU, read the station sign. It creaked back and forth in the wind. BIRKENAU.

When the train slowed, then stopped, and the doors pushed open from the outside, the living got out. The dead were already gathered up to their G-d.

My companion followed the men and boys, but I—I flew right above the weeping women and their weeping children, as I have done all these years.

There was another Angel of Death that day, standing in the midst of the madness. He hardly moved, only his finger seemed alive, an organism in itself, choosing the dead, choosing the living.

"Please, Herr General," a boy cried out. "I am strong enough to work."

But the finger moved, and having writ, moved on. To the right, boy. To the arms of Lilith, Belilah, Lillake.

"Will we get out?" a child whispered to its mother.

"We will get out," she whispered back.

But I had been here many times before. "You will only get out of here through the chimney," I said.

Neither mother nor child nor General himself heard.

There were warning signs at the camp. BEWARE, they said. TENSION WIRE, they said.

There were other signs, too. Pits filled with charred bones. Prisoners whose faces were imprinted with the bony mask of death.

JEDEM DAS SEINE. Each one gets what he deserves.

In the showers, the naked mothers held their naked children to them. They were too tired to scream, too tired to cry. They had no tears left.

Only one child, a seven-year-old, stood alone. Her face was angry. She was not resigned. She raised her fist and looked at the heavens and then, a little lower, at me.

Surprised, I looked back.

The showers began their rain of poison. Coughing, praying, calling on G-d to save them, the women died with their children in their arms.

The child alone did not cough, did not pray, did not call on G-d. She held out her two little hands to me. *To me.*

"Imma," she said. "Mother."

I trembled, flew down, and took her in my arms. Then we flew through the walls as if they were air.

So I beg you, as you love life, as you master Death, let my brother be the sole harvester. I have served my five thousand years; not once did I complain. But give me a mother's span with my child, and I will serve you again till the end of time. The child alone chose me in all those years. You could not be so cruel a god as to part us now.

The Singer and the Song

Once in the service of the High King of Elb there was a musician named Lark. He could play the plekta till its three strings rang like thirty. He could blow the tenor netto till it wailed like a woman in labor. And when he sang, his voice was so pure, it was said that he spoke a hundred truths in a single breath.

Everyone loved Lark, but none more than the young prince of Elb. Whenever he heard Lark sing, the prince would put his small hand in the musician's, look up at him, and say: "Oh, Lark, you are the fairest and truest of all the men in my father's kingdom."

On hearing that, Lark would squat down on his heels so that he could look the boy right in the eye. "Do not confuse the singer with the song, my prince" he would say.

The prince did not believe him, of course. Princes believe what they will. But many years later, on the day the poor folk of the land rose up against the High King, Lark made a song for their victory. In it he rhymed "tyrant" in a dozen different ways, which one could do in the old tongue.

"I thought you were true," whispered the prince to Lark, when they took the entire royal family out of the dungeon to be hanged. "I thought you were the fairest in the kingdom," the prince said as the rope was put around his neck.

But Lark did not answer. He only smiled at the prince. For *he* had never confused the king with the crown, the rope with justice, or the singer with the song.

Salvage

The old poet lay in the bow of his ship, dying of space sickness and homesickness and a touch of alien flu. There was nothing to be done for him but to make him comfortable, which meant listening to his ramblings and filling his arm with a strange liquid from his own stores. He had been the only one left alive in the ship when we found it and at first we had thought him dead, too. Only at my touch, he had roused up, pointed a stalk at us, and recited in a bardic chant some alien click-clacks that, run through the translator, turned out to be a spell against goblins and ghoulies and things that go bump in the night.

Whatever night is.

Ghoulies was his name for us.

He had immediately fallen back into a deep sleep from which he roused periodically to harangue whoever had a free moment, calling us *worms* and *devils* and *satan's spawn*. Most of us decided to leave his mouthings untranslated since what spewed out of the machine made little sense and we had not time to properly salvage it. The boxes, after all, were not yet full.

But one of the younglings, a two-year named Necros 29, chose to sit with the poet-traveler and translate his every word. Necros 29 called it salvage, but I wondered. He comes from a family of puzzlers, though, and they are slow to mature and mate. It may be that that side of the line runs true, for it was he who first understood that the creature was a poet, or at least a speaker-of-poems. It was soon clear that the alien did not make up his poems as would any true poet, but rather carried the words of others in his head. Disgusting thought, a crime against nature, this salvage of the mind. If we saved up all our poems, our heads would soon be so crowded with them there would be no room left for savoring new ones. What a strange race we had come upon, whose equipment is new and whose thoughts are so borrowed and old.

But Necros, being a puzzler, kept at his task while we scavenged the ship thoroughly. It was full of salvage and the bones of the poet's companions were especially fine.

"He calls upon the names of many gods," commented Necros to me during report, "and that is fine for a poet. But he also says many not-found things."

"Such as?" I asked. My great-great-grandsire, Mordos Prime, had been a puzzler on his matriarchal side, though my mother denies it when asked. Occasionally I am drawn to such things, though basically I am of a solider nature.

"He speaks of night, a darkness that ends and comes again."

I passed the bones through my mouth and into the salvage sack before I spoke. They were, as I have said, very fine indeed. As the sack's teeth ground the bones into dust, I said, "Is night then a birthing cave? Is it the winking of far stars against the Oneness of space?"

Many who heard me laughed, their sections wiggling greatly with their amusement.

Necros shook his head and his eyestalks trembled. "I do not think so. But I will listen to him further. I think there may be some strong salvage in his thoughts."

"Pah, it is worthless stuff," remarked my old mate, the long cylinder of his head shaking. His salvage sack was full and grinding away, and the rolling action of it under his belly excited me. But now was the time of work, not pleasure. The boxes were not yet full and it would be days more of grinding before our organs descended enough to touch.

I went back across the boarding platform that linked the silent ship to ours. I emptied my sack of the fine silt, spreading it thinly over the mating box. Days? It would be weeks if we did not fill the boxes faster. As Prime of this ship it was my duty to direct young Necros away from the live poet to the dead and salvageable parts. It is all very well to salvage a culture when the boxes are full, but—and I remembered my old mate's rolling sack—there is an order, after all, and poetry would have to wait.

Mouthing a small lump of unground bone out of the box, I swallowed it again. Then I turned back and crossed over the platform to the alien ship.

"Necros!" I called out as I crawled. "Come. I would talk with you."

He came at once though with a slight reluctance on his face, his stalks drooping and his first section slightly faded. I think he already knew what I had to say.

"The boxes are thin," I said. "There is no time for him." I gestured with a stalk towards the alien who raised on one side and was babbling again.

"Fe-fi-fo-fum," spewed the translator. Nonsense in any language is still nonsense. "Be he live or be he dead, I'll grind his bones to make my bread."

"What in the universe is bread?" I asked.

Necros touched me, mouth to mouth, then raised his chin, showing me his neck section, the fine lumps of his heart beating a rhythm through the translucent skin. He could not have been more subservient.

"I will work long into the third work period," he said. "Do you not see that it is such things—bread, night, seasons—that we must salvage from him. *Only with salvage*," he reminded me, "*is growth.*"

I thought of the silty boxes where we would soon lie down and mate, starting the next generation wiggling through our bodies and out our mouths. "Yes," I said at last, "you are right this time. But still you will have to work the extra period to make up for it."

He quivered sectionally and scurried back to the alien. At his touch, the alien fainted, though I suspected that he would revive again soon.

Necros 29 kept his word. He worked the extra load, and so much salvage quickened him. He entered maturity early yet lost none of the enthusiasm of a youngling. It was dreadful to see.

Once he came to me wriggling with joy. "I have come to something new," he said. "Something not-found which is now found. It is called *haiku*." He savored the word and gave it directly into my mouth.

I let the word slide down slowly, section by section, to my sack and the slow grinding began. Then it stopped. "I do not comprehend this word, *haiku*," I said. "It means no more than his fe-fi's."

Necros shivered deliciously. "It is a poem that is worked in sections," he said.

"A poem in sections?" It *was* a new idea—and quite fine.

"There are seventeen sections broken into bodies of five-seven-five. And there are rules."

"That is the first your poet has shown that he understands order," I said thoughtfully. "Perhaps I was right to let you salvage him."

Necros nodded, showing his neck section for good measure. "These are the rules. First the poem must rouse emotion."

"Well, of course. Any youngling knows that." I turned partly away from him, to show my displeasure.

"Wait, there is more. Second, the poem must show spiritual insight." He nodded his head and his sections moved like a wave, enticing.

"Still, that is not new."

Necros drew out the last. "And finally there must be some use of the seasons."

"Fe-fi's again."

"I am comprehending that piece of alienness slowly. Digestion is difficult. The grinding continues."

"Perhaps," I replied coolly. "it should not continue."

"But I am working triple," Necros said, twisting his head back in such alarm that the lumps of heart were pounding madly in front of my mouth. "And we have salvaged all but the ship's shell and the room where the poet lies." His voice was strained by his effort to show me his chin.

"It is true that the boxes grow full and my desires descend," I admitted. "How long will this salvage take?"

He shrugged. "The poet's voice weakens. He speaks again and again of *the night.*" He dared to lower his chin. "*Night* is, I am beginning to think, the ultimate alien season. Perhaps I will comprehend it soon."

"Perhaps you will," I said, turning without giving him any promises.

. . .

The next work section I was sleeping, with my body pressed along the sleek gray ship's side, dreaming of mating. I had grown so much with the salvage that I was now nearly half the length of the alien vessel, and my movements were slow.

Necros found me there and quivered in all his sections. I heard a deep grinding in his sack which he coyly kept from my sight.

"The poet is dead," he said, "and I have salvaged him. But before he died, I made up one of his own strange poems and sang it into the translator. He liked it. Listen, I too think it quite fine."

We all stopped our work to listen, raising our chins slightly. To listen well is of the highest priority. It is how one acknowledges order.

Necros recited:

> *The old poet fades,*
> *Transfigured into the night,*
> *Not-true becomes true.*

What do you think? Does it capture the alien? Is it true salvage?"

A small one-year shook his head. "I still do not know what *night* is."

"Look out beyond the ship," said Necros. "What is it you see?"

"I see our great Oneness."

Necros nodded, letting ripples of pleasure run the entire length of his body. "Yes, that is what I thought, too. But I comprehend it is what he, the alien, would call *night*."

I smiled. "Then your poem should have said: *Transfigured into Oneness*."

Necros shivered deliciously and his sack began its melodi-ous grinding again. "But they are the same, Oneness/Night. So Not-true becomes True. Surely you see that. Truly it is written that: *With salvage all becomes One.*"

And indeed, finally, we all comprehend. It was fine salvage. The best. The hollow ship rang with our grinding.

"You shall share my box this section," I said.

But so full of his triumph, Necros did not at first realize the great honor I had bestowed upon him. He chattered away. "Next time I must try to use all the alien seasons in a poem. *Seasons.* I must think more about the word and digest it again, for I am not at all sure what it means. It has sections, though, like a beautiful body." And he blushed and looked at me. "They are called Winter, Spring, Summer, Fall."

I ran them into my mouth and agreed. "They are indeed meaty," I said. "Next time we meet such aliens we will all sal-vage their poems." Then I spoke the haiku back to him, once quickly before it was forgotten:

> *The old poet fades,*
> *Transfigured into the night.*
> *Not-true becomes true.*

Smiling, I led the way back across the platform to the boxes, leaving the one-years who were not yet ready to mate to finish salvaging the ship's hull.

Lost Girls

"I t isn't fair!" Darla complained to her mom for the third time during their bedtime reading. She meant it wasn't fair that Wendy only did the housework in Neverland and that Peter Pan and the boys got to fight Captain Hook.

"Well, I can't change it," Mom said in her even, lawyer voice. "That's just the way it is in the book. Your argument is with Mr. Barrie, the author, and he's long dead. Should I go on?"

"Yes. No. I don't know," Darla said, coming down on both sides of the question, as she often did.

Mom shrugged and closed the book, and *that* was the end of the night's reading.

Darla watched impassively as her mom got up and left the room, snapping off the bedside lamp as she went. When she closed the door there was just a rim of light from the hall showing around three sides of the door, making it look like something out of a science fiction movie. Darla pulled the covers up over her nose. Her breath made the space feel like a little oven.

"Not fair at all," Darla said to the dark, and she didn't just mean the book. She wasn't the least bit sleepy.

But the house made its comfortable night-settling noises around her: the breathy whispers of the hot air through the vents, the ticking of the grandfather clock in the hall, the sound of the maple branch scritch-scratching against the clapboard siding. They were a familiar lullaby, comforting and soothing. Darla didn't mean to go to sleep, but she did.

Either that or she stepped out of her bed and walked through the closed door into Neverland.

Take your pick.

It didn't feel at all like a dream to Darla. The details were too exact. And she could *smell things.* She'd never smelled anything in a dream before. So Darla had no reason to believe that what happened to her next was anything but real.

One minute she had gotten up out of bed, heading for the bathroom, and the very next she was sliding down the trunk of a very large, smooth tree. The trunk was unlike any of the maples in her yard, being a kind of yellowish color. It felt almost slippery under her hands and smelled like bananas gone slightly bad. Her nightgown made a sound like *whooosh* as she slid along.

When she landed on the ground, she tripped over a large root and stubbed her toe.

"Ow!" she said.

"Shhh!" cautioned someone near her.

She looked up and saw two boys in matching ragged cutoffs and T-shirts staring at her. "Shhh! yourselves," she said, wondering at the same time who they were.

But it hadn't been those boys who spoke. A third boy, behind her, tapped her on the shoulder and whispered, "If you aren't quiet, *He* will find us."

She turned, ready to ask who *He* was. But the boy, dressed in green tights and a green shirt and a rather silly green hat, and smelling like fresh lavender, held a finger up to his lips. They were perfect lips. Like a movie star's. Darla knew him at once.

"Peter," she whispered. "Peter Pan."

He swept the hat off and gave her a deep bow. "Wendy," he countered.

"Well, Darla, actually," she said.

"Wendy Darla," he said. "Give us a thimble."

She and her mom had read that part in the book already, where Peter got kiss and thimble mixed up, and she guessed what it was he really meant, but she wasn't about to kiss him. She was much too young to be kissing boys. Especially boys she'd just met. And he had to be more a man than a boy, anyway, no matter how young he looked. The copy of *Peter Pan* she and her mother had been reading had belonged to her grandmother originally. Besides, Darla wasn't sure she liked Peter. Of course, she wasn't sure she *didn't* like him. It was a bit confusing. Darla hated things being confusing, like her parents' divorce and her dad's new young wife and their twins who were—and who weren't exactly—her brothers.

"I don't have a thimble," she said, pretending not to understand.

"I have," he said, smiling with persuasive boyish charm. "Can I give it to you?"

But she looked down at her feet in order not to answer, which was how she mostly responded to her dad these days, and that was that. At least for the moment. She didn't want to think any further ahead, and neither, it seemed, did Peter.

He shrugged and took her hand, dragging her down a path that smelled of moldy old leaves. Darla was too surprised to protest. And besides, Peter was lots stronger than she was. The two boys followed. When they got to a large dark brown tree whose odor reminded Darla of her grandmother's wardrobe, musty and ancient, Peter stopped. He let go of her hand and jumped up on one of the twisted roots that were looped over and around one another like woody snakes. Darla was suddenly reminded of her school principal when he towered above the students at assembly. He was a tall man but the dais he stood on made him seem even taller. When you sat in the front row, you could look up his nose. She could look up Peter's nose now. Like her principal, he didn't look so grand that way. Or so threatening.

"Here's where we live," Peter said, his hand in a large sweeping motion. Throwing his head back, he crowed like a rooster; he no longer seemed afraid of making noise. Then he said, "You'll like it."

"Maybe I will. Maybe I won't," Darla answered, talking to her feet again.

Peter's perfect mouth made a small pout as if that weren't the response he'd been expecting. Then he jumped down into a dark space between the roots. The other boys followed him. Not to be left behind, in case that rooster crow really had called something awful to them, Darla went after the boys into the dark place. She found what they had actually gone through was a door that was still slightly ajar.

The door opened on to a long, even darker passage that wound into the very center of the tree; the passage smelled damp, like bathing suits left still wet in a closet. Peter and the boys seemed to know the way without any need of light. But Darla was constantly afraid of stumbling and she was glad when someone reached out and held her hand.

Then one last turn and there was suddenly plenty of light from hundreds of little candles set in holders that were screwed right into the living heart of the wood. By the candlelight she saw it was Peter who had hold of her hand.

"Welcome to Neverland," Peter said, as if this were supposed to be a big surprise.

Darla took her hand away from his. "It's smaller than I thought it would be," she said. This time she looked right at him.

Peter's perfect mouth turned down again. "It's big enough for us," he said. Then as if a sudden thought had struck him, he smiled. "But too small for *Him*." He put his back to Darla and shouted, "Let's have a party. We've got us a new Wendy."

Suddenly, from all corners of the room, boys came tumbling and stumbling and dancing, and pushing one another to get a look at her. They were shockingly noisy and all smelled like unwashed socks. One of them made fart noises with his mouth. She wondered if any of them had taken a bath recently. They were worse—Darla thought—than her Stemple cousins, who were so awful their parents never took them anywhere anymore, not out to a restaurant or the movies or anyplace at all.

"Stop it!" she said.

The boys stopped at once.

"I told you," Peter said. "She's a regular Wendy, all right. She's even given me a thimble."

Darla's jaw dropped at the lie. *How could he?*

She started to say "I did not!" but the boys were already cheering so loudly her protestations went unheard.

"Tink," Peter called, and one of the candles detached itself from the heartwood to flutter around his head, "tell the Wendys we want a Welcome Feast."

The Wendys? Darla bit her lip. *What did Peter mean by that?*

The little light flickered on and off. *A kind of code*, Darla thought. She assumed it was the fairy Tinker Bell, but she couldn't really make out what this Tink looked like except for that flickering, fluttering presence. But as if understanding Peter's request, the flicker took off toward a black corner and, shedding but a little light, flew right into the dark.

"Good old Tink," Peter said, and he smiled at Darla with

such practice, dimples appeared simultaneously on both sides of his mouth.

"What kind of food . . ." Darla began.

"Everything parents won't let you have," Peter answered. "Sticky buns and tipsy cake and Butterfingers and brownies and . . ."

The boys gathered around them, chanting the names as if they were the lyrics to some kind of song, adding, ". . . apple tarts and gingerbread and chocolate mousse and trifle and . . ."

"And stomachaches and sugar highs," Darla said stubbornly. "My dad's a nutritionist. I'm only allowed healthy food."

Peter turned his practiced dimpled smile on her again. "Forget your father. You're in Neverland now, and no one need ever go back home from here."

At that Darla burst into tears, half in frustration and half in fear. She actually liked her dad, as well as loved him, despite the fact that he'd left her for his new wife, and despite the fact of the twins, who were actually adorable as long as she didn't have to live with them. The thought that she'd been caught in Neverland with no way to return was so awful, she couldn't help crying.

Peter shrugged and turned to the boys. *"Girls!"* he said with real disgust.

"All Wendys!" they shouted back at him.

Darla wiped her eyes, and spoke right to Peter. "My name is *not* Wendy," she said clearly. "It's Darla."

Peter looked at her, and there was nothing nice or laughing or young about his eyes. They were dark and cold and very very old.

Darla shivered.

Here you're a Wendy," he said.

"And with that, the dark place where Tink had disappeared grew increasingly light, as a door opened and fifteen girls carrying trays piled high with cakes, cookies, biscuits, buns, and other kinds of goodies marched single file into the hall. They were led by a tall, slender, pretty girl with brown hair that fell straight to her shoulders.

The room suddenly smelled overpoweringly of that sickly sweetness of children's birthday parties at school, when their mothers brought in sloppy cupcakes greasy with icing. Darla shuddered.

"Welcome Feast!" shouted the boy who was closest to the door. He made a deep bow.

"Welcome Feast!" they all shouted, laughing and gathering around a great center table.

Only Darla seemed to notice that not one of the Wendys was smiling.

The Feast went on for ages, because each of the boys had to stand up and give a little speech. Of course, most of them only said, "Welcome, Wendy!" and "Glad to meet you!" before sitting down again. A few elaborated a little bit more. But Peter more than made up for it with a long, rambling talk about duty and dessert and how no one loved them out in the World Above as much as he did here in Neverland, and how the cakes proved that.

The boys cheered and clapped at each of Peter's pronouncements, and threw buns and scones across the table at one another as a kind of punctuation. Tink circled Peter's head continuously like a crown of stars, though she never really settled.

But the girls, standing behind the boys like banquet waitresses, did not applaud. Rather they shifted from foot to foot, looking alternately apprehensive and bored. One, no more than four years old, kept yawning behind a chubby hand.

After a polite bite of an apple tart, which she couldn't swallow but spit into her napkin, Darla didn't even try to pretend. The little pie had been much too sweet, not tart at all. And even though Peter kept urging her between the welcomes to eat something, she just couldn't. That small rebellion seemed to annoy him enormously and he stood up once again, this time on the tabletop, to rant on about how some people lacked gratitude, and how difficult it was to provide for many, especially with *Him* about.

Peter never actually looked at Darla as he spoke, but she knew—and everyone else knew—that he meant *she* was the ungrateful one. That bothered her some, but not as much as it might have. She even found herself enjoying the fact that he was annoyed, and that realization almost made her smile.

When Peter ended with "No more Feasts for them with Bad Attitudes!" the boys leaped from their benches and overturned the big table, mashing the remaining food into the floor. Then they all disappeared, diving down a variety of bolt-holes, with Tink after them, leaving the girls alone in the big candlelit room.

"Now see what you've done," said the oldest girl, the pretty one with the straight brown hair. Obviously the leader of the Wendys, she wore a simple dark dress—*like a uniform,* Darla thought, *a school uniform that's badly stained.* "It's going to take forever to get that stuff off the floor. Ages and ages. Mops and buckets. And nothing left for us to eat."

The other girls agreed loudly.

"*They* made the mess," Darla said sensibly. "Let *them* clean it up! That's how it's done at my house."

There was a horrified silence. For a long moment none of the girls said a word, but their mouths opened and shut like fish on beaches. Finally the littlest one spoke.

"Peter won't 'ike it."

"Well, I don't *'ike* Peter!" Darla answered quickly. "He's nothing but a long-winded bully."

"But," said the little Wendy, "you gave him a thimble." She actually said "simble."

"No," Darla said. "Peter lied. I didn't."

The girls all seemed dumbstruck by that revelation. Without a word more, they began to clean the room, first righting the table and then laboriously picking up what they could with their fingers before resorting, at last, to the dreaded buckets and mops. Soon the place smelled like any institution after a cleaning, like a school bathroom or a hospital corridor, Lysol-fresh with an overcast of pine.

Shaking her head, Darla just watched them until the littlest Wendy handed her a mop.

Darla flung the mop to the floor. "I won't do it," she said. "It's not fair."

The oldest Wendy came over to her and put her hand on Darla's shoulder. "Who ever told you that life is fair?" she asked. "Certainly not a navvy, nor an upstairs maid, nor a poor man trying to feed his family."

"Nor my da," put in one of the girls. She was pale skinned, sharp nosed, gap toothed, homely to a fault. "He allas said life was a crapshoot and all usn's got was snake-eyes."

"And not my father," said another, a whey-faced, doughy-looking eight-year-old. "He used to always say that the world didn't treat him right."

"What I mean is that it's not fair that *they* get to have adventures and you get to clean the house," Darla explained carefully.

"Who will clean it if we don't?" Wendy asked. She picked up the mop and handed it back to Darla. "Not *them*. Not ever. So if we want it done, we do it. Fair is not the matter here." She went back to her place in the line of girls mopping the floor.

With a sigh that was less a capitulation and more a show of

solidarity with the Wendys, Darla picked up her own mop and followed.

When the room was set to rights again, the Wendys—with Darla following close behind—tromped into the kitchen, a cheerless, windowless room they had obviously tried to make homey. There were little stick dollies stuck in every possible niche and hand-painted birch bark signs on the wall.

SMILE, one sign said, YOU ARE ON CANDIED CAMERA. And another: WENDYS ARE WONDERFUL. A third, in very childish script, read: WENDYS ARE WINERS. Darla wondered idly if that was meant to be WINNERS or WHINERS, but she decided not to ask.

Depressing as the kitchen was, it was redolent with bakery smells that seemed to dissipate the effect of a prison. Darla sighed, remembering her own kitchen at home, with the windows overlooking her mother's herb garden and the rockery where four kinds of heather flowered till the first snows of winter.

The girls all sat down—on the floor, on the table, in little bumpy, woody niches. There were only two chairs in the kitchen, a tatty overstuffed chair whose gold brocaded covering had seen much better days, and a rocker. The rocker was taken by the oldest Wendy; the other chair remained empty.

At last, seeing that no one else was going to claim the stuffed chair, Darla sat down on it, and a collective gasp went up from the girls.

"'At's Peter's chair," the littlest one finally volunteered.

"Well, Peter's not here to sit in it," Darla said. But she did not relax back against the cushion, just in case he should suddenly appear.

"I'm hungry, Wendy," said one of the girls, who had two gold braids down to her waist. "Isn't there *anything* left to eat?" She addressed the girl in the rocker.

"You are always hungry, Madja," Wendy said. But she smiled, and it was a smile of such sweetness, Darla was immediately reminded of her mom, in the days before the divorce and her dad's new wife.

"So you *do* have names, and not just Wendy," Darla said.

They looked at her as if she were stupid.

"Of course we have names," said the girl in the rocker. "I'm the only one *truly* named Wendy. But I've been here from the first. So that's what Peter calls us all. That's Madja," she said, pointing to the girl with the braids. "And that's Lizzy," the youngest girl. "And that's Martha, Pansy, Nina, Nancy, Heidi, Betsy, Maddy, JoAnne, Shula, Connie, Corrie, Barbara . . ." She went around the circle of girls.

Darla interrupted. "Then why doesn't Peter—"

"Because he can't be bothered remembering," said Wendy. "And we can't be bothered reminding him."

"And it's all right," said Madja. "Really. He has so much else to worry about. Like—"

"*Him!*" They all breathed the word together quietly, as if saying it aloud would summon the horror to them.

"Him? You mean Hook, don't you?" asked Darla. "Captain Hook."

The look they gave her was compounded of anger and alarm. Little Lizzy put her hands over her mouth as if she had said the name herself.

"Well, isn't it?"

"You are an extremely stupid girl," said Wendy. "As well as a dangerous one." Then she smiled again—that luminous smile—at all the other girls, excluding Darla, as if Wendy had not just said something that was both rude and horrible. "Now, darlings, how many of you are as hungry as Madja?"

One by one, the hands went up, Lizzy's first. Only Darla kept her hand down and her eyes down as well.

"Not hungry in the slightest?" Wendy asked, and everyone went silent.

Darla felt forced to look up and saw that Wendy's eyes were staring at her, glittering strangely in the candlelight.

It was too much. Darla shivered and then, all of a sudden, she wanted to get back at Wendy, who seemed as much of a bully as Peter, only in a softer, sneakier way. *But how to do it?* And then she recalled how her mom said that telling a story in a very quiet voice always made a jury lean forward to concentrate that much more. *Maybe,* Darla thought, *I could try that.*

"I remember . . ." Darla began quietly. ". . . I remember a story my mom read to me about a Greek girl who was stolen away by the king of the underworld. He tricked her into eating six seeds and so she had to remain in the underworld six months of every year because of them."

The girls had all gone quiet and were clearly listening. It *works!* Darla thought.

"Don't be daft," Wendy said, her voice loud with authority.

"But Wendy, I remember that story, too," said the whey-faced girl, Nancy, in a kind of whisper, as if by speaking quietly she could later deny having said anything at all.

"And I," put in Madja, in a similarly whispery voice.

"And the fairies," said Lizzy. She was much too young to worry about loud or soft, so she spoke in her normal tone of voice. "If you eat anything in their hall, my mum allas said . . . you never get to go home again. Not ever. I miss my mum." Quite suddenly she began to cry.

"Now see what you've done," said Wendy, standing and stamping her foot. Darla was shocked. She'd never seen anyone over four years old do such a thing. "They'll all be blubbing now, remembering their folks, even the ones who'd been badly beaten at home or worse. And not a sticky bun left to comfort them with. You—girl—ought to be ashamed!"

"Well, it isn't *my* fault!" said Darla, loudly, but she stood, too. The thought of Wendy towering over her just now made her feel edgy and even a bit afraid. "And my name isn't *girl*. It's Darla!"

They glared at one another.

Just then there was a brilliant whistle. A flash of light circled the kitchen like a demented firefly.

"It's Tink!" Lizzy cried, clapping her hands together. "Oh! Oh! It's the signal. 'Larm! 'Larm!"

"Come on, you lot," Wendy cried. "Places, all." She turned her back to Darla, grabbed up a soup ladle, and ran out of the room.

Each of the girls picked up one of the kitchen implements and followed. Not to be left behind, Darla pounced on the only thing left, a pair of silver sugar tongs, and pounded out after them.

They didn't go far, just to the main room again. There they stood silent guard over the bolt-holes. After a while—not quite fifteen minutes, Darla guessed—Tink fluttered in with a more melodic *all clear* and the boys slowly slid back down into the room.

Peter was the last to arrive.

"Oh, Peter, we were so worried," Wendy said.

The other girls crowded around. "We were scared silly," Madja added.

"Weepers!" cried Nancy.

"Knees all knocking," added JoAnne.

"Oh, this is really *too* stupid for words!" Darla said. "All we did was stand around with kitchen tools. Was I supposed to brain a pirate with these?" She held out the sugar tongs as she spoke.

The hush that followed her outcry was enormous. Without

another word, Peter disappeared back into the dark. One by one, the Lost Boys followed him. Tink was the last to go, flickering out like a candle in the wind.

"Now," said Madja with a pout, "we won't even get to hear about the fight. And it's the very best part of being a Wendy."

Darla stared at the girls for a long moment. "What you all need," she said grimly, "is a backbone transplant." And when no one responded, she added, "It's clear the Wendys need to go out on strike." Being the daughter of a labor lawyer had its advantages. She knew all about strikes.

"What the Wendy's *need*," Wendy responded sternly, "is to give the cupboards a good shaking-out." She patted her hair down and looked daggers at Darla. "But first, cups of tea all 'round." Turning on her heel, she started back toward the kitchen. Only four girls remained behind.

Little Lizzy crept over to Darla's side. "What's a strike?" she asked.

"Work stoppage," Darla said. "Signs and lines."

Nancy, Martha, and JoAnne, who had also stayed to listen, looked equally puzzled.

"Signs?" Nancy said.

"Lines?" Joanne said.

"*Hello . . .*" Darla couldn't help the exasperation in her voice. "What year do you all live in? I mean, haven't you ever heard of strikes? Watched CNN? Endured social studies?"

"Nineteen fourteen," said Martha.

"Nineteen thirty-three," said Nancy.

"Nineteen seventy-two," said Joanne.

"Do you mean to say that none of you are . . " Darla couldn't think of what to call it, so added lamely, "new?"

Lizzy slipped her hand into Darla's. "You are the onliest new Wendy we've had in years."

"Oh," Darla said. "I guess that explains it." But she wasn't sure.

"Explains what?" they asked. Before Darla could answer, Wendy called from the kitchen doorway, "Are you lot coming? Tea's on." She did not sound as if she were including Darla in the invitation.

Martha scurried to Wendy's side, but Nancy and JoAnne hesitated a moment before joining her. That left only Lizzy with Darla.

"Can I help?" Lizzy asked. "For the signs. And the 'ines? I be a good worker. Even Wendy says so."

"You're my only . . ." Darla said, smiling down at her and giving her little hand a squeeze. "My *on*liest worker. Still, as my mom always says, Start with one, you're halfway done."

Lizzy repeated the rhyme. "Start with one, you're halfway done. Start with one . . ."

"Just remember it. No need to say it aloud," Darla said.

Lizzy looked up at her, eyes like sky blue marbles. "But I 'ike the way that poem sounds."

"Then 'ike it quietly. We have a long way to go yet before we're ready for any chants." Darla went into the kitchen hand-in-hand with Lizzy, who skipped beside her, mouthing the words silently.

Fourteen Wendys stared at them. Not a one was smiling. Each had a teacup—unmatched, chipped, or cracked—in her hand.

"A long way to go where?" Wendy asked in a chilly voice.

"A long way before you can be free of this yoke of oppression," said Darla. *Yoke of oppression* was a favorite expression of her mother's.

"We are not yoked," Wendy said slowly. "And we are not oppressed."

"What's o-oppressed?" asked Lizzy.

"Made to do what you don't want to do," explained Darla, but she never took her eyes off of Wendy. "Treated harshly. Ruled unjustly. Governed with cruelty." Those were the three definitions she'd had to memorize for her last social studies exam. She never thought she'd ever actually get to use them in the real world. *If,* she thought suddenly, *this world is real.*

"No one treats us harshly or rules us unjustly. And the only cruel ones in Neverland are the pirates," Wendy explained carefully, as if talking to someone feebleminded or slow.

None of the other Wendys said a word. Most of them stared into their cups, *a little*—Darla thought—*like the way I always stare down at my shoes when Mom or Dad wants to talk about something that hurts.*

Lizzy pulled her hand from Darla's. "I think it harsh that we always have to clean up after the boys." Her voice was tiny but still it carried.

"And unjust," someone put in.

"Who said that?" Wendy demanded, staring around the table. "Who *dares* to say that Peter is unjust?"

Darla pursued her lips, wondering how her mom would answer such a question. She was about to lean forward to say something when JoAnne stood in a rush.

"I said it. And it is unjust. I came to Neverland to get away from that sort of thing. Well . . . and to get away from my stepfather, too," she said. "I mean, I don't mind cleaning up my own mess. And even someone else's, occasionally. But . . ." She sat down as quickly as she had stood, looking accusingly into her cup, as if the cup had spoken and not she.

"*Well!*" Wendy said, sounding so much like Darla's home ec teacher that Darla had to laugh out loud.

As if the laugh freed them, the girls suddenly stood up one after another, voicing complaints. And as each one rose, little

Lizzy clapped her hands and skipped around the table, chanting, "Start with one, you're halfway done! Start with one, you're halfway done!"

Darla didn't say a word more. She didn't have to. She just listened as the first trickle of angry voices became a stream and the stream turned into a flood. The girls spoke of the boys' mess and being under-appreciated and wanting a larger share of the food. They spoke about needing to go outside every once in a while. They spoke of longing for new stockings and a bathing room all to themselves, not one shared with the boys, who left rings around the tub and dirty underwear everywhere. They spoke of the long hours and the lack of fresh air, and Barbara said they really could use every other Saturday off, at least. It seemed once they started complaining they couldn't stop.

Darla's mom would have understood what had just happened, but Darla was clearly as stunned as Wendy by the rush of demands. They stared at one another, almost like comrades.

The other girls kept on for long minutes, each one stumbling over the next to be heard, until the room positively rocked with complaints. And then, as suddenly as they had begun, they stopped. Red-faced, they all sat down again, except for Lizzy, who still capered around the room, but now did it wordlessly.

Into the sudden silence, Wendy rose. "How *could* you . . ." she began. She leaned over the table, clutching the top, her entire body trembling. "After all Peter has done for you, taking you in when no one else wanted you, when you had been tossed aside by the world, when you'd been crushed and corrupted and canceled. How *could* you?"

Lizzy stopped skipping in front of Darla. "Is it time for signs and 'ines now?" she asked, her marble-blue eyes wide.

Darla couldn't help it. She laughed again. Then she held out her arms to Lizzy, who cuddled right in. "Time indeed," Darla said. She looked up at Wendy. "Like it or not, Miss Management, the Lost Girls are going out on strike."

Wendy sat in her rocker, arms folded, a scowl on her face. She looked like a four-year-old having a temper tantrum. But of course it was something worse than that.

The girls ignored her. They threw themselves into making signs with a kind of manic energy and in about an hour they had a whole range of them, using the backs of their old signs, pages torn from cookbooks, and flattened flour bags.

WENDYS WON'T WORK, one read. EQUAL PLAY FOR EQUAL WORK, went another. MY NAME'S NOT WENDY! said a third, and FRESH AIR IS ONLY FAIR a fourth. Lizzy's sign was decorated with stick figures carrying what Darla took to be swords, or maybe wands. Lizzy had spelled out—or rather misspelled out—what became the girls' marching words: WE AIN'T LOST, WE'RE JUST MIZ-PLAYST.

It turned out that JoAnne was musical. She made up lyrics to the tune of "Yankee Doodle Dandy" and taught them to the others:

> We ain't lost, we're just misplaced,
> The outside foe we've never faced.
> Give us a chance to fight and win
> And we'll be sure to keep Neverland neat as a pin.

The girls argued for awhile over that last line, which Betsy said had too many syllables and the wrong sentiment, until Magda suggested, rather timidly, that if they actually wanted a chance to fight the pirates, maybe the boys should take a turn at cleaning the house. "Fair's fair," she added.

That got a cheer. "Fair's fair," they told one another, and Patsy scrawled that sentiment on yet another sign.

The cheer caused Wendy to get up grumpily from her chair and leave the kitchen in a snit. She must have called for the boys then, because no sooner had the girls decided on an amended line (which still had too many syllables but felt right otherwise) —

And you can keep Neverland neat as a pin!

—than the boys could be heard coming back noisily into the dining room. They shouted and whistled and banged their fists on the table, calling out for the girls and for food. Tink's high-pitched cry overrode the noise, piercing the air. The girls managed to ignore it all until Peter suddenly appeared in the kitchen doorway.

"What's this I hear?" he said, smiling slightly to show he was more amused than angry. Somehow that only made his face seem both sinister and untrustworthy.

But his appearance in the doorway was electrifying. For a moment not one of the girls could speak. It was as if they had all taken a collective breath and were waiting to see which of them had the courage to breathe out first.

Then Lizzy held up her sign. "We're going on strike," she said brightly.

"And what, little Wendy, is that?" Peter asked, leaning forward and speaking in the kind of voice grown-ups use with children. He pointed at her sign. "Is it . . ." he said slyly, "like a thimble?"

"Silly Peter," said Lizzy, "it's signs and 'ines."

"I see the signs, all right," said Peter. "But what do they mean? WENDYS WON'T WORK. Why, Neverland counts on Wendys working. And I count on it, too. You Wendys are the most important of what we have made here."

"Oh," said Lizzy, turning to Darla, her face shining with pleasure. "*We're* the mostest important . . ."

Darla sighed heavily. "If you are so important, Lizzy, why can't he remember your name? If you're so important, why do you have all the work and none of the fun?"

"Right!" cried JoAnne suddenly, and immediately burst into her song. It was picked up at once by the other girls. Lizzy, caught up in the music, began to march in time all around the table with her sign. The others, still singing, fell in line behind her. They marched once around the kitchen and then right out into the dining room. Darla was at the rear.

At first the Lost Boys were stunned at the sight of the girls and their signs. Then they, too, got caught up in the song and began to pound their hands on the table in rhythm.

Tink flew around and around Wendy's head, flickering on and off and on angrily, looking for all the world like an electric hair-cutting machine. Peter glared at them all until he suddenly seemed to come to some conclusion. Then he leaped onto the dining room table, threw back his head, and crowed loudly.

At that everyone went dead silent. Even Tink.

Peter let the silence prolong itself until it was almost painful. At last he turned and addressed Darla and, through her, all the girls. "What is it you want?" he asked. "What is it you truly want? Because you'd better be careful what you ask for. In Neverland wishes are granted in very strange ways."

"It's not," Darla said carefully, "what I want. It's what *they* want.

In a tight voice, Wendy cried out. "They never wanted for anything until *she* came, Peter. They never needed or asked . . ."

"What we want . . ." JoAnne interrupted, "is to be equals."

Peter wheeled about on the table and stared down at Joanne and she, poor thing, turned gray under his gaze. "No one is asking you," he said pointedly.

"We want to be equals!" Lizzy shouted. "To the boys. To Peter!"

The dam burst again, and the girls began shouting and singing and crying and laughing all together. "Equal . . . equal . . . equal . . ."

Even the boys took it up.

Tink flickered frantically, then took off up one of the bolt-holes, emerging almost immediately down another, her piercing alarm signal so loud that everyone stopped chanting, except for Lizzy, whose little voice only trailed off after a bit.

"So," said Peter, "you want equal share in the fighting? Then here's your chance."

Tink's light was sputtering with excitement and she whistled nonstop.

"Tink says Hook's entire crew is out there, waiting. And, boy! are they angry. You want to fight them? Then go ahead." He crossed his arms over his chest and turned his face away from the girls. "I won't stop you."

No longer gray but now pink with excitement, JoAnne grabbed up a knife from the nearest Lost Boy. "I'm not afraid!" she said. She headed up one of the bolt-holes.

Weaponless, Barbara, Pansy, and Betsy followed right after.

"But that's not what I meant them to do," Darla said. "I mean, weren't we supposed to work out some sort of compromise?"

Peter turned back slowly and looked at Darla, his face stern and unforgiving. "I'm Peter Pan. I don't have to compromise in Neverland." Wendy reached up to help him off the tabletop.

The other girls had already scattered up the holes, and only Lizzy was left. And Darla.

"Are you coming to the fight?" Lizzy asked Darla, holding out her hand.

Darla gulped and nodded. They walked to the bolt-hole

hand-in-hand. Darla wasn't sure what to expect, but they began rising up as if in some sort of air elevator. Behind them one of the boys was whining to Peter, "But what are we going to do without them?"

The last thing Darla heard Peter say was, "Don't worry. There are always more Wendys where they came from."

The air outside was crisp and autumny and smelled of apples. There was a full moon, orange and huge. *Harvest moon,* Darla thought, which was odd since it had been spring in her bedroom.

Ahead she saw the other girls. *And* the pirates. Or at least she saw their silhouettes. It obviously hadn't been much of a fight. The smallest of the girls—Martha, Nina, and Heidi—were already captured and riding atop their captors' shoulders. The others, with the exception of Joanne, were being carried off fireman-style. JoAnne still had her knife and she was standing off one of the largest of the men; she got in one good swipe before being disarmed, and lifted up.

Darla was just digesting this when Lizzy was pulled from her.

"Up you go, little darlin'," came a deep voice.

Lizzy screamed. "Wendy! Wendy!"

Darla had no time to answer her before she, too, was gathered up in enormous arms and carted off.

In less time than it takes to tell of it, they were through the woods and over a shingle, dumped into boats, and rowed out to the pirate ship. There they were hauled up by ropes and—except for Betsy, who struggled so hard she landed in the water and had to be fished out, wrung out, and then hauled up again—it was a silent and well-practiced operation.

The girls stood in a huddle on the well-lit deck and awaited their fate. Darla was glad no one said anything. She felt awful. She hadn't meant them to come to this. Peter had been right. Wishes in Neverland were dangerous.

"Here come the captains," said one of the pirates. It was the first thing anyone had said since the capture.

He must mean captain, singular, thought Darla. But when she heard footsteps nearing them and dared to look up, there were, indeed, two figures coming forward. One was an old man about her grandfather's age, his white hair in two braids, a three-cornered hat on his head. She looked for the infamous hook but he had two regular hands, though the right one was clutching a pen.

The other captain was . . . a woman.

"Welcome to Hook's ship," the woman said. "I'm Mrs. Hook. Also known as Mother Jane. Also known as Pirate Lil. Also called The Pirate Queen. We've been hoping we could get you away from Peter for a very long time." She shook hands with each of the girls and gave Lizzy a hug.

"I need to get to the doctor, ma'am," said one of the pirates. "That little girl . . ." he pointed to JoAnne ". . . gave me quite a slice."

JoAnne blanched and shrank back into herself.

But Captain Hook only laughed. It was a hearty laugh, full of good humor. "Good for her. You're getting careless in your old age, Smee," he said. "Stitches will remind you to stay alert. Peter would have got your throat, and even here on the boat that could take a long while to heal."

"Now," said Mrs. Hook, "it's time for a good meal. Pizza, I think. With plenty of veggies on top. Peppers, mushrooms, carrots, onions. But no anchovies. I have never understood why anyone wants a hairy fish on top of pizza."

"What's pizza?" asked Lizzy.

"Ah . . . something you will love, my dear," answered Mrs.

Hook. "Things never do change in Peter's Neverland, but up here on Hook's ship we move with the times."

"Who will do the dishes after?" asked Betsy cautiously.

The crew rustled behind them.

"I'm on dishes this week," said one, a burly, ugly man with a black eyepatch.

"And I," said another. She was as big as the ugly man, but attractive in a rough sort of way.

"There's a duty roster on the wall by the galley," explained Mrs. Hook. "That's ship talk for the kitchen. You'll get used to it. We all take turns. A pirate ship is a very democratic place."

"What's demo-rat-ic?" asked Lizzy.

They all laughed. "You will have a long time to learn," said Mrs. Hook. "Time moves more swiftly here than in the stuffy confines of a Neverland tree. But not so swiftly as out in the world. Now let's have that pizza, a hot bath, and a bedtime story, and then tomorrow we'll try and answer your questions."

The girls cheered, JoAnne loudest of them all.

"I *am* hungry," Lizzy added, as if that were all the answer Mrs. Hook needed.

"But I'm not," Darla said. "And I don't want to stay here. Not in Neverland or on Hook's ship. I want to go home."

Captain Hook came over and put his good hand under her chin. Gently he lifted her face into the light. "Father beat you?" he asked.

"Never," Darla said.

"Mother desert you?" he asked.

"Fat chance," said Darla.

"Starving? Miserable? Alone?"

"No. And no. And *no.*"

Hook turned to his wife and shrugged. She shrugged back, then asked, "Ever think that the world was unfair, child?"

"Who hasn't?" asked Darla, and Mrs. Hook smiled.

"Thinking it and meaning it are two very different things," Mrs. Hook said at last. "I expect you must have been awfully convincing to have landed at Peter's door. Never mind. Have pizza with us, and then you can go. I want to hear the latest from outside, anyway. You never know what we might find useful. Pizza was the last really useful thing we learned from one of the girls we snagged before Peter found her. And that—I can tell you—has been a major success."

"Can't I go home with Darla?" Lizzy asked.

Mrs. Hook knelt down till she and Lizzy were face-to-face. "I am afraid that would make for an awful lot of awkward questions," she said.

Lizzy's blue eyes filled up with tears.

"My mom is a lawyer," Darla put in quickly. "Awkward questions are her specialty."

The pizza was great, with a crust that was thin and delicious. And when Darla awoke to the ticking of the grandfather clock in the hall and the sound of the maple branch *scritch-scratching* against the clapboard siding, the taste of the pizza was still in her mouth. She felt a lump at her feet, raised up, and saw Lizzy fast asleep under the covers at the foot of the bed.

"I sure hope Mom is as good as I think she is," Darla whispered. Because there was no going back on this one—fair, unfair, or anywhere in between.

Belle Bloody Merciless Dame

n elf, they say, has no real emotions, cannot love, cannot cry. Do not believe them, that relative of the infinite Anon. Get an elf at the right time, on a Solstice for example, and you will get all the emotions you want.

Only you may not like what you get.

Sam Herriot, for example, ran into one of the elves of the Western Ridings on a Sunday in June. He'd forgotten—if he'd ever actually known—it was the Summer Solstice. He'd had a skinful at the local pub, mostly Tennants, that Bud wannabe, thin and pale amber, and was making his unsteady way home through the dark alley of Kirk Wynd.

And there was this girl, tall, skinny, actually quite a bit anorexic, Sam thought, leaning against the gray stone wall. Her long ankle-length skirt was rucked up in front and she was scratching her thin thigh lazily with bright red nails, making runnels in her skin that looked like veins, or like track marks. He thought she was some bloody local junkie, you see, out trolling for a john to make enough money for another round of the whatever.

And Sam, being drunk but not that drunk, thought he'd accommodate her, even though he preferred his women plump, two handsful he liked to say, hefting his hands palms upward. He had several unopened safes in his pocket, and enough extra pounds in his wallet because he hadn't had to pay for any of the drinks that night. His Mam didn't expect him home early since it had been his bachelor party. And with Jill gone home to spend the last week before their marriage with her own folks, there was no one to wait up for him. So he thought, "What the hell!" and continued down the alley toward the girl.

She didn't look up. But he was pretty sure she knew he was there; it was the way she got quiet all of a sudden, stopped scratching her leg. A kind of still anticipation.

So he went over to her and said, "Miss?" being polite just in case, and only then did she look up and her eyes were not normal eyes. More like a cat's eyes, with yellow pupils that sat up and down rather than side to side. Only, being drunk, he thought that they were just a junkie's eyes.

She smiled at him, and it was a sudden sweet and ravenous smile, if you can imagine those two things together. He took it for lust, which it was, of a sort. Even had he been sober, he wouldn't have known the difference.

She held out her hand, and he took it, drawing her toward him and she said, "Not here," with a peculiar kind of lilt to her voice. And he asked, "Where?"

Then without quite realizing the how of it, he suddenly found himself sitting on a hillside with her, though the nearest one he knew of was way out of town, about a quarter of a mile, near the Boarside Steadings.

He thought, *I'm really drunk, not remembering walking all this way.* But that didn't stop him from kissing her, putting his tongue up against her teeth until she opened her mouth and sucked him in so quickly, so deeply he nearly passed out. So he drew back for a breath, tasting her saliva like some herbal tea, and watched as she shrugged out of the top of her blouse, some filmy little number, no buttons or anything.

She was naked underneath.

"God!" he said, and he really meant it as a sudden prayer because she was painfully thin. He could actually count her ribs. And she had this odd third nipple, right on the breastbone between the other two. He'd heard that some girls did, but he'd never actually seen anything like it before.

He wondered, suddenly, about Jill and their wedding in a couple of days, and it sobered him a bit, making his own eyes go a bit dead for a moment.

That's when the girl stood up on those long skinny legs and walked over to him, pressing him backward, whispering in some strange, liquid language. Suddenly it all made sense to him. She was a foreigner, not British at all.

"Aren't you cold, lass?" he asked, thinking that maybe he should just cover her up, here on the hillside, and never mind the other stuff at all. Because Jill would kill him if she knew, the girl so skinny and foreign and odd.

But the girl put her hands on his shoulders and pushed him back till he lay on the cold grass staring up at her. It was past midnight and the sky still pearly, this being Scotland where summer days spin across the twenty-four hours with hardly any dark at all. He could see faint stars around her head, and they looked as if they were moving. Then he realized it wasn't stars at all, but something white and fluttering behind her. *Moths,* he thought. Or *gulls.* Only much too big for either.

She lay down on top of him and kissed him again, hard and

soft, sighing and weeping. Her hot tears filled his own eyes till he could not see at all. But all the while the wings—not moths, not gulls—wrapped around him. He did not feel the cold.

He woke hours later on the hillside and thought they must have had sex, or had something at any rate, though he couldn't remember any of it, for his trousers were soaked through, back and front. He felt frantically in his pocket. The safes were still there, untouched. His wallet, too. His mouth felt bruised, his head ached from all the beer, and he could feel the heat of a hickey rising on the left side of his neck.

But the girl was gone.

He stood slowly and looked around. Far off was the sea looking, in the morning light, silvery and strange. He was miles from town, not Boarside Steadings at all, and there was no sign of the thin girl, though how she could have disappeared, or when, he did not know. But leaving him here, alone, on the bloody hillside, drained and tired, feeling older than time itself must have given her some bloody big laugh. Well, he hoped she got sick, hoped she got the clap, hoped she got herself pregnant, little tart. And all he had to show for it was a great white feather, as if from some bloody stupid fairy wing.

And brushing himself off, he started down the cold hillside toward—he hoped—home.

Words of Power

L ate Blossoming Flower, the only child of her mother's
old age, stared sulkily into the fire. A homely child, with
a nose that threatened to turn into a beak and a mouth
that seldom smiled, she was nonetheless cherished by
her mother and the clan. Her loneness, the striking rise of her
nose, the five strands of white hair that stroked through her
shiny black hair, were all seen as the early signs of great power,
the power her mother had given up when she had chosen to
bear a child.

"I would never have made such a choice," Late Blossoming
Flower told her mother. "I would never give up *my* power."

Her mother, who had the same fierce nose, the white streak
of hair, and the bitter smile but was a striking beauty, replied
gently, "You do not have that power yet. And if I had not given
up mine, you would not be here now to make such a statement
and to chide me for my choice." She shook her head. "Nor
would you now be scolded for forgetting to do those things
which are yours by duty."

Late Blossoming Flower bit back the reply that was no reply but merely angry words. She rose from the fireside and went out of the cliff house to feed the milk beast. As she climbed down the withy ladder to the valley below, she rehearsed that conversation with her mother as she had done so often before. Always her mother remained calm, her voice never rising into anger. It infuriated Flower, and she nursed that sore like all the others, counting them up as carefully as if she were toting them on a notch stick. The tally by now was long indeed.

But soon, she reminded herself, soon she would herself be a woman of power, though she was late coming to it. All the signs but one were on her. Under the chamois shirt her breasts had finally begun to bud. There was hair curling in the secret places of her body. Her waist and hips were changing to create a place for the Herb Belt to sit comfortably, instead of chafing her as it did now. And when at last the moon called to her and her first blood flowed, cleansing her body of man's sin, she would be allowed to go on her search for her own word of power and be free of her hated, ordinary chores. Boys could not go on such a search, for they were never able to rid themselves of the dirty blood-sin. But she took no great comfort in that, for not all girls who sought found. Still, Late Blossoming Flower knew she was the daughter of a woman of power, a woman so blessed that even though she had had a child and lost the use of the Shaping Hands, she still retained the Word That Changes. Late Blossoming Flower never doubted that when she went on her journey she would find what it was she sought.

The unfed milk beast lowed longingly as her feet touched the ground. She bent and gathered up bits of earth, cupped the fragments in her hand, said the few phrases of the *Ke-waha,* the prayer to the land, then stood.

"I'm not *that* late," she said sharply to the agitated beast, and went to the wooden manger for maize.

• • •

It was the first day after the rising of the second moon, and the florets of the night-blooming panomom tree were open wide. The sickly sweet smell of the tiny clustered blossoms filled the valley, and all the women of the valley dreamed dreams.

The women of power dreamed in levels. Late Blossoming Flower's mother passed from one level to another with the ease of long practice, but her daughter's dream quester had difficulty going through. She wandered too long on the dreamscape paths, searching for a ladder or a rope or some other familiar token of passage.

When Late Blossoming Flower had awakened, her mother scolded her for her restless sleep.

"If you are to be a true woman of power, you must force yourself to lie down in the dream and fall asleep. Sleep within sleep, dream within dream. Only then will you wake at the next level." Her head had nodded gently every few words and she spoke softly, braiding her hair with quick and supple hands. "You must be like a gardener forcing an early bud to bring out the precious juices."

"Words. Just words," said Late Blossoming Flower. "And none of *those* words has power." She had risen from her pallet, shaking her own hair free of the loose night braiding, brushing it fiercely before plaiting it up again. She could not bear to listen to her mother's advice any longer and had let her thoughts drift instead to the reed hut on the edge of the valley, where old Sand Walker lived. A renegade healer, he lived apart from the others and, as a man, was little thought of. But Late Blossoming Flower liked to go and sit with him and listen to his stories of the time before time, when power had been so active in the world it could be plucked out of the air as easily as fruit from a tree. He said that dreams eventually explained themselves and that to discipline the dream figure was to bind its power. To

Late Blossoming Flower that made more sense than all her mother's constant harping on the Forcing Way.

So intent was she on visiting the old man that day, she had raced through her chores, scanting the milk beast and the birds who squatted on hidden nests. She had collected only a few eggs and left them in the basket at the bottom of the cliff. Then, without a backward glance at the withy ladders spanning the levels or the people moving busily against the cliff face, she raced down the path toward Sand Walker's home.

As a girl child she had that freedom, given leave for part of each day to walk the many trails through the valley. On these walks she was supposed to learn the ways of the growing flowers, to watch the gentler creatures at their play, to come to a careful understanding of the way of predator and prey. It was time for her to know the outer landscape of her world as thoroughly as she would, one day, know the inner dream trails. But Late Blossoming Flower was a hurrying child. As if to make up for her late birth and the crushing burden of early power laid on her, she refused to take the time.

"My daughter," her mother often cautioned her, "a woman of true power must be in love with silence. You must learn all the outward sounds in order to approach the silence that lies within."

But Flower wanted no inner silence. She delighted in tuneless singing and loud sounds: the sharp hoarse cry of the night herons sailing across the marsh; the crisp howl of the jackals calling under the moon; even the scream of the rabbit in the teeth of the wolf. She sought to imitate *those* sounds, make them louder, sing them again in her own mouth. What was silence compared to sound?

And when she was with old Sand Walker in his hut, he sang with her. And told stories, joking stories, about the old women and their silences.

"Soon enough," Sand Walker said, "soon enough it will be silent and dark. In the grave. Those old *bawenahs*"—he used the word that meant the unclean female vulture—"those old *bawenahs* would make us rehearse for our coming deaths with their binding dreams. Laugh *now,* child. Sing out. Silence is for the dead ones, though they call themselves alive and walk the trails. But you and I, ho"—he poked her in the stomach lightly with his stick—"we know the value of noise. It blocks out thinking, and thinking means pain. Cry out for me, child. Loud. Louder."

And as if a trained dog, Late Blossoming Flower always dropped to her knees at this request and howled, scratching at the dirt and wagging her bottom. Then she would fall over on her back with laughter and the old man laughed with her.

All this was in her mind as she ran along the path toward Sand Walker's hut.

A rabbit darted into her way, then zagged back to escape her pounding feet. A few branches, emboldened by the coming summer, strayed across her path and whipped her arm, leaving red scratches. Impatient with the marks, she ignored them.

At the final turning the old man's hut loomed up. He was sitting, as always, in the doorway, humming, and eating a piece of yellowed fruit, the juices running down his chin. At the noise of her coming he looked up and grinned.

"Hai!" he said, more sound than greeting.

Flower skidded to a stop and squatted in the dirt beside him.

"You look tired," he said. "Did you dream?"

"I tried. But dreaming is so slow," Flower admitted.

"Dreaming is not living. You and I—we live. Have a bite?" He offered her what was left of the fruit, mostly core.

She took it so as not to offend him, holding the core near

her mouth but not eating. The smell of the overripe, sickly sweet fruit made her close her eyes, and she was startled into a dream.

The fruit was in her mouth and she could feel its sliding passage down her throat. It followed the twists of her inner pathways, dropping seeds as it went, until it landed heavily in her belly. There it began to burn, a small but significant fire in her gut.

Bending over to ease the cramping, Flower turned her back on the old man's hut and crept along the trail toward the village. The trees along the trail and the muddle of gray-green wildflowers blurred into an indistinct mass as she went, as if she were seeing them through tears, though her cheeks were dry and her eyes clear.

When she reached the cliffside she saw, to her surprise, that the withy ladders went down into a great hole in the earth instead of up toward the dwellings on the cliff face.

It was deathly silent all around her. The usual chatter of children at their chores, the chant of women, the hum-buzz of men in the furrowed fields were gone. The cliff was as blank and as smooth as the shells of the eggs she had gathered that morning.

And then she heard a low sound, compounded of moans and a strange hollow whistling, like an old man's laughter breathed out across a reed. Turning around, she followed the sound. It led her to the hole. She bent over it, and as she did, the sound resolved itself into a single word: bawenah. *She saw a pale, shining face looking up at her from the hole, its mouth a smear of fruit. When the mouth opened, it was as round and as black as the hole. There were no teeth. There was no tongue. Yet still the mouth spoke:* bawenah.

Flower awoke and stared at the old man. Pulpy fruit stained his scraggly beard. His eyes were filmy. Slowly his tongue emerged and licked his lips.

She turned and without another word to him walked home. Her hands cupped her stomach, pressing and releasing, all the way back, as if pressure alone could drive away the cramps.

Her mother was waiting for her at the top of the ladder, hands folded on her own belly. "So," she said, "it is your woman time."

Flower did not ask how she knew. Her mother was a woman of great power still and such knowledge was well within her grasp, though it annoyed Flower that it should be so.

"Yes," Flower answered, letting a small whine creep into her voice. "But you did not tell me it would hurt so."

"With some," her mother said, smiling and smoothing back the white stripe of hair with her hand, "with some, womanhood comes easy. With some it comes harder." Then, as they walked into their rooms, she added with a bitterness uncharacteristic of her, "Could your *healer* not do something for you?"

Flower was startled at her mother's tone. She knew that her association with the old man had annoyed her mother. But Flower had never realized it would hurt her so much. She began to answer her mother, then bit back her first angry reply. Instead, mastering her voice, she said, "I did not think to ask him for help. He is but a man. *I* am a woman."

"You are a woman today, truly," her mother said. She went over to the great chest she had carved before Flower's birth, a chest made of the wood of a lightning-struck panomom tree. The chest's sides were covered with carved signs of power: the florets of the tree with their three-foil flowers, the mouse and hare who were her mother's personal signs, the trailing arbet vine which was her father's, and the signs for the four moons: quarter, half, full, and closed faces.

When she opened the chest, it made a small creaking protest. Flower went over to look in. There, below her first cradle dress and leggings, nestled beside a tress of her first, fine baby hair, was the Herb Belt she had helped her mother make. It had fifteen pockets, one for each year she had been a girl.

They went outside, and her mother raised her voice in that wild ululation that could call all the women of power to her. It echoed around the clearing and across the fields to the gathering streams beyond, a high, fierce yodeling. And then she called out again, this time in a gentler voice that would bring the women who had borne and their girl children with them.

Flower knew it would be at least an hour before they all gathered; in the meantime she and her mother had much to do.

They went back into the rooms and turned around all the objects they owned, as a sign that Flower's life would now be turned around as well. Bowls, cups, pitchers were turned. Baskets of food and the drying racks were turned. Even the heavy chest was turned around. They left the bed pallets to the very last, and then, each holding an end, they walked the beds around until the ritual was complete.

Flower stripped in front of her mother, something she had not done completely in years. She resisted the impulse to cover her breasts. On her leggings were the blood sign. Carefully her mother packed those leggings into the panomom chest. Flower would not wear them again.

At the bottom of the chest, wrapped in a sweet-smelling woven-grass covering, was a white chamois dress and leggings. Flower's mother took them out and spread them on the bedding, her hand smoothing the nap. Then, with a pitcher of water freshened with violet flowers, she began to wash her daughter's body with a scrub made of the leaves of the sandarac tree. The nubby sandarac and the soothing rinse of the violet water were to remind Flower of the fierce and gentle sides of womanhood. All the while she scrubbed, Flower's mother chanted the songs of Woman: the seven-fold chant of Rising, the Way of Power, and the Praise to Earth and Moon.

The songs reminded Flower of something, and she tried to think of what it was as her mother's hands cleansed her of the sins of youth. It was while her mother was braiding her hair, plaiting in it reed ribbons that ended in a dangle of shells, that Flower remembered. The chants were like the cradle songs her mother had sung her when she was a child, with the same rise and fall, the same liquid sounds. She suddenly wanted to cry for the loss of those times and the pain she had given her mother, and she wondered why she felt so like weeping when anger was her usual way.

The white dress and leggings slipped on easily, indeed fit her perfectly, though she had never tried them on before, and that, too, was a sign of her mother's power.

And what of her own coming power, Flower wondered as she stood in the doorway watching the women assemble at the foot of the ladder. The women of power stood in the front, then the birth women, last of all the girls. She could name them all, her friends, her sisters in the tribe, who only lately had avoided her because of her association with the old man. She tried to smile at them, but her mouth would not obey her. In fact, her lower lip trembled and she willed it to stop, finally clamping it with her teeth.

"She is a woman," Flower's mother called down to them. The ritual words. They had known, even without her statement, had known from that first wild cry, what had happened. "Today she has come into her power, putting it on as a woman dons her white dress, but she does not yet know her own way. She goes now, as we all go at our time, to the far hills and beyond to seek the Word That Changes. She may find it or not, but she will tell of that when she has returned."

The women below began to sway and chant the words of the Searching Song, words which Flower had sung with them for fifteen years without really understanding their meaning. Fifteen years—far longer than any of the other girls—standing at the ladder's foot and watching another Girl-Become-Woman go off on her search. And that was why—she saw it now—she had fallen under Sand Walker's spell.

But now, standing above the singers, waiting for the Belt and the Blessing, she felt for the first time how strongly the power called to her. This was *her* moment, *her* time, and there would be no other. She pictured the old man in his hut and realized that if she did not find her word she would be bound to him forever.

"Mother," she began, wondering if it was too late to say all the things she should have said before, but her mother was coming toward her with the Belt and suddenly it was too late. Once the Belt was around her waist, she could not speak again until the Word formed in her mouth, with or without its accompanying power. Tears started in her eyes.

Her mother saw the tears, and perhaps she mistook them for something else. Tenderly she placed the Belt around Flower's waist, setting it on the hips, and tying it firmly behind her. Then she turned her daughter around, the way every object in the house had been turned, till she faced the valley again where all the assembled women could read the fear on her face.

> Into the valley, in the fear we all face,
> Into the morning of your womanhood,
> Go with our blessing to guide you,
> Go with our blessing to guard you,
> Go with our blessing and bring back your word.

The chant finished, Flower's mother pushed her toward the ladder and went back into the room and sat on the chest to do her own weeping.

Flower opened her eyes, surprised, for she had not realized that she had closed them. All the women had disappeared, back into the fields, into the woods; she did not know where, nor was she to wonder about them. Her journey had to be made alone. Talking to anyone on the road this day would spell doom to them both, to her quest for her power, to the questioner's very life.

As she walked out of the village, Flower noticed that everything along the way seemed different. Her power had, indeed, begun. The low bushes had a shadow self, like the moon's halo, standing behind. The trees were filled with eyes, peering out of the knotholes. The chattering of animals in the brush was a series of messages, though Flower knew that she was still unable to decipher them. And the path itself sparkled as if water rushed over it, tumbling the small stones.

She seemed to slip in and out of quick dreams that were familiar pieces of her old dreams stitched together in odd ways. Her childhood was sloughing off behind her with each step, a skin removed.

Further down the path, where the valley met the foothills leading to the far mountains, she could see Sand Walker's hut casting a long, dark, toothy shadow across the trail. Flower was not sure if the shadows lengthened because the sun was at the end of its day or because this was yet another dream. She closed her eyes, and when she opened them again, the long shadows were still there, though not nearly as dark or as menacing.

When she neared the hut, the old man was sitting silently out front. His shadow, unlike the hut's black shadow, was a strange shade of green.

She did not dare greet the old man, for fear of ruining her quest and because she did not want to hurt him. One part of her was still here with him, wild, casting green shadows, awake. He had no protection against her power. But surely she might give him one small sign of recognition. Composing her hands in front of her, she was prepared to signal him with a finger, when without warning he leaped up, grinning.

"*Ma-hane,* white girl," he cried, jumping into her path. "Do not forget to laugh, you in your white dress and leggings. If you do not laugh, you are one of the dead ones."

In great fear she reached out a hand toward him to silence him before he could harm them both, and power sprang unbidden from her fingertips. She had forgotten the Shaping Hands. And though they were as yet untrained and untried, still they were a great power. She watched in horror as five separate arrows of flame struck the old man's face, touching his eyes, his nostrils, his mouth, sealing them, melting his features like candle wax. He began to shrink under the fire, growing smaller and smaller, fading into a gray-green splotch that only slowly resolved itself into the form of a *sa-hawa,* a butterfly the color of leaf mold.

Flower did not dare speak, not even a word of comfort. She reached down and shook out the crumpled shirt, loosing the butterfly. It flapped its wings, tentatively at first, then with more strength, and finally managed to flutter up toward the top of the hut.

Folding the old man's tattered shirt and leggings with gentle hands, Flower laid them on the doorstep of his hut, still watching the fluttering *sa-hawa.* When she stood again, she had to shade her eyes with one hand to see it. It had flown away from the hut and was hovering between patches of wild onion in a small meadow on the flank of the nearest foothill.

Flower bit her lip. How could she follow the butterfly? It was going up the mountainside and her way lay straight down

the road. Yet how could she not follow it? Sand Walker's transformation had been her doing. No one else might undo what she
had so unwillingly, unthinkingly created.

To get to the meadow was easy. But if the butterfly went
further up the mountainside, what could she do? There was only
a goat track, and then the sheer cliff wall. As she hesitated, the
sa-hawa rose into the air again, leaving the deep green spikes of
onions to fly up toward the mountain itself.

Flower looked quickly down the trail, but the shadows of
oncoming evening had closed that way. Ahead, the Path of
Power—her Power—was still brightly lit.

Oh, Mother, she thought. *Oh, my mothers, I need your blessing indeed.* And so thinking, she plunged into the underbrush after
the *sa-hawa,* heedless of the thorns tugging at her white leggings or the light on the Path of Power that suddenly and inexplicably went out.

The goat path had not been used for years, not by goats or by
humans either. Briars tangled across it. Little rock slides
blocked many turnings, and in others the pebbly surface slid
away beneath her feet. Time and again she slipped and fell; her
knees and palms bruised, and all the power in her Shaping
Hands seemed to do no good. She could not call on it. Once
when she fell she bit her underlip so hard it bled. And always,
like some spirit guide, the little gray-green butterfly fluttered
ahead, its wings glowing with five spots as round and marked as
fingerprints.

Still Flower followed, unable to call out or cry out because a
new woman on her quest for her Power must not speak until she
has found her word. She still hoped, a doomed and forlorn hope,
that once she had caught the *sa-hawa* she might also catch her
Power or at least be allowed to continue on her quest. And she

would take the butterfly with her and find at least enough of the Shaping Hands to turn him back into his own tattered, laughing, dismal self.

She went on. The only light now came from the five spots on the butterfly's wings and the pale moon rising over the jagged crest of First Mother, the left-most mountain. The goat track had disappeared entirely. It was then the butterfly began to rise straight up, as if climbing the cliff face.

Out of breath, Flower stopped and listened, first to her own ragged breathing, then to the pounding of her heart. At last she was able to be quiet enough to hear the sounds of the night. The butterfly stopped, too, as if it was listening as well.

From far down the valley she heard the rise and fall of the running dogs, howling at the moon. Little chirrups of frogs, the pick-buzz of insect wings, and then the choughing of a night-bird's wings. She turned her head for a moment, fearful that it might be an eater-of-bugs. When she looked back, the *sa-hawa* was almost gone, edging up the great towering mountain that loomed over her.

Flower almost cried out then, in frustration and anger and fear, but she held her tongue and looked for a place to start the climb. She had to use hands and feet instead of eyes, for the moonlight made this a place of shadows—shadows within shadows—and only her hands and feet could see between the dark and dark.

She felt as if she had been climbing for hours, though the moon above her spoke of a shorter time, when the butterfly suddenly disappeared. Without the lure of its phosphorescent wings, Flower was too exhausted to continue. All the tears she had held back for so long suddenly rose to swamp her eyes. She snuffled loudly and crouched uncertainly on a ledge. Then, huddling against the rockface, she tried to stay awake, to draw warmth and courage from the mountain. But without wanting to, she fell asleep.

In the dream she spiraled up and up and up into the sky without ladder or rope to pull her, and she felt the words of a high scream fall from her lips, a yelping *kya*. She awoke terrified and shaking in the morning light, sitting on a thin ledge nearly a hundred feet up the mountainside. She had no memory of the climb and certainly no way to get down.

And then she saw the *sa-hawa* next to her and memory flooded back. She cupped her hand, ready to pounce on the butterfly, when it fluttered its wings in the sunlight and moved from its perch. Desperate to catch it, she leaned out, lost her balance, and began to fall.

"Oh, Mother," she screamed in her mind, and a single word came back to her. *Aki-la*. Eagle. She screamed it aloud.

As she fell, the bones of her arms lengthened and flattened, cracking sinew and marrow. Her small, sharp nose bone arched outward and she watched it slowly form into a black beak with a dull yellow membrane at the base. Her body, twisting, seemed to stretch, catching the wind, first beneath, then above; she could feel the swift air through her feathers and the high, sweet whistling of it rushing past her head. Spiraling up, she pumped her powerful wings once. Then, holding them flat, she soared.

Aki-la. Golden eagle, she thought. It was her Word of Power, the Word That Changes, hers and no one else's. And then all words left her and she knew only wind and sky and the land spread out far below.

How long she coursed the sky in her flat-winged glide she did not know. For her there was no time, no ticking off of moment after moment, only the long sweet soaring. But at last her stomach marked the time for her and, without realizing it, she was scanning the ground for prey. It was as if she had two sights now, one the sweeping farsight that showed her the land as a series of patterns and the other that closed up the space whenever she saw movement or heat in the grass that meant some small creature was moving below.

At the base of the mountain she spied a large mouse and her wings knew even before her mind, even before her stomach. They cleaved to her side and she dove down in one long, perilous stoop toward the brown creature that was suddenly still in the short grass.

The wind rushed by her as she dove, and a high singing filled her head, wordless visions of meat and blood.

Kya, she called, and followed it with a whistle. *Kya,* her hunting song.

Right before reaching the mouse, she threw out her wings and backwinged, extending her great claws as brakes. But her final sight of the mouse, larger than she had guessed, standing upright in the grass as if it had expected her, its black eyes meeting her own and the white stripe across its head gleaming in the early sun, stayed her. Some memory, some old human thought teased at her. Instead of striking the mouse, she landed gracefully by its side, her great claws gripping the earth, remembering ground, surrendering to it.

Aki-la. She thought the word again, opened her mouth, and spoke it to the quiet air. She could feel the change begin again. Marrow and sinew and muscle and bone responded, reversing themselves, growing and shrinking, molding and forming. It hurt, yet it did not hurt; the pain was delicious.

And still the mouse sat, its bright little eyes watching her until the transformation was complete. Then it squeaked a word, shook itself all over, as if trying to slough off its own skin and bones, and grew, filling earth and sky, resolving itself into a familiar figure with the fierce stare of an eagle and the soft voice of the mouse.

"Late Blossoming Flower," her mother said, and opened welcoming arms to her.

"I have found my word," Flower said as she ran into them. Then, unaccountably, she put her head on her mother's breast and began to sob.

"You have found much more," said her mother. "For see—I have tested you, tempted you to let your animal nature overcome your human nature. And see—you stopped before the hunger for meat, the thirst for blood, mastered you and left you forever in your eagle form."

"But I might have killed you," Flower gasped. "I might have eaten you. I was an eagle and you were my natural prey."

"But you did not," her mother said firmly. "Now I must go home."

"Wait," Flower said. "There is something . . . something I have to tell you."

Her mother turned and looked at Flower over her shoulder. "About the old man?"

Flower looked down.

"I know it already. There he is." She pointed to a gray-green butterfly hovering over a blossom. "He is the same undisciplined creature he always was."

"I must change him back. I must learn how, quickly, before he leaves."

"He will not leave," said her mother. "Not that one. Or he would have left our village long ago. No, he will wait until you learn your other powers and change him back so that he might sit on the edge of power and laugh at it as he has always done, as he did to me so long ago. And now, my little one who is my little one no longer, use your eagle wings to fly. I will be waiting at our home for your return."

Flower nodded, and then she moved away from her mother and held out her arms. She stretched them as far apart as she could. Even so—even farther—would her wings stretch. She looked up into the sky, now blue and cloudless and beckoning.

"*Aki-la!*" she cried, but her mouth was not as stern as her mother's or as any of the other women of power, for she knew how to laugh. She opened her laughing mouth again. "*Aki-la.*"

She felt the change come on her, more easily this time, and she threw herself into the air. The morning sun caught the wash of gold at her beak, like a necklace of power. *Kya,* she screamed into the waiting wind, *kya,* and, for the moment, forgot mother and butterfly and all the land below.

Great Gray

The cold spike of winter wind struck Donnal full in the face as he pedaled down River Road toward the marsh. He reveled in the cold just as he reveled in the ache of his hands in the wool gloves and the pull of muscle along the inside of his right thigh.

At the edge of the marsh, he got off the bike, tucking it against the sumac, and crossed the road to the big field. He was lucky this time. One of the Great Grays, the larger of the two, was perched on a tree. Donnal lifted the field glasses to his eyes and watched as the bird, undisturbed by his movement, regarded the field with its big yellow eyes.

Donnal didn't know a great deal about birds, but the newspapers had been full of the *invasion,* as it was called. Evidently Great Gray owls were Arctic birds that only every hundred years found their way in large numbers to towns as far south as Hatfield. As if a Massachusetts town on the edge of the Berkshires was south. The red-back vole population in the north had crashed and the young Great Grays had fled their own hunger and the talons of the older birds. And here they were, daytime owls, fattening themselves on the mice and voles common even in winter in Hatfield.

Donnal smiled, and watched the bird as it took off, spreading its six-foot wings and sailing silently over the field. He knew there were other Great Grays in the Valley—two in Amherst, one in the Northampton Meadows, three reported in Holyoke, and some twenty others between Hatfield and Boston. But he felt that the two in Hatfield were his alone. So far no one else had discovered them. He had been biking out twice a day for over a week to watch them, a short three miles along the meandering road.

A vegetarian himself, even before he'd joined the Metallica commune in Turner's Falls, Donnal had developed an unnatural desire to watch animals feeding, as if that satisfied any of his dormant carnivorous instincts. He'd even owned a boa at one time, purchasing white mice for it at regular intervals. It was one of the reasons he'd been asked to leave the commune. The other, hardly worth mentioning, had more to do with a certain sexual ambivalence having to do with children. Donnal never thought about *those* things anymore. But watching the owls feeding made him aware of how much superior he was to the hunger of mere beasts.

"It makes me understand what is meant by a little lower than the angels," he'd remarked to his massage teacher that morning, thinking about angels with great gray wings.

This time the owl suddenly plummeted down, pouncing on something which it carried in its talons as it flew back to the tree. Watching through the field glasses, Donnal saw it had a mouse. He shivered deliciously as the owl plucked at the mouse's neck, snapping the tiny spinal column. Even though he was much too far away to hear anything, Donnal fancied a tiny dying shriek and the satisfying *snick* as the beak crunched through bone. He held his breath in three great gasps as the owl swallowed the mouse whole. The last thing Donnal saw was the mouse's tail stuck for a moment out of the beak like a piece of gray velvet spaghetti.

Afterward, when the owl flew off, Donnal left the edge of the field and picked his way across the crisp snow to the tree. Just as he hoped, the pellet was on the ground by the roots.

Squatting, the back of his neck prickling with excitement, Donnal took off his gloves and picked up the pellet. For a minute he just held it in his right hand, wondering at how light and how dry the whole thing felt. Then he picked it apart. The mouse's skull was still intact, surrounded by bits of fur. Reaching into the pocket of his parka, Donnal brought out the silk scarf he'd bought a week ago at the Mercantile just for this purpose. The scarf was blood red with little flecks of dark blue. He wrapped the skull carefully in the silk and slipped the packet into his pocket, then turned a moment to survey the field again. Neither of the owls was in sight.

Patting the pocket thoughtfully, he drew his gloves back on and strode back toward his bike. The wind had risen and snow was beginning to fall. He let the wind push him along as he rode, almost effortlessly, back to the center of town.

Donnal had a room in a converted barn about a quarter of a mile south of the center. The room was within easy walking to his massage classes and only about an hour's bike ride into Northampton, even closer to the grocery store. His room was dark and low and had a damp, musty smell as if it still held the memory of cows and hay in its beams. Three other families shared the main part of the barn, ex-hippies like Donnal, but none of them from the commune. He had found the place by biking through each of the small Valley towns, their names like some sort of English poem: Hadley, Whately, Sunderland, Deerfield, Heath, Goshen, Rowe. Hatfield, on the flat, was outlined by the Connecticut River on its eastern flank. There had been acres of potatoes, their white flowers waving in the breeze, when he first cycled through. He took it as an omen and when he found that the center had everything he would need—a pizza parlor, a bank, a convenience store, and a video store—had made up his mind to stay. There was a notice about the room for rent tacked up in the convenience store. He went right over and was accepted at once.

Stashing his bike in one of the old stalls, Donnal went up the rickety backstairs to his room. His boots lined up side by side by the door, he took the red scarf carefully out of his pocket. Cradling it in two hands, he walked over to the mantel which he'd built from a long piece of wood he'd found in the back, sanding and polishing the wood by hand all summer long.

He bowed his head a moment, remembering the owl flying on its silent wings over the field, pouncing on the mouse, picking at the animals's neck until it died, then swallowing it whole. Then he smiled and unwrapped the skull.

He placed it on the mantel and stepped back, silently counting. There were seventeen little skulls there now. Twelve were mice, four were voles. One, he was sure, was a weasel's.

Lost in contemplation, he didn't hear the door open, the quick intake of breath. Only when he had finished his hundredth repetition of the mantra and turned did Donnal realize that little Jason was staring at the mantel.

"You . . ." Donnal began, the old rhythm of his heart spreading a heat down his back. "You are not supposed to come in without knocking, Jay. Without being . . ." He took a deep breath and willed the heat away. "Invited."

Jason nodded silently, his eyes still on the skulls.

"Did you hear me?" Donnal forced his voice to be soft but he couldn't help noticing that Jason's hair was as velvety as mouse skin. Donnal jammed his hands into his pockets. "Did you?"

Jason looked at him then, his dark eyes wide, vaguely unfocused. He nodded but did not speak. He never spoke.

"Go back to your apartment," Donnal said, walking the boy to the door. He motioned with his head, not daring to remove his hands from his pockets. "Now."

Jason disappeared through the door and Donnal shut it carefully with one shoulder, then leaned against it. After a moment, he drew his hands out of his pockets. They were trembling and moist.

He stared across the room at the skulls. They seemed to glow, but it was only a trick of the light, nothing more.

Donnal lay down on his futon and thought about nothing but the owls until he fell asleep. It was dinnertime when he finally woke. As he ate he thought—and not for the first time—how hard winter was on vegetarians.

"But owls don't have that problem," he whispered aloud.

His teeth crunched through the celery with the same sort of *snick-snack* he thought he remembered hearing when the owl had bitten into the mouse's neck.

The next morning was one of those crisp, bright, clear winter mornings with the sun reflecting off the snowy fields with such an intensity that Donnal's eyes watered as he rode along River Road. By the water treatment building, he stopped and watched a cardinal flicking through the bare ligaments of sumac. His disability check was due and he guessed he might have a client or two as soon as he passed his exams at the Institute. He had good hands for massage and the extra money would come in handy. He giggled at the little joke: *hands . . . handy.* Extra money would mean he could buy the special tapes he'd been wanting. He'd use them for the accompaniment for massages and for his own meditations. Maybe even have cards made up: *Donnal McIvery, Licensed Massage Therapist,* the card would say. *Professional Massage. By Appointment Only.*

He was so busy thinking about the card, he didn't notice the car parked by the roadside until he was upon it. And it took him a minute before he realized there were three people—two men and a woman—standing on the other side of the car, staring at the far trees with binoculars.

Donnal felt hot then cold with anger. They were looking at *his* birds, *his* owls. He could see that both of the Great Grays were sitting in the eastern field, one on a dead tree down in the swampy area of the marsh and one in its favorite perch on a swamp maple. He controlled his anger and cleared his throat. Only the woman turned.

"Do you want a look?" she asked with a kind of quavering eagerness in her voice, starting to take the field glasses from around her neck.

Unable to answer, his anger still too strong, Donnal shook his head and, reaching into his pocket, took his own field glasses out. The red scarf came with it and fell to the ground. His cheeks flushed as red as the scarf as he bent to retrieve it. He knew there was no way the woman could guess what he used the scarf for, but still he felt she knew. He crumpled it tightly into a little ball and stuffed it back in his pocket. It was useless now, desecrated. He would have to use some of his disability check to buy another. He might have to miss a lesson because of it; because of *her.* Hatred for the woman flared up and it was all he could do to breathe deeply enough to force the feeling down, to calm himself. But his hands were shaking too much to raise the glasses to his eyes. When at last he could, the owls had flown, the people had gotten back into the car and driven away. Since the scarf was useless to him, he didn't even check for pellets, but got back on his bike and rode home.

Little Jason was playing outside when he got there and followed Donnal up to his room. He thought about warning the boy away again, but when he reached into his pocket and pulled out the scarf, having for the moment forgotten the scarf's magic was lost to him, he was overcome with the red heat. He could feel great gray wings growing from his shoulders, bursting through his parka, sprouting quill, feather, vane. His mouth tasted blood. He heard the *snick-snack* of little neck bones being broken. Such a satisfying sound. When the heat abated, and his eyes cleared, he saw that the boy lay on the floor, the red scarf around his neck, pulled tight.

For a moment Donnal didn't understand. Why was Jason lying there; why was the scarf set into his neck in just that way? Then when it came to him that his own strong hands had done it, he felt a strange satisfaction and he breathed as slowly as when he said his mantras. He laid the child out carefully on his bed and walked out of the room, closing the door behind.

He cashed the check at the local bank, then pedaled into Northampton. The Mercantile had several silk scarves, but only one red one. It was a dark red, like old blood. He bought it and folded it carefully into a little packet, then tucked it reverently into his pocket.

When he rode past the barn where he lived, he saw that there were several police cars parked in the driveway and so he didn't stop. Bending over the handlebars, he pushed with all his might, as if he could feel the stares of townsfolk.

The center was filled with cars, and two high school seniors, down from Smith Academy to buy candy, watched as he flew past. The wind at his back urged him on as he pedaled past the Main Street houses, around the meandering turns, past the treatment plant and the old barns marked with the passage of high school graffiti.

He was not surprised to see two vans by the roadside, one with out-of-state plates; he knew why they were there. Leaning his bike against one of the vans, he headed toward the swamp, his feet making crisp tracks on the crusty snow.

There were about fifteen people standing in a semicircle around the dead tree. The largest of the Great Grays sat in the crotch of the tree, staring at the circle of watchers with its yellow eyes. Slowly its head turned from left to right, eyes blinked, then another quarter turn.

The people were silent, though every once in a while one would move forward and kneel before the great bird, then as silently move back to place.

Donnal was exultant. These were not birders with field glasses and cameras. These were worshipers. Just as he was. He reached into his pocket and drew out the kerchief. Then slowly, not even feeling the cold, he took off his boots and socks, his jacket and trousers, his underpants and shirt. No one noticed him but the owl, whose yellow eyes only blinked but showed no fear.

He spoke his mantra silently and stepped closer, the scarf between his hands, moving through the circle to the foot of the tree. There he knelt, spreading the cloth to catch the pellet when it fell and baring his neck to the Great Gray's slashing beak.

Under the Hill

The day Big Nose Harry got tossed down the mine shaft for stealing from his boss, Joey the Needle, was All Hallows Eve. Or, as they say in the upper world, Halloween

He had been blindfolded and gagged and his hands and feet tied, just to make things more difficult.

But not impossible.

If they'd wound the rope widdershins, or if he had been tied with the binding of the three narrows—hands, wrists, knees—I couldn't have helped him.

Or if it had been a real mine shaft.

A real mine shaft and Big Nose Harry would have been in trouble. That would have landed him in with the dwarves, which would have been uncomfortable in the extreme.

Or in with the trolls.

Enough said.

But Big Nose Harry had been taken for a ride and dropped Under the Hill, which may have looked to the humans who dropped him there like a mine shaft, but certainly isn't.

Which is how I got him.

And which is what I told him as I took off the gag.

And after a while, when he'd stopped all that screaming and started listening, he realized that we might be of mutual benefit to one another.

One hand, he said, *washing the other.* A typical human way of looking at things. But close enough to what I already had in mind.

So I took off his blindfold. Which for a while made things worse.

But when they got better again—him being a natural hero, which is someone who can overcome his tendency to scream and turn it to good use—I untied him as well.

I knew he couldn't get out from Under the Hill again unless I helped. And—as I told him—if I even *began* to suspect he was a runner, I could always sell him to the Queen. She's perpetually short of good teinds around this time of year.

And him being a good soldier—except for that one mis-step with Joey the Needle—he got the point real quick.

Allegiances Under the Hill as well as Over can be bought. Of course they can. The threat of death or dismemberment is a powerful coin.

He shook his hands to get out the pins and needles. Those are his words. I didn't see any such thing. But then humans have different sight than the fey. If he believed he had pins or needles, it was not my duty to set him right.

When he finished shaking, he spit in his hand and said, "Put it there!"

Of course I took his hand.

Saliva, like blood, is a great binder.

"So whadda we do now?" he asked, looking around.

His eyes goggled, like a great frog's. I had put a glamour on the place before taking off his blindfold. Standard procedure, of course. What he saw was a room all gilded on top and sparkling below. Roots running riot with gems, and mushrooms looking like diamonds ready to be plucked.

Beginner stuff. Nothing exotic. But it always works with humans and Harry was no exception.

"I mean whadda you do for fun in this joint?" he added.

"Work comes first," I reminded him.

He nodded and put his finger to the side of his not inconsiderable nose.

"Got you," he replied.

I'm sure he did, though it didn't stop him from putting one of the "diamonds" in his pocket. I didn't plan to be around when it turned back into a toad.

We had to wait till moonrise, of course. My magic doesn't work as well in the bright light of day. And of course, this being All Hallow's Eve, I was as strong as I ever get during the year. I didn't tell Harry that of course. No use giving him any power over me.

Didn't tell him my true name either.

And I made him carry the pot, handle slung over his right arm. Left, of course, would have invited disaster.

Where we were heading was back to Joey the Needle's place, a little social club on seventh street situated between a garage and a sandwich shop.

Revenge for Big Nose Harry. This we both knew.

Revenge for me as well.

But that was my own little secret.

Joey the Needle had not always been a kingpin. He was a small numbers man from Bayonne. But about a year ago he had come into big money and with it bought his way right up to the top.

"Just found it lying around," he liked to say.

Only where he found it was underground when he was burying one of his boss's ex-employees, a man who had asked for too much of a raise.

Where Joey the Needle found the money was in my safe hole.

How was I to know he was going to dig in the middle of a swamp? There'd been no rainbows that day, no need to keep an eye on the pot. My tea leaves hadn't said anything about theft. Only about sewing.

Sewing.

Needle.

I didn't make the connection until much later. Tea leaves are like that. Useless really. I understand coffee grounds are purer. But I can't stand the taste.

So there I was sitting in my cozy condo Under the Hill, several dozen leagues away from the safe hole. I was reading a book called "Touch Magic" and laughing uproariously at the funny parts.

The alarm went off.

By the time I got on my seven leaguers and went to see what had triggered the bell, my entire pot was gone. Not even a copper penny left.

I'd barely time to write down the license number of the Honda Civic that was making its swift getaway.

It took me weeks to convince a drunken Irish cop to trace that license for me. Weeks more to locate the Needle. Things are hard these days when only drunks and old ladies believe in us. We fey can't just get up and go easily into the city amongst the iron and steel girded walls.

So Big Nose Harry ending up in my place was a gift, really.

But we fey know that eventually these gifts always come our way.

Of course we don't always know what to do with a gift once we have it. Though this time I already had a glimmer of an idea.

Well, more than a glimmer.

It depended upon Harry's greed and Joey's uneasiness.

In other words, it depended upon human nature.

We went in my cart, pulled by a one-horned nanny goat, as I could no more have gotten into a car (all those metal parts) than fly.

A glamour convinced Harry we were in a Porsche.

He was impressed. "Nice wheels."

I agreed. "German '97" I said. I wasn't lying. It was a 1797, and the wheels had been made by a wheelwright known throughout the Black Forest.

As we went along—jouncing a bit more than a Porsche, but I didn't want to expend any more of my magical capital than necessary, even if it was Halloween—I explained my plan to Harry.

"I can make you look exactly like the Needle," I said.

"Are you a face lift doc or sumpin?" he asked.

"Sumpin . . . er, something like that," I answered, "only I take half as long and it doesn't hurt."

He smiled. "I like that."

"I thought you would."

"And this face change will help me exactly how?" He rubbed a finger on his nose again.

Rather on than in, I thought. Really, humans are a disgusting race. Inventing metal solely to kill one another off.

"Think, Harry," I said, and then make it a command by placing my left hand over my right. "Think!"

And then he got it. "If I look like him, everyone will think I *am* him." He grinned.

"And . . ."

Really, humans are not very bright either. Better not to burden him with the knowledge that, with the glamour in place, only twelve humans at any one time would see him that way. I doubted he could count that high.

"And I can tell everyone what to do and . . ."

I could see I was going to have to take a more active role than is normal. That's never a good idea. Humans need to believe they make all the decisions in any interactions with the fey. But we were almost into town and he still hadn't got it.

"And you can have control of the Needle's money and his—"

"His *safe!*" shouted Harry happily. "I can open his big Underwood 777!"

Rather you than me, I thought. According to my sources, that safe was pure iron. Even being in the same room with it was going to give me a headache you wouldn't believe.

"And see what's inside," I finished up for him.

"Yeah," he said with the same kind of look the Queen gives her teinds, just before shoving them into the Pit of Hell.

We pulled up in front of the little sandwich shop an hour after moonrise. The space right by the social club door was just being taken up by an enormous stretch limo. At the rate Joey the Needle was going through my gold, there'd be precious little left for me.

I got out of the cart and tossed what looked like keys to Harry. Actually they were three beans sewn together.

"Gee, thanks, Boss," he said.

"No, Harry, no. *You're* the boss now," I said, turning him so he could see his transformation in the plate glass window.

And there, right below *EATS MAMA'S EATS* was Joey the Needle, looking dapper and disgustingly thin.

Harry saluted the image. It saluted him back. He turned and checked it out over his right shoulder. It did the same. He waved. It waved.

After a few seconds of such posturing, Harry got it.

"Hey!" he said in a fair imitation of Joey's reedy voice, "I'm him. The Needle."

"No, Harry," I said, "you're you. But everyone else will think you're Joey. Now remember, we have only a short time to do this before the glamour goes."

"How short?" he asked.

"Cock's crow," I said.

"Hunh?"

"Sunrise."

"Ah geeze," he said.

"Exactly."

We went in.

Now I'm not saying that all humans are dim bulbs, but the ones at the social club were not the brightest of creatures. Perhaps their names had something to do with it. Call yourself Sammy Two Shoes or Tim the Tongue or Grasshopper Vic or Slow Hand Charley and you're asking for a bad geas. The Powers simply don't fool around when it comes to names. An ancestor of mine called himself Rumplestiltskin and look where that got him!

So when we walked in, and Harry—now Joey—was being greeted by the gang, I told them I was Ben Armstrong from Chicago. Pick a name, pick one that gives you strength.

"Muscle, eh?" asked Tim the Tongue. When he spoke, his tongue—with its silver stud—flicked in and out like some dotty reptile.

I nodded.

"Chicago, eh?" Grasshopper Vic asked. "I got me an uncle in Chicago." He set down his violin case, opened it, drew out a gun and began to clean it.

"Put that thing away," Harry/Joey said. "Before somebody gets hurt."

"Some *body* did," Slow Hand Charley said.

They all laughed.

See—dim bulbs.

Grasshopper put his gun away and asked, casually, "So why're you back, Boss. Thought you were off for a weekend trip to Vegas."

Harry/Joey turned to me.

No use hoping *he'd* come up with an answer.

"Changed his mind," I said.

"But I thought him and Miss Foofy was getting hitched there," Sammy Two Shoes said.

Come in the middle of a story, my old mother used to say, and you lose the plot.

"Changed his mind about . . ." I hesitated.

But Harry/Joey jumped in, surprising me with his quickness. "Changed his mind about using the credit card. I want to use what's in the safe."

There was a moment of silence.

"Safe money, you know," I added, smiling.

They all laughed.

"Okay, Boss," the Tongue said.

We went into the back room where the safe was kept, picking up a trio of hangers-on along the way: Jimmy Four Eyes, Willy the Weeper, and Cricket Danny Pucci whose shoes squeaked as he walked.

"Do you always open the safe with this big a crowd?" I whispered into Harry/Joey's ear.

"Yeah," Harry/Joey whispered out of the side of his mouth. "It's an Underwood 777."

As if that explained it.

The Underwood 777 was big and black, with touches of green and brass. It had a large dial with numbers and letters picked out in gold. I could feel the unshielded iron all the way at the door and my knees went weak. Putting my hands on the frame, I hung in there. The touch of the wood kept me standing.

Just.

Meanwhile, the gang members had made a big half-circle around the safe.

Harry/Joey went over to the Underwood 777 and cracked his knuckles. They sounded like a skeleton reassembling itself: *clickety-clickety-clack.*

Then he straightened up again.

"Get me a beer," he ordered hoarsely, and Grasshopper Vic raced out to do his bidding.

Then Harry/Joey turned to me and gestured. "Armstrong, commere."

I couldn't leave the doorframe. Not and keep standing.

"I said, commere."

I shook my head. It was about all I could manage.

Harry/Joey snapped his fingers and Jimmy Four Eyes and Willy the Weeper came over to me. Each one grabbed an arm and carried me across the room, depositing me in front of Harry/Joey.

Right by the safe.

"When I say commere, you gotta commere," said Harry/Joey. "I am the boss. Right?"

They all nodded their heads, but I could no longer manage even that.

"All of youse outta here. Now!" said Harry/Joey. "Cepting Armstrong. Him I want here."

"But the safe . . . " Sammy Two shoes began.

"Outta Here!"

"Now," I added softly.

They all left.

Harry/Joey bent down and stared at me. "Whadda I do now?"

I looked up at his befuddled expression. "Open the safe."

"I don't know the combination," he said.

"Well don't look at me," I told him. "I'm not likely to have it. Who *does* know it?"

"Only the Needle knows."

"*You* are the Needle now."

"Only this Needle knows nothing," he said.

Before we got stuck entirely on N's, something I couldn't stop while that close to the iron safe, I whispered, "Get me into the next room and I'll think of something."

"What's wrong wit' you?" he asked.

"The opposite of iron deficiency," I said.

"Iron *a*fficiency?" he asked.

"Close enough."

So he picked me up and carried me back across the safe room. As we reached the door, my strength began to return, and with it my magic and with that my brains.

"Put me down," I instructed him, and he did.

"This is what you have to do . . ." I began, looking up at him.

But Harry/Joey had this peculiar expression. He was staring bumfuddled at something across the big room.

Striding through the front door of the social club was another Needle—the real one—accompanied by three thugs who made up in mass what they clearly lacked in any gray matter.

Harry/Joey dropped me and straightened up.

"Thought I'd better get some safe money," the real Needle said.

"But, Boss . . ." began Sammy and Danny and Arnold and Willy together. Their heads jerked back and forth, forth and back between the two Needles so quickly, I was surprised they didn't develop whiplash.

"Stand tall," I whispered to my Needle. And such was my renewed strength, he did.

"What's goin' on here?" cried Harry/Joey. "Who's this imposer?"

"Imposter," I whispered.

"Whatever," he whispered back.

The real Needle looked over and goggled. It did not improve his looks or his standing with the men in the social club. "Who'er you?" he managed to get out.

But my Harry/Joey was ready for that one.

"I," he said, "am Joey the Needle. Whaddare you doin' in my place?"

The real Needle was stuck for an answer.

Then Harry/Joey shouted, "Grab him!"

Well even the torpedoes who'd come in with the Needle were confused now. But they could count. And we outnumbered them nine to three. Well ten if you count me, but I didn't.

"Bring him into the safe room," Harry/Joey said. "Let's see if he can open it."

They carried the squirming Needle in. "Of course I can open it you dimwits," he said.

They dumped him in front of the safe and he opened it as quick as that, three turns to the right, one to the left.

"So, you planned to come in disguised as me and open my safe," said Harry/Joey, crossing his arms, a huge scowl on his face.

Really, I was impressed with his quick thinking.

"Maybe we need to get rid of him, Boss?" asked Will the Weeper.

"Yes!" said Harry/Joey and the Needle at the same time, which confused everyone, to say the least.

Just then a voice from the other room cried in a tremulous whine, "Sweetie pie. Honeydew. Where are you."

"Miss Fuffy!" both the Needles cried.

And then she came into the safe room on ridiculously high heels, practically tripping over the threshold and into my arms.

"Honeybunch," she cooed, looking straight at the Real Needle.

"You know it's me?" he asked.

"Who else?" she said, shrugging out of my grasp and peering at each of the thugs in turn.

I counted rapidly.

Four thugs at the beginning.

A trio joining them.

Two Needles and three torpedoes made twelve.

But Miss Fuffy on her stiletto heels made thirteen humans, and with that, the glamour was over.

So here we sit, Big Nose Harry and me, back to back, tied tightly together. We were thrown down in this big hole in the Jersey swamps just a couple of minutes ago.

"Don't worry," I tell him. "The ropes weren't turned widdershins and we weren't tied with the binding of the narrows. I can get us out."

Unless, I think, there are trolls.

Or dwarves.

Or . . .

But even I don't want to think about barrow-wights.

"So once we're out," Harry/Joey says, "what then?"

I smile and fiddle with the ropes. "Now I know the combination of the Needle's safe," I tell him. "And next Halloween . . ."

I can tell by the way he screams that he is not amused.

Godmother Death

You think you know this story. You do not.

You think it comes from Ireland, from Norway, from Spain. It does not. You have heard it in Hebrew, in Swedish, in German. You have read it in French, in Italian, in Greek.

It is not a story, though many mouths have made it that way. It is true.

How do I know? Death, herself, told me. She told me in that whispery voice she saves for special tellings. She brushed her thick black hair away from that white forehead, and told me.

I have no reason to disbelieve her. Death does not know how to lie. She has no need to.

It happened this way, only imagine it in Death's own soft breeze of a voice. Imagine she is standing over your right shoulder speaking this true story in your ear. You do not turn to look at her. I would not advise it. But if you do turn, she will smile at you, her smile a child's smile, a woman's smile, the grin of a crone. But she will not tell *her* story anymore. She will tell yours.

It happened this way, as Death told me. She was on the road, between Cellardyke and Crail. Or between Claverham and Clifton. Or between Chagford and anywhere. Does it matter the road? It was small and winding; it was cobbled and pot-holed; it led from one place of human habitation to another. Horses trotted there. Dogs marked their places. Pig drovers and cattle drovers and sheepherders used those roads. So why not Death?

She was visible that day. Sometimes she plays at being mortal. It amuses her. She has had a long time trying to amuse herself. She wore her long gown kirtled above her knee. She wore her black hair up in a knot. But if you looked carefully, she did not walk like a girl of that time. She moved too freely for that, her arms swinging. She stepped on her full foot, not on the toes, not mincing. She could copy the clothes, but she never remembered how girls really walk.

A man, frantic, saw her and stopped her. He actually put his hand on her arm. It startled her. That did not happen often, that Death is startled. Or that a man puts a hand on her.

"Please," the man said. "My Lady." She was clearly above him, though she had thought she was wearing peasant clothes. It was the way she stood, the way she walked. "My wife is about to give birth to our child and we need someone to stand god-mother. You are all who is on the road."

Godmother? It amused her. She had never been asked to be one. "Do you know who I am?" she asked.

"My Lady?" The man suddenly trembled at his temerity. Had he touched a high lord's wife? Would she have him executed? No matter. It was his first child. He was beyond thinking.

Death put a hand up to her black hair and pulled down her other face. "Do you know me now?"

He knew. Peasants are well acquainted with Death in that form. He nodded.

"And want me still?" Death asked.

He nodded and at last found his voice. "You are greater than God or the Devil, Lady. You would honor us indeed."

His answer pleased her, and so she went with him. His wife was couched under a rowan tree, proof against witches. The babe was near to crowning when they arrived.

"I have found a great lady to stand as godmother," the man said. "But do not look up at her face, wife." For suddenly he feared what he had done.

His wife did not look, except out of the corner of her eye. But so seeing Death's pale, beautiful face, she was blinded in that eye forever. Not because death had blinded the woman, that was not her way. But fear—and perhaps the sugar sickness—did what Death would not.

The child, a boy, was born with a caul. Death ripped it open with her own hand, then dropped the slimed covering onto the morning grass where it shimmered for a moment like dew.

"Name him Haden," Death said. "And when he is a man I shall teach him a trade." Then she was gone, no longer amused. Birth never amused for her long.

Death followed the boy's progress one year closely, another not at all. She sent no gifts. She did not stand for him at the church font. Still, the boy's father and his half-blind mother did well for themselves; certainly better than peasants had any reason to expect. They were able to purchase their own farm, able to send their boy to a school. They assumed it was because of Death's patronage, when in fact she had all but forgotten them and her godson. You cannot expect Death to care so about a single child, who has seen so many.

Yet on the day Haden became a man, on the day of his majority, his father called Death. He drew her sign in the sand, the same that he had seen on the chain around her neck. He said her name and the boy's.

And Death came.

One minute the man was alone and the next he was not. Death was neither winded nor troubled by her travel, though she still wore the khakis of an army nurse. She had not bothered to change from her last posting.

"Is it time?" she asked, who was both in and out of time. "Is he a man, my godson?" She knew he was not dead. *That* she would have known.

"It is time, Lady," the man said, carefully looking down at his feet. *He* was not going to be blinded like his wife.

"Ah." She reached up and took off the nurse's cap and shook down her black hair. The trouble with bargains, she mused, was that they had to be kept.

"He shall be a doctor," she said after a moment.

"A doctor?" the man had thought no further than a great farm for his boy.

"A doctor," Death said. "For doctors and generals know me best. And I have recently seen too much of generals." She did not tell him of the Crimea, of the Dardanelles, of the riders from beyond the steppes. "A doctor would be nice."

Haden was brought to her. He was a smart lad, but not overly smart. He had strong hands and a quick smile.

Death dismissed the father and took the son by the hand, first warming her own hand. It was an effort she rarely made.

"Haden, you shall be a doctor of power," she said. "Listen carefully and treat this power well."

Haden nodded. He did not look at her, not right at her. His

mother had warned him, and though he was not sure he believed, he believed.

"You will become the best-known doctor in the land, my godson," Death said. "For each time you are called to a patient, look for me at the bedside. If I stand at the head of the bed, the patient will live, no matter what you or any other doctor will do. But if I stand at the foot, the patient will die. And there is nought anyone can do—no dose and no diagnoses—to save him."

Haden nodded again. "I understand, godmother."

"I think you do," she said, and was gone.

In a few short years, Haden became known throughout his small village, and a few more years and his reputation had spread through the county. A few more and he was known in the kingdom. If he said a patient would live, that patient would rise up singing. If he said one would die, even though the illness seemed but slight, then that patient would die. It seemed uncanny, but he was *always* right. He was more than a doctor. He was—some said—a seer.

Word came at last to the king himself.

Ah—now you think I have been lying to you, that this is only a story. It has a king in it. And while a story with Death might be true, a story with a king in it is always a fairy tale. But remember, this comes from a time when kings were as common as corn. Plant a field and you got corn. Plant a kingdom and you got a king. It is that simple.

The king had a beautiful daughter. Nothing breeds as well as money, except power. Of course a king's child would be beautiful.

She was also dangerously ill, so ill in fact that the king promised his kingdom—not half but all—to anyone who could save her. The promise included marriage, for how else could he hand the kingdom off. She was his only child, and he would not beggar her to save her life. That was *worse* than death.

Haden heard of the offer and rode three days and three nights, trading horses at each inn. When he came to the king's palace he was, himself, thin and weary from travel; there was dirt under his fingernails. His hair was ill kempt. But his reputation had preceded him.

"Can she be cured?" asked the king. He had no time or temper for formalities.

"Take me to her room," Haden said.

So the king and the queen together led him into the room.

The princess's room was dark with grief and damp with crying. The long velvet drapes were pulled close against the light. The place smelled of Death's perfume, that soft, musky odor. The tapers at the door scarcely lent any light.

"I cannot see," Haden said, taking one of the tapers. Bending over the bed, he peered down at the princess and a bit of hot wax fell on her cheek. She opened her eyes and they were the color of late wine, a deep plum. Haden gasped at her beauty.

"Open the drapes," he commanded, and the king himself drew the curtains aside.

Then Haden saw that Death was sitting at the foot of the great four-poster bed, buffing her nails. She was wearing a black shift, cut entirely too low in the front. Her hair fell across her shoulders in black waves. The light from the windows shone through her and she paid no attention to what was happening in the room, intent on her nails.

Haden put his finger to his lips and summoned four serving men to him. Without a word, instructing them only with his hands, he told them to turn the bed around quickly. And such was his reputation, they did as he bade.

Then he walked to the bed's head, where Death was finishing her final nail. He was so close, he might have touched her.

But instead, he lifted the princess's head and helped her sit up. She smiled, not at him but through him, as if he were as transparent as Death.

"She will live, sire," Haden said.

Both Death and the maiden looked at Haden straight on, startled, Death because she had been fooled, and the princess because she had not noticed him before. Only then did the princess smile at Haden, as she would to a footman, a serving-man, a cook. She smiled at him, but Death did not.

"A trick will not save her," said Death. "I will have all in the end." She shook her head. "I do not say this as a boast. Nor as a promise. It simply is what it is."

"I know," Haden said.

"What do you know?" asked the king, for he could not see or hear Death.

Haden looked at the king and smiled a bit sadly. "I know she will live and that if you let me, I will take care of her the rest of her life."

The king did not smile. A peasant's son, even though he is a doctor, even though he is famous throughout the kingdom, does not marry a princess. In a story, perhaps. Not in the real world. Unlike Death, kings do not have to keep bargains. He had Haden thrown into the dungeon.

There Haden spent three miserable days. On the fourth he woke to find Godmother Death sitting at his bedfoot. She was dressed as if for a ball, her hair in three braids that were caught up on the top of her head with a jeweled pin. Her dress, of some white silken stuff, was demurely pleated and there were rosettes at each shoulder. She looked sixteen or sixteen hundred. She looked ageless.

"I see you at my bedfoot," Haden said. "I suppose that means that today I die."

She nodded.

"And there is no hope for me?"

"I can be tricked only once," Death said. "The king will hang you at noon."

"And the princess?"

"Oh, I am going to her wedding," Death said, standing and pirouetting gracefully so that Haden could see how pretty the dress was, front and back.

"Then I shall see her in the hereafter," Haden said. "She did not look well at all. Ah—then I am content to die."

Death, who was a kind godmother after all, did not tell him that it was not the princess who was to die that day. Nor was the king to die, either. It was just some old auntie for whom the excitement of the wedding would prove fatal. Death would never lie to her godson, but she did not always tell the entire truth. Like her brother Sleep, she liked to say things on the slant. Even Death can be excused just one weakness.

At least, that is what she told me, and I have no reason to doubt the truth of it. She was sitting at my bedfoot, and—sitting there—what need would she have to lie?

Dedicated to the memory of
Charles Mikolaycak

Creationism:

An Illustrated Lecture in Two Parts

In the beginning
(click)

God created the heavens and the earth.
The earth was without form.
(click)

which is not to say entirely formless, but rather still lumpy and without fixed landmarks. And void, or empty, or unpopulated.
(click)

Darkness was over the face of the deep and under it as well. And as the spirit of God hovered over the face of the dark deep, rather like a hovercraft, only without any actual flow systems, the voice of God said, "Let there be Light."
(click)

Which we take to mean the sun appeared in the sky, though appear may be rather too sudden a word for what obviously. . . .
(click)

And there was light and it was good.

Then God divided the light from the darkness, a rather neat trick, and called the Light Day and the darkness He called Night.

(click)

and there was evening and morning, the first day.

Then God checked his list and said, "Let there be a firmament in the midst of the waters, a kind of metaphysical dike, dividing them." And He called the firmament Heaven. Or Lower Atmosphere. There are two schools of thought on this.

(click)

(click)

And there was evening and there was morning, the second day.

And God said, "Let the waters under the Heaven be gathered together in one place and let dry lands appear, which are easy to map."

(click)

And which appear in any child's telescope. And He called the dry land Earth and the gathered waters Seas or Oceans or Mares, there are three schools of thought on this.

(click)

(click)

(click)

And He bade the Earth put forth grasses and seeds and trees bearing fruit and mushroom and fungi and trailing vines. And God saw that it was good.

(clickclickclickclickclickclick)

And there was evening and morning and that was the third day.

On the fourth day God put a multitude of lights in the Heaven further dividing day and night and southern hemisphere from northern. And He distinguished the seasons, making one half Earth freeze and one half Earth bake, an interesting approach to world building.

(click)

Which led, as we shall see, to an odd prolificity of life, the hemispheres each with their own distinguishable creatures. And it was evening and morning, the fourth day.

Then God said, "Let the waters swarm with swarms of living creatures.

(click)

And let birds fly in the Heavens."

(click)

And He created great monsters of the sea which could not live on land and great monsters of the land which could not live in the seas, a great wasting of monsters, whose bones litter both land and sea.

(click)
(click)

Then God saw that it was good, and told the creatures to be fruitful and multiply

(click)

though He forgot to tell them how to stop multiplying, a rather more useful skill one would think. And there was evening and there was morning, the fifth day.

Then God said, "Let Earth bear living creatures, wild animals of every kind," by which He meant creatures other than the great monsters, who were already overbreeding on the shores and polluting the seas with their monster bones.

(click)

So He brought forth cattle and serpents and herds of horses

(click)
(click)

(*click*)

and wombats, snail darters, and the chicken-eating frog.
(*clickclickclick*)

And God saw—though we may wonder why—that it was good.

(*click*)

And then God said, "Fuck it. I'm not going to make man in my image. I have total recall, both forward and back. I know what a mess he will make of my Earth. And just when I've gotten all my firmaments and Mares and snail darters and lights just right." And He squeezed His fingers together

(*click*)

which made
mush of the piece of clay he had been molding,

(*click*)

and threw it down in the middle of the central continent where it formed an odd ridge of mountains

(*click*)

which we today call *God's Pile.*

(*click*)

And He made our lovely planet instead, ninth away from the sun.

(*click*)

Lights, please.

Now, before I deal with the second part of my lecture, the scientific approach to creation, are there any questions?

—*for Salman Rushdie*

Allerleirauh

Her earliest memory was of rain on a thatched roof, and surely it was a true one, for she had been born in a country cottage two months before time, to her father's sorrow and her mother's death. They had sheltered there, out of the storm, and her father had never forgiven himself nor the child who looked so like her mother. *So* like her, it was said, that portraits of the two as girls might have been exchanged and not even Nanny the wiser.

So great had been her father's grief at the moment of his wife's death, he might even have left the infant there, still bright with birth blood and squalling. Surely the crofters would have been willing, for they were childless themselves. His first thought was to throw the babe away, his wife's Undoing as he called her ever after, though her official name was Allerleirauh. And he might have done so had she not been the child of a queen. A royal child, whatever the crime, is not to be tossed aside so lightly, a feather in the wind.

But he had made two promises to the blanched figure that

lay on the rude bed, the woolen blankets rough against her long, fair legs. White and red and black she had been then. White of skin, like the color of milk after the whey is skimmed out. Red as the toweling that carried her blood, the blood they could not staunch, the life leaching out of her. And black, the color of her eyes, the black seas he used to swim in, the black tendrils of her hair.

"Promise me." Her voice had stumbled between those lips, once red, now white.

He clasped her hands so tightly he feared he might break them, though it was not her bones that were brittle, but his heart. "I promise," he said. He would have promised her anything, even his own life, to stop the words bleeding out of that white mouth. "I promise."

"Promise me you will love the child," she said, for even in her dying she knew his mind, knew his heart, knew his dark soul. "Promise."

And what could he do but give her that coin, the first of two to close her dead eyes?

"And promise me you will not marry again, lest she be . . ." and her voice trembled, sighed, died.

"Lest she be as beautiful as thee," he promised wildly in the high tongue, giving added strength to his vow. "Lest she have thy heart, thy mind, thy breasts, thy eyes . . ." and his rota continued long past her life. He was speaking to a dead woman many minutes and would not let himself acknowledge it, as if by naming the parts of her he loved, he might keep her alive, the words bleeding out of him as quickly as her lost blood.

"She is gone, my lord," said the crofter's wife, not even sure of his rank except that he was clearly above her. She touched his shoulder for comfort, a touch she would never have ventured in other circumstances, but tragedy made them kin.

The king's litany continued as if he did not hear, and indeed he did not. For all he heard was the breath of death, that absence made all the louder by his own sobs.

"She is dead, Sire," the crofter said. He had known the king all along, but had not mentioned it till that one moment. Blunter than his wife, he was less sure of the efficacy of touch. "Dead."

And this one final word the king heard.

"*She is not dead!*" he roared, bringing the back of his hand around to swat the crofter's face as if he were not a giant of a man but an insect. The crofter shuddered and was silent, for majesty does make gnats of such men, even in their own homes. Even there.

The infant, recognizing no authority but hunger and cold, began to cry at her father's voice. On and on she bawled, a high, unmusical strand of sound till the king dropped his dead wife's hand, put his own hands over his ears, and ran from the cottage screaming, "I shall go mad!"

He did not, of course. He ranged from distracted to distraught for days, weeks, months, and then the considerations of kingship recalled him to himself. It was his old self recalled: the distant, cold, considering king he had been before his marriage. For marriage to a young, beautiful, foreign-born queen had changed him. He had been for those short months a better man, but not a better ruler. So the counselors breathed easier, certainly. The barons and nobles breathed easier, surely. And the peasants—well, the peasants knew a hard hand either way, for the dalliance of kings has no effect on the measure of rain nor the seasons in the sun, no matter what the poets write or the minstrels pluck upon their strings.

Only two in the kingdom felt the brunt of his neglect. Allerleirauh, of course, who would have loved to please him; but she scarcely knew him. And her Nanny, who had been her mother's Nanny, and was brought across the seas to a strange land. Where Allerleirauh knew hunger, the nurse knew hate. She blamed the king as he blamed the child for the young queen's death, and she swore in her own dark way to bring sorrow to him and his line.

The king was mindful in his own way of his promises. Kingship demands attention to be paid. He loved his daughter with the kindness of kings, which is to say he ordered her clothed and fed and educated to her station. But he did not love her with his heart. How could he, having seen her first cloaked in his wife's blood? How could he, having named her Undoing?

He had her brought to him but once a year, on the anniversary of his wife's death, that he might remind himself of her crime. That it was also the anniversary of Allerleirauh's birth, he did not remark. She thought he remembered, but he did not.

So the girl grew unremarked and unloved, more at home in the crofter's cottage where she had been born. And remembering each time she sat there in the rain—learning the homey crafts from the crofter's stout wife—that first rain.

The king did not marry again, though his counselors advised it. Memory refines what is real. Gold smelted in the mind's cauldron is the purer. No woman could be as beautiful to him as the dead queen. He built monuments and statues, commissioned poems and songs. The palace walls were hung with portraits that resembled her, all in color—the skin white as snow, the lips red as blood, the hair black as raven's wings. He lived in a mausoleum and did not notice the live beauty for the dead one.

Years went by, and though each spring messengers went through the kingdom seeking a maiden "white and black and red," the king's own specifications, they came home each summer's end to stare disconsolately at the dead queen's portraits.

"Not one?" the king would ask.

"Not one," the messengers replied. For the kingdom's maidens had been blonde or brown or redheaded. They had been pale or rosy or tan. And even those sent abroad found not a maid who looked like the statues or spoke like the poems or resembled in the slightest what they had all come to believe the late queen had been.

So the king went through spring and summer and into snow, still unmarried and without a male heir.

In desperation, his advisers planned a great three-day ball, hoping that—dressed in finery—one of the rejected maidens of the kingdom might take on a queenly air. Notice was sent that all were to wear black the first night, red the second, and white the third.

Allerleirauh was invited, too, though not by the king's own wishes. She was told of the ball by her nurse.

"I will make you three dresses," the old woman said. "The first dress will be as gold as the sun, the second as silver as the moon, and the third one will shine like the stars." She hoped that in this way, the princess would stand out. She hoped in this way to ruin the king.

Now if this were truly a fairy tale (and what story today with a king and queen and crofter's cottage is not?) the princess would go outside to her mother's grave. And there, on her knees, she would learn a magic greater than any craft, a woman's magic compounded of moonlight, elopement, and deceit. The neighboring kingdom would harbor her, the neighboring prince would marry her, her father would be brought to his senses, and the moment of complete happiness would be the moment of story's end. Ever after is but a way of saying: "There is nothing more to tell." It is but a dissembling. There is always more to tell. There is no happy *ever* after. There is happy *on occasion* and happy *every once in a while.* There is happy *when the memories do not overcome the now.*

But this is not a fairy tale. The princess is married to her father and, always having wanted his love, does not question the manner of it. Except at night, late at night, when he is away from her bed and she is alone in the vastness of it.

The marriage is sanctioned and made pure by the priests, despite the grumblings of the nobles. One priest who dissents is murdered in his sleep. Another is burned at the stake. There is no third. The nobles who grumble lose their lands. Silence becomes the conspiracy; silence becomes the conspirators.

Like her mother, the princess is weak-wombed. She dies in childbirth surrounded by that silence, cocooned in it. The child she bears is a girl, as lovely as her mother. The king knows he will not have to wait another thirteen years.

It is an old story.

Perhaps the oldest.

Sun/Flight

They call me the nameless one. My mother was the sea, and the sun itself fathered me. I was born fully clothed and on my boyish cheeks the beginnings of a beard. Whoever I was, wherever I came from, had been washed from me by the waves in which I was found.

And so I have made many pasts for myself. A honey-colored mother cradling me. A father with his beard short and shaped like a Minoan spade. Sisters and brothers have I gifted myself. And a home that smelled of fresh-strewn reeds and olives ripening on the trees. Sometimes I make myself a king's son, god-born, a javelin in my hand and a smear of honeycake on my lips. Other times I am a craftsman's child, with a length of golden string threaded around my thumbs. Or the son of a *dmos,* a serf, my back arched over the furrows where little birds search for seeds like farmers counting the crop. With no remembered pasts, I can pick a different one each day to suit my mood, to cater my need.

But most of the time I think myself the child of the birds, for when the fishermen pulled me up from the sea, drowned of my past, I clutched a single feather in my hand. The feather was golden, sun-colored, and when it dried it was tufted with yellow rays. I carried it with me always, my talisman, my token back across the Styx. No one knew what bird had carried this feather in its wing or tail. The shaft is strong and white and the barbs soft. The little fingers of down are no-color at all; they change with the changing light.

So I am no-name, son of no-bird, pulled from the waters of the sea north and east of Delos, too far for swimming, my only sail the feather in my hand.

The head of the fishermen who rescued me was a morose man called Talos who would have spoken more had he no tongue at all. But he was a good man, for all that he was silent. He gave me advice but once, and had I listened then, I would not be here, now, in a cold and dark cavern listening to voices from my unremembered past and fearing the rising of the sun.

When Talos plucked me from the water, he wrung me out with hands that were horned from work. He made no comment at all about my own hands, whose softness the water-wrinkles could not disguise. He brought me home to his childless wife. She spread honey-balm on my burns, for my back and right side were seared as if I had been drawn from the flames instead of from the sea. The puckered scars along my side are still testimony to that fire. Talos was convinced I had come from the wreckage of a burning ship, though no sails or spars were ever found. But the only fire I could recall was red and round as the sun.

Of fire and water was I made, Talos' wife said. Her tongue ran before her thoughts always. She spoke twice, once for herself and once for her speechless husband. "Of sun and sea, my only child," she would say, fondly stroking my wine-dark hair, touching the feather I kept pinned to my *chiton.* "Bird child. A gift of the sky, a gift from the sea."

So I stayed with them. Indeed, where else could I, still a boy, go? And they were content. Except for the scar seaming my side, I was thought handsome. And my fingers were clever with memories of their own. They could make things of which I had no conscious knowledge: miniature buildings of strange design, with passages that turned back upon themselves; a mechanical bull-man that could move about and roar when wound with a hand-carved key.

"Fingers from the gods," Talos' wife said. "Such fingers. You're father must have been Hephaestus, though you have Apollo's face." And she added god after god to my string, a litany that comforted her until Talos' warning grunt stemmed the rising tide of her words.

At last my good looks and my clever fingers brought me to the attention of the local lord, I the nameless one, the child of sun and sea and sky. That lord was called Circinus. He had many slaves and many bondsmen, but only one daughter, Perdix.

She was an ox-eyed beauty, with a long neck. Her slim, boy-ish body, her straight, narrow nose, reminded me somehow of my time before the waves, though I could not quite say how. Her name was signed from every man's lips, but no one dared speak it aloud.

Lord Circinus asked for my services and, reluctantly, Talos and his wife let me go. He merely nodded a slow acceptance. She wept all over my shoulder before I left, a second drowning. But I, eager to show the Lord Circinus my skills, paid them scant attention.

It was then that Talos unlocked his few words for me.

"Do not fly too high, my son," he said. And like his wife, re-peated himself. "Do not fly too high."

He meant Perdix, of course, for he had seen my eyes on her. But I was just newly conscious of my body's desires. I could not, did not listen.

That was how I came into Lord Circinus' household, bringing nothing but the clothes I wore, the feather of my past, and the strange talent that lived in my hands. In Lord Circinus' house I was given a sleeping room and a workroom and leave to set the pattern of my days.

Work was my joy and my excuse. I began simply, making clay-headed dolls, with wooden trunks and jointed limbs, testing out the tools that Circinus gave me. But soon I moved away from such childish things and constructed a dancing floor of such intricately mazed panels of wood, I was rewarded with a pocket of gold.

I never looked boldly upon the Lady Perdix. It was not my place. But I glanced longways, from the corners of my eyes. And somehow she must have known. For it was not long before she found my workroom and came to tease me with her boy's body and quick tongue. Like my stepfather Talos, I had no magic in my answers, only in my fingers, and Perdix always laughed at me twice: once for my slow speech and once for the quick flush that quickly burned my cheeks after each exchange.

I recall the first time she came upon me as I worked on a mechanical bird that could fly in short bursts towards the sun. She entered the workroom and stood by my side watching for a while. Then she put her right hand over mine. I could feel the heat from her hand burn me, all the way up my arm, though this burning left no visible scar.

"My Lady," I said. So I had been instructed to address her. She was a year younger than I. "It is said that a woman should wait upon a man's moves."

"If that were so," she answered swiftly, "all women would be called Penelope. But I would have woven a different ending to *that* particular tale." She laughed. "Too much waiting without an eye upon her, makes a maid mad."

Her wordy cleverness confounded me and I blushed. But she lifted her hand from mine and, still laughing, left the room.

It was a week before she returned. I did not even hear her enter, but when I turned around she was sitting on the floor with her skirts rolled halfway up her thighs. Her tanned legs flashed unmistakable signs at me that I dared not answer.

"Do you think it better to wait for a god or wait upon a man?" she asked, as if a week had not come between her last words and these.

I mumbled something about a man having but one form and a god many, and concluded lamely that perhaps, then, waiting for a god would be more interesting.

"Oh, yes," she said, "many girls have waited for a god to come. But not I. Men can be made gods, you know."

I did not know, and confessed it.

"My cousin Danae," she said, "said that great Zeus had come into her lap in a shower of gold. But I suspect it was a more mundane lover. After all, it has happened many times before that a man has showered gold into a girl's skirts and she opens her legs to him. That does not make *him* a god, or his coming gold." She laughed that familiar low laugh and added under her breath, "Cousin Danae always did have a quick answer for her mistakes."

"Like you, my Lady?" I asked.

She answered me with a smile and stood up slowly. As I watched, she walked towards me, stopping only inches away. I could scarcely breathe. She took the feather off the workbench where it lay among my tools and ran it down my chest. I was dressed only in a linen loincloth, my *chiton* set aside, for it was summer and very very hot.

I must have sighed. I know I bit my lip. And then she dropped the feather and it fluttered slowly to the floor. She used her fingers in the feather's place, and they were infinitely more knowing than my own. They found the pattern of my scar and traced it slowly as a blind child traces the raised fable on a vase.

I stepped through the last bit of space between us and put my arms around her as if I were fitting the last piece of my puzzle into a maze. For a moment we stood as still as any frieze; then she pushed me backwards and I tumbled down. But I held on to her, and she fell on top of me, fitting her mouth to mine.

Perdix came to my room that night, and the next I went to hers. And she made me a god. And so it continued night after night, a pattern as complicated as any I could devise, and as simple, too. I could not conceive of it ending.

But end it did.

One night she did not tap lightly at my door and slip in, a shadow in a night of shadows. I thought perhaps her moon time had come, until the next morning in the hallway near my workroom when I saw her whisper into the ear of a new slave. He had skin almost as dark as the wings of the bittern, and wild black hair. His nostrils flared like a beast's. Perdix placed her hand on his shoulder and turned him to face me. When I flushed with anger and with pain, they both laughed, he taking his cue from her, a scant beat behind.

Night could not come fast enough to hide my shame. I lay on my couch and thought I slept. A dream voice from the labyrinth that is my past cried out to me, in dark and brutish tones. I rose, not knowing I rose, and took my carving knife in hand. Wrapped only in night's cloak, the feather stuck in my hair, I crept down the corridors of the house.

I sniffed the still air. I listened for every sound. And then I heard it truly, the monster from my dream, agonizing over its meal. It screamed and moaned and panted and wept, but the tears that fell from its bullish head were as red as human blood.

I saw it, I tell you, in her room crouched over her, devouring my lady, my lost Perdix. My knife was ready, and I fell upon its back, black Minotaur of my devising. But it slid from the bed and melted away in the darkness, and my blade found her waiting heart instead.

She made no sound above a sigh.

My clever fingers, so nimble, so fast, could not hold the wound together, could not seam it closed. She seemed to be leaking away through my clumsy hands.

Then I heard a rush of wings, as if her soul had flown from the room. And I knew I had to fly after her and fetch her back before she left this world forever. So I took the feather from my hair and, dipping it into the red ocean of her life, printed great bloody wings, feathered tracings, along my shoulders and down my arms. And I flew high, high after her and fell into the bright searing light of dawn.

When they found me in the morning, by her bedside, crouched naked by her corpse, scarred with her blood, they took me, all unprotesting, to Lord Circinus. He had me thrown into this dark cave.

Tomorrow, before the sun comes again, I will be brought from this place and tied to a post sunk in the sand.

Oh, the cleverness of it, the cleverness. It might have been devised by my own little darling, my Perdix, for her father never had her wit. The post is at a place beyond the high water mark and I will be bound to it at the ebb. All morning my father, the sun, will burn me, and my father the rising tide will melt the red feathers of blood that decorate my chest and arms and side. And I will watch myself go back into the waters from which I was first pulled, nameless but alive.

Of fire and water I came, of fire and water I return. Talos was right. I flew too high. Truly there is no second fooling of the Fates.

Dick W. and His Pussy; or, Tess and Her Adequate Dick

Once upon a time—I say that up front so you will know this is a fairy tale and not just another wish-fulfillment fantasy—there was a boy named Adequate Dick. Unfortunate, but true. His mother, being no better than she should have been, but a beauty nonetheless, named him after that which had brought her much fame though little fortune.

When she saw that having a child narrowed her client base, she abandoned him. Simply dropped him off at the nearest dock: Whittington Pier. If she had dropped him *off* the dock instead of *at* it, this story would have been considerably shorter.

Adequate Dick knocked about the port for quite some time, about fifteen years to be exact, eventually taking the dock's name as his own, after much pier counseling. He was handsome; in that, he took after his mother. But in all other ways he was like his dad: adequate.

At last one day he was hired by a kind merchant who was always on the lookout for cheap labor.

"Will you come and work for me, Adequate Dick Whitting-ton Pier?" asked the merchant.

"I will," said Adequate Dick.

They shook hands but signed no papers. In those days no one could write, though most had handshakes down pat.

Now, the boy quickly came to the attention of the merchant's pretty daughter, Tess, who had a fondness for lower-class Dicks. She gave him money and considerable other favors, which Adequate Dick, being well named and handsome but not particularly favored in the brains department, took as a compliment.

He took a few other things as well: her silver ring, a glass vase, a small nude portrait done on ivory. He didn't take Tess's virtue. She had none left for him to take.

The merchant knew that cheap labor has a way of drifting, and so to keep his servants happy and at home, he gave them certain allowances. He allowed them once a year to give him something of theirs to take on his voyage, something the merchant might sell to make their fortunes. None of them ever got rich this way, of course. But, as if it were a sixteenth-century lottery, the chance of becoming millionaires overnight kept all the servants trying and at home. *Very* trying and *quite* at home.

Adequate Dick had nothing to give the merchant but a cat named Pussy (and the things he had taken from Tess, but those he would not part with). But when it was his turn, he handed over his pet without a thought. "Pussy could make my fortune," he thought, thereby proving himself his mother's boy. The vegetable does not fall very far from the tree.

Tess could have warned him that his chances for a fortune were slim at best. But she didn't want him leaving anyway. "Why waste a perfectly adequate Dick?" was her motto.

. . .

So far—I can hear you saying—this sounds like a folktale, what with the merchant and his pretty daughter, a servant and his cat. Or maybe it sounds like the plot of an eighteenth-century picaresque novel. Or a grainy, naughty black-and-white French film. But how can it be a fairy tale? It has no fairies in it. Or magic.

And you would be right. Right—but impatient.

Wait for it.

The merchant's ship ran aground on a small island kingdom and he was thought lost to the world. The household, like a boat, began to founder; the servants to look for other work. Adequate Dick, being last hired, was first fired, so he went off toward the familiar docks to seek his fortune. Without—of course—his Pussy. Either one.

So what of Tess?

She tried to take over her father's firm. She was the merchant's only child, after all. But the men who worked for her complained.

"She has," they said, "no Adequate Dick. And who can run a business without one?" It was true. Her Adequate Dick had gone back to his piers.

Then a miracle!

You must allow me a miracle.

Surely miracles will do in a tale when magic is nowhere to be found. Miracles *are* magic processed by faith and a lack of a scientific imagination.

The merchant returned home unexpectedly, but just in time it seems, with much gold in his ship's hold. The island kingdom where he had run aground had itself been overrun by rats. That he had Pussy to sell was a great fortune. Or a miracle. Or a serendipity. Or a fairy tale. Or the kind of luck a Donald Trump would envy. (Speaking of adequate Dicks.)

So he sold Dick's Pussy. But little did he know the consequences of such a sale. For miracles are not singular. They lean on one another, like art on art. No sooner was Pussy sold than Tess—far away in London—found herself changed beyond measure. That is, she could measure the change. It occurred between her legs.

Was she surprised? Not really. It was merely form following function.

The merchant returned home rich beyond counting.

"Where is that Adequate Dick?" he asked when he entered the door.

"Oh, Father!" Tess cried. "He has gone. But something rare has occurred. Something better than Adequate."

Her father did not listen. He was not a man to believe in the miraculous beyond the swelling of a purse. "Better get him back, then," he said. "He has wealth and treasure."

"As do I," thought Tess, pausing to spit accurately by the stoop. Then she ran down the road to call Adequate Dick home, crying: "Turn again, Whittington Pier." She had never called him by his first name outside her bedroom.

He heard her, and he turned.

And returned.

Now that he was rich, Tess could marry him, though, given the circumstances, she never slept with him again. He was no longer of the lower classes and he was—after all—only an *adequate* Dick.

She had better.

Become a Warrior

Both the hunted and the hunter pray to God.

The moon hung like a bloody red ball over the silent battlefield. Only the shadows seemed to move. The men on the ground would never move again. And their women, sick with weeping, did not dare the field in the dark. It would be morning before they would come like crows to count their losses.

But on the edge of the field there was a sudden tiny movement, and it was no shadow. Something small was creeping to the muddy hem of the battleground. Something knelt there, face shining with grief. A child, a girl, the youngest daughter of the king who had died that evening surrounded by all his sons.

The girl looked across the dark field and, like her mother, like her sisters, like her aunts, did not dare put foot on to the bloody ground. But then she looked up at the moon and thought she saw her father's face there. Not the father who lay with his innards spilled out into contorted hands. Not the one who had braided firesticks in his beard and charged into battle screaming. She thought she saw the father who had always sung her to sleep against the night terrors. The one who sat up with her when Great Graxyx haunted her dreams.

"I will do for you, Father, as you did for me," she whispered to the moon. She prayed to the goddess for the strength to accomplish what she had just promised.

Then foot by slow foot, she crept onto the field, searching in the red moon's light for the father who had fallen. She made slits of her eyes so she would not see the full horror around her. She breathed through her mouth so that she would not smell all the deaths. She never once thought of the Great Graxyx who lived—so she truly believed—in the black cave of her dressing room. Or any of the hundred and six gibbering children Graxyx had sired. She crept across the landscape made into a horror by the enemy hordes. All the dead men looked alike. She found her father by his boots.

She made her way up from the boots, past the gaping wound that had taken him from her, to his face which looked peaceful and familiar enough, except for the staring eyes. He had never stared like that. Rather his eyes had always been slotted, against the hot sun of the gods, against the lies of men. She closed his lids with trembling fingers and put her head down on his chest, where the stillness of the heart told her what she already knew.

And then she began to sing to him.

She sang of life, not death, and the small gods of new things. Of bees in the hive and birds on the summer wind. She sang of foxes denning and bears shrugging off winter. She sang of fish in the sparkling rivers and the first green uncurlings of fern in spring. She did not mention dying, blood, or wounds, or the awful stench of death. Her father already knew this well and did not need to be recalled to it.

And when she was done with her song, it was as if his corpse gave a great sigh, one last breath, though of course he was dead already half the night and made no sound at all. But she heard what she needed to hear.

By then it was morning and the crows came. The human crows as well as the black birds, poking and prying and feeding on the dead.

So she turned and went home and everyone wondered why she did not weep. But she had left her tears out on the battle-field.

She was seven years old.

Dogs bark, but the caravan goes on.

Before the men who had killed her father and who had killed her brothers could come to take all the women away to serve them, she had her maid cut her black hair as short as a boy's. The maid was a trembling sort, and the hair cut was ragged. But it would do.

She waited until the maid had turned around and leaned down to put away the shears. Then she put her arm around the woman and with a quick knife's cut across her throat killed her, before the woman could tell on her. It was a mercy, really, for she was old and ugly and would be used brutally by the soldiers before being slaughtered, probably in a slow and terrible manner. So her father had warned before he left for battle.

Then she went into the room of her youngest brother, dead in the field and lying by her father's right hand. In his great wooden chest she found a pair of trews that had probably been too small for him, but were nonetheless too long for her. With the still-bloody knife she sheared the legs of the trews a hand's width, rolled and sewed them with a quick seam. All the women of her house could sew well, even when it had to be done quickly. Even when it had to be done through half-closed eyes. Even when the hem was wet with blood. Even then.

When she put on the trews, they fit, though she had to pull the drawstring around the waist quite tight and tie the ribbands twice around her. She shrugged into one of her brother's shirts as well, tucking it down into the waistband. Then she slipped her bloody knife into the shirt sleeve. She wore her own riding boots, which could not be told from a boy's, for her brother's boots were many times too big for her.

Then she went out through the window her brother always used when he set out to court one of the young and pretty maids. She had watched him often enough though he had never known she was there, hiding beside the bed, a dark little figure as still as the night.

Climbing down the vine, hand over hand, was no great trouble either. She had done it before, following after him. Really, what a man and a maid did together was most interesting, if a bit odd. And certainly noisier than it needed to be.

She reached the ground in moments, crossed the garden, climbed over the outside wall by using a turned tree as her ladder. When she dropped to the ground, she twisted her ankle a bit, but she made not the slightest whimper. She was a boy now. And she knew they did not cry.

In the west a cone of dark dust was rising up and advancing on the fortress, blotting out the sky. She knew it for the storm that many hooves make as horses race across the plains. The earth trembled beneath her feet. Behind her, in their rooms, the women had begun to wail. The sound was thin, like a gold filiment thrust into her breast. She plugged her ears that their cries could not recall her to her old life, for such was not her plan.

Circling around the stone skirting of the fortress, in the

shadow so no one could see her, she started around toward the east. It was not a direction she knew. All she knew was that it was away from the horses of the enemy.

Once she glanced back at the fortress that had been the only home she had ever known. Her mother, her sisters, the other women stood on the battlements looking toward the west and the storm of riders. She could hear their wailing, could see the movement of their arms as they beat upon their breasts. She did not know if that were a plea or an invitation.

She did not turn to look again.

To become a warrior, forget the past.

Three years she worked as a serving lad in a fortress not unlike her own but many days' travel away. She learned to clean and to carry, she learned to work after a night of little sleep. Her arms and legs grew strong. Three years she worked as the cook's boy. She learned to prepare geese and rabbit and bear for the pot, and learned which parts were salty, which sweet. She could tell good mushrooms from bad and which greens might make the toughest meat palatable.

And then she knew she could no longer disguise the fact that she was a girl for her body had begun to change in ways that would give her away. So she left the fortress, starting east once more, taking only her knife and a long loop of rope which she wound around her waist seven times.

She was many days hungry, many days cold, but she did not turn back. Fear is a great incentive.

She taught herself to throw the knife and hit what she aimed at. Hunger is a great teacher.

She climbed trees when she found them in order to sleep safe at night. The rope made such passages easier.

She was so long by herself, she almost forgot how to speak. But she never forgot how to sing. In her dreams she sang to her father on the battlefield. Her songs made him live again. Awake she knew the truth was otherwise. He was dead. The worms had taken him. His spirit was with the goddess, drinking milk from her great pap, milk that tasted like honey wine.

She did not dream of her mother or of her sisters or of any of the women in her father's fortress. If they died, it had been with little honor. If they still lived, it was with less.

So she came at last to a huge forest with oaks thick as a goddess' waist. Over all was a green canopy of leaves that scarcely let in the sun. Here were many streams, rivulets that ran cold and clear, torrents that crashed against rocks, and pools that were full of silver trout whose meat was sweet. She taught herself to fish and to swim, and it would be hard to say which gave her the greater pleasure. Here, too, were nests of birds, and that meant eggs. Ferns curled and then opened, and she knew how to steam them, using a basket made of willow strips and a fire from rubbing sticks against one another. She followed bees to their hives, squirrels to their hidden nuts, ducks to their watered beds.

She grew strong, and brown, and—though she did not know it—very beautiful.

Beauty is a danger, to women as well as to men. To warriors most of all. It steers them away from the path of killing. It softens the soul.

When you are in a tree, be a tree.

She was three years alone in the forest and grew to trust the sky, the earth, the river, the trees, the way she trusted her knife. They did not lie to her. They did not kill wantonly. They gave her shelter, food, courage. She did not remember her father except as some sort of warrior god, with staring eyes, looking as she had seen him last. She did not remember her mother or sisters or aunts at all.

It had been so long since she had spoken to anyone, it was as if she could not speak at all. She knew words, they were in her head, but not in her mouth, on her tongue, in her throat. Instead she made the sounds she heard every day—the grunt of boar, the whistle of duck, the trilling of thrush, the settled cooing of the wood pigeon on its nest.

If anyone had asked her if she was content, she would have nodded.

Content.

Not happy. Not satisfied. Not done with her life's work.

Content.

And then one early evening a new sound entered her domain. A drumming on the ground, from many miles away. A strange halloing, thin, insistent, whining. The voices of some new animal, packed like wolves, singing out together.

She trembled. She did not know why. She did not remember why. But to be safe from the thing that made her tremble, she climbed a tree, the great oak that was in the very center of her world.

She used the rope ladder she had made, and pulled the ladder up after. Then she shrank back against the trunk of the tree to wait. She tried to be the brown of the bark, the green of the leaves, and in this she almost succeeded.

It was in the first soft moments of dark, with the woods outlined in muzzy black, that the pack ran yapping, howling, belling into the clearing around the oak.

In that instant she remembered dogs.

There were twenty of them, some large, lanky grays; some stumpy browns with long muzzles; some stiff-legged spotted with pushed-in noses; some thick-coated; some smooth. Her father, the god of war, had had such a motley pack. He had hunted boar and stag and hare with such. They had found him bear and fox and wolf with ease.

Still, she did not know why the dog pack was here, circling her tree. Their jaws were raised so that she could see their iron teeth, could hear the tolling of her death with their long tongues.

She used the single word she could remember. She said it with great authority, with trembling.

"Avaunt!"

At the sound of her voice, the animals all sat down on their haunches to stare up at her, their own tongues silenced. Except for one, a rat terrier, small and springy and unable to be still. He raced back up the path toward the west like some small spy going to report to his master.

Love comes like a thief, stealing the heart's gold away.

It was in the deeper dark that the dogs' master came, with his men behind him, their horses' hooves thrumming the forest paths. They trampled the grass, the foxglove's pink bells and the purple florets of self-heal, the wine-colored burdock flowers and the sprays of yellow goldenrod equally under the horses' heavy feet. The woods were wounded by their passage. The grass did not spring back nor the flowers raise up again.

She heard them and began trembling anew as they thrashed their way across her green haven and into the very heart of the wood.

Ahead of them raced the little terrier, his tail flagging them on, till he led them right to the circle of dogs waiting patiently beneath her tree.

"Look, my lord, they have found something," said one man.

"Odd they should be so quiet," said another.

But the one they called lord dismounted, waded through the sea of dogs, and stood at the very foot of the oak, his feet crunching on the fallen acorns. He stared up, and up, and up through the green leaves and at first saw nothing but brown and green.

One of the large gray dogs stood, walked over to his side, raised its great muzzle to the tree, and howled.

The sound made her shiver anew.

"See, my lord, see—high up. There is a trembling in the foliage," one of the men cried.

"You fool," the lord cried, "that is no trembling of leaves. It is a girl. She is dressed all in brown and green. See how she makes the very tree shimmer." Though how he could see her so well in the dark, she was never to understand. "Come down, child, we shall not harm you."

She did not come down. Not then. Not until the morning fully revealed her. And then, if she was to eat, if she was to relieve herself, she had to come down. So she did, dropping the rope ladder, and skinning down it quickly. She kept her knife tucked up in her waist, out where they could see it and be afraid.

They did not touch her but watched her every movement, like a pack of dogs. When she went to the river to drink, they watched. When she ate the bit of journeycake the lord offered her, they watched. And even when she relieved herself, the lord watched. He would let no one else look then, which she knew honored her, though she did not care.

And when after several days he thought he had tamed her, the lord took her on his horse before him and rode with her back to the far west where he lived. By then he loved her, and knew that she loved him in return, though she had yet to speak a word to him.

"But then, what have words to do with love," he whispered to her as they rode.

He guessed by her carriage, by the way her eyes met his, that she was a princess of some sort, only badly used. He loved her for the past which she could not speak of, for her courage which showed in her face, and for her beauty. He would have loved her for much less, having found her in the tree, for she was something out of a story, out of a prophecy, out of a dream.

"I loved you at once," he whispered. "When I knew you from the tree."

She did not answer. Love was not yet in her vocabulary. But she did not say the one word she could speak: *avaunt*. She did not want him to go.

When the cat wants to eat her kittens, she says they look like mice.

His father was not so quick to love her.

His mother, thankfully, was long dead.

She knew his father at once, by the way his eyes were slotted against the hot sun of the gods, against the lies of men. She knew him to be a king if only by that.

And when she recognized her mother and her sisters in his retinue, she knew who it was she faced. They did not know her, of course. She was no longer seven but nearly seventeen. Her life had browned her, bronzed her, made her into such steel as they had never known. She could have told them but she had only contempt for their lives. As they had contempt now for her, thinking her some drudge run off to the forest, some sinister throwling from a forgotten clan.

When the king gave his grudging permission for their marriage, when the prince's advisers set down in long scrolls what she should and should not have, she only smiled at them. It was a tree's smile, giving away not a bit of the bark.

She waited until the night of her wedding to the prince, when they were couched together, the servants a-giggle outside their door. She waited until he had covered her face with kisses, when he had touched her in secret places that made her tremble, when he had brought blood between her legs. She waited until he had done all the things she had once watched her brother do to the maids, and she cried out with pleasure as she had heard them do. She waited until he was asleep, smiling happily in his dreams, because she did love him in her warrior way.

Then she took her knife and slit his throat, efficiently and without cruelty, as she would a deer for her dinner.

"Your father killed my father," she whispered, soft as a love token in his ear as the knife carved a smile on his neck.

She stripped the bed of its bloody offering and handed it to the servants who thought it the effusions of the night. Then she walked down the hall to her father-in-law's room.

He was bedded with her mother, riding her like one old wave atop another.

"Here!" he cried as he realized someone was in the room. "You!" he said when he realized who it was.

Her mother looked at her with half opened eyes and, for the first time, saw who she really was, for she had her father's face, fierce and determined.

"No!" her mother cried. "Avaunt!" But it was a cry that was ten years too late.

She killed the king with as much ease as she had killed his son, but she let the knife linger longer to give him a great deal of pain. Then she sliced off one of his ears and put it gently in her mother's hand.

In all this she had said not one word. But wearing the blood of the king on her gown, she walked out of the palace and back to the woods, though she was many days getting there.

No one tried to stop her, for no one saw her. She was a flower in the meadow, a rock by the roadside, a reed by the river, a tree in the forest.

And a warrior's mother by the spring of the year.

Memoirs of a Bottle Djinn

The sea was as dark as old blood, not the wine color poets sing of. In the early evening it seemed to stain the sand. As usual this time of year the air was heavy, ill-omened.

I walked out onto the beach below my master's house whenever I could slip away unnoticed, though it was a dangerous practice. Still, it was one necessary to my well-being. I had been a sailor for many more years than I had been a slave, and the smell of the salt air was not a luxury for me but a necessity.

If a seabird had washed up dead at my feet, its belly would have contained black worms and other evil auguries, so dark and lowering was the sky. So I wondered little at the bottle that the sea had deposited before me, certain it contained noxious fumes at best, the legacy of its long cradling in such a salty womb.

In my country poets sing the praises of wine and gift its color to the water along the shores of Hellas, and I can think of no finer hymn. But in this land they believe their prophet forbade them strong drink. They are a sober race who reward themselves in heaven even as they deny themselves on earth. It is a system of which I do not approve, but then I am a Greek by birth and a heathen by inclination despite my master's long importuning. It is only by chance that I have not yet lost an eye, an ear, or a hand to my master's unforgiving code. He finds me amusing, but it has been seven years since I have had a drink.

I stared at the bottle. If I had any luck at all, the bottle had fallen from a foreign ship and its contents would still be potable. But then, if I had any luck at all, I would not be a slave in Araby, a Greek sailor washed up on these shores the same as the bottle at my feet. My father, who was a cynic like his father before him, left me with a cynic's name—Antithias—a wry heart, and an acid tongue, none proper legacies for a slave. But as blind Homer wrote, "Few sons are like their father; many are worse." I guessed that the wine, if drinkable, would come from an inferior year. And with that thought, I bent to pick it up.

The glass was a cloudy green, like the sea after a violent storm. Like the storm that had wrecked my ship and cast me onto a slaver's shore. There were darker flecks along the bottom, a sediment that surely foretold an undrinkable wine. I let the bottle warm between my palms.

Since the glass was too dark to let me see more, I waited past my first desire and was well into my second, letting it rise up in me like the heat of passion. The body has its own memories, though I must be frank: passion, like wine, was simply a fragrance remembered. Slaves are not lent the services of houri nor was one my age and race useful for breeding. It had only been by feigning impotence that I had kept that part of my anatomy intact—another of my master's unforgiving laws. Even in the dark of night, alone on my pallet, I forwent the pleasures of the hand for there were spies everywhere in his house and the eunuchs were a notably gossipy lot. Little but a slave's tongue lauding morality stood between gossip and scandal, stood between me and the knife. Besides, the women of Araby tempted me little. They were like the bottle in my hand—beautiful and empty. A wind blowing across the mouth of each could make them sing but the tunes were worth little. I liked my women like my wine—full-bodied and tanged with history, bringing a man into poetry. So I had put my passion into work these past seven years, slave's work though it was. Blind Homer had it right, as usual: "Labor conquers all things." Even old lusts for women and wine.

Philosophy did not conquer movement, however, and my hand found the cork of the bottle before I could stay it. With one swift movement I had plucked the stopper out. A thin strand of smoke rose into the air. A very bad year indeed, I thought, as the cork crumbled in my hand.

Up and up and up the smoky rope ascended and I, bottle in hand, could not move, such was my disappointment. Even my father's cynicism and his father's before him had not prepared me for such a sudden loss of all hope. My mind, a moment before full of anticipation and philosophy, was now in blackest despair. I found myself without will, reliving in my mind the moment of my capture and the first bleak days of my enslavement.

That is why it was several minutes before I realized that the smoke had begun to assume a recognizable shape above the bottle's gaping mouth: long, sensuous legs glimpsed through diaphanous trousers; a waist my hands could easily span; breasts beneath a short embroidered cotton vest as round as ripe pomegranates; and a face . . . the face was smoke and air. I remembered suddenly a girl in the port of Alexandria who sold fruit from a basket and gave me a smile. She was the last girl who had smiled upon me when I was a free man and I, not knowing the future, had ignored her, so intent was I on my work. My eyes clouded over at the memory, and when they were clear again, I saw that same smile imprinted upon the face of the djinn.

"I am what you would have me be, master," her low voice called down to me.

I reached up a hand to help her step to earth, but my hand went through hers, mortal flesh through smoky air. It was then, I think, that I really believed she was what I guessed her to be.

She smiled. "What is your wish, master?"

I took the time to smile back. "How many wishes do I get?"

She shook her head but still she smiled, that Alexandrian smile, all lips without a hint of teeth. But there was a dimple in her left cheek. "One, my master, for you drew the cork but once."

"And if I draw it again?"

"The cork is gone." This time her teeth showed as did a second dimple, on the right.

I sighed and looked at the crumbled mess in my hand, then sprinkled the cork like seed upon the sand. "Just one."

"Does a slave need more?" she asked in that same low voice.

"You mean that I should ask for my freedom?" I laughed and sat down on the sand. The little waves that outrun the big ones tickled my feet, for I had come out barefoot. I looked across the water. "Free to be a sailor again at my age? Free to let the sun peel the skin from my back, free to heave my guts over the stern in a blinding rain, free to wreck once more upon a slaver's shore?"

She drifted down beside me and, though her smoky hand could not hold mine, I felt a breeze across my palm that could

have been her touch. I could see through her to the cockleshells
and white stones pocking the sand.

"Free to make love to Alexandrian women," she said. "Free
to drink strong wine."

"Free to have regrets in the morning either way," I replied.
Then I laughed.

She laughed back. "What about the freedom to indulge in a
dinner of roast partridge in lemons and eggplant. What about
hard-boiled eggs sprinkled with vermilion. What about cinna-
mon tripes?" It was the meal my master had just had.

"Rich food like rich women gives me heartburn," I said.

"The freedom to fill your pockets with coins?"

Looking away from her, over the clotted sea, I whispered to
myself, "'Accursed thirst for gold! What dost thou not compel
mortals to do,'" a line from the *Aeneid.*

"Virgil was a wise man," she said quietly. "For a Roman!"
Then she laughed.

I turned to look at her closely for the first time. A woman
who knows Virgil, be she djinn or mortal, was a woman to be-
hold. Though her body was still composed of that shifting,
smoky air, the features on her face now held steady. She no
longer looked like the Alexandrian girl, but had a far more so-
phisticated beauty. Lined with kohl, her eyes were gray as smoke
and her hair the same color. There were shadows along her
cheeks that emphasized the bone and faint smile lines crinkling
the skin at each corner of her generous mouth. She was not as
young as she had first appeared, but then I am not so young myself.

"Ah, Antithias," she said, smiling at me, "even djinns age,
though corked up in a bottle slows down the process immeasur-
ably."

I spoke Homer's words to her then: "In youth and beauty,
wisdom is but rare." I added in my own cynic's way, "If ever."

"You think me wise, then?" she asked, then laughed and her laughter was like the tinkling of camel bells. "But a gaudy parrot is surely as wise, reciting another's words as his own."

"I know no parrots who hold Virgil and Homer in their mouths," I said, gazing at her not with longing but with a kind of wonder. "No djinn either."

"You know many?"

"Parrots, yes; djinn, no. You are my first."

"Then you are lucky, indeed, Greek, that you called up one of the worshippers of Allah and not one of the followers of Iblis."

I nodded. "Lucky, indeed."

"So, to your wish, master," she said.

"You call me master, I who am a slave," I said. "Do *you* not want the freedom you keep offering me? Freedom from the confining green bottle, freedom from granting wishes to any *master* who draws the cork?"

She brushed her silvery hair back from her forehead with a delicate hand. "You do not understand the nature of the djinn," she said. "You do not understand the nature of the bottle."

"I understand rank," I said. "On the sea I was between the captain and the rowers. In that house," and I gestured with my head to the palace behind me, "I am below my master and above the kitchen staff. Where are you?"

Her brow furrowed as she thought. "If I work my wonders for centuries, I might at last attain a higher position within the djinn," she said.

It was my turn to smile. "Rank is a game," I said. "It may be conferred by birth, by accident, or by design. But rank does not honor the man. The man honors the rank."

"You are a philosopher," she said, her eyes lightening.

"I am a Greek," I answered. "It is the same thing."

She laughed again, holding her palm over her mouth coquettishly. I could no longer see straight through her though an occasional piece of driftweed appeared like a delicate tattoo on her skin.

"Perhaps we both need a wish," I said, shifting my weight. One of my feet touched hers and I could feel a slight jolt, as if lightning had run between us. Such things happen occasionally on the open sea.

"Alas, I cannot wish, myself," she said in a whisper. "I can only grant wishes."

I looked at her lovely face washed with its sudden sadness and whispered back, "Then I give my wish to you."

She looked directly into my eyes and I could see her eyes turn golden in the dusty light. I could at the same time somehow see beyond them, not into the sand or water, but to a different place, a place of whirlwinds and smokeless fire.

"Then, Antithias, you will have wasted a wish," she said. Shifting her gaze slightly, she looked behind me, her eyes opening wide in warning. As she spoke, her body seemed to melt into the air and suddenly there was a great white bird before me, beating its feathered pinions against my body before taking off towards the sky.

"Where are you going?" I cried.

"To the Valley of Abqar," the bird called. "To the home of my people. I will wait there for your wish, Greek. But hurry. I see both your past and your future closing in behind you."

I turned and, pouring down the stone steps of my master's house, were a half-dozen guards and one shrilling eunuch pointing his flabby hand in my direction. They came towards me screaming, though what they were saying I was never to know for their scimitars were raised and my Arabic deserts me in moments of sheer terror.

I think I screamed; I am not sure. But I spun around again

towards the sea and saw the bird winging away into a halo of light.

"Take me with you," I cried. "I desire no freedom but by your side."

The bird shuddered as it flew, then banked sharply, and headed back towards me, calling, "Is that your wish, master?"

A scimitar descended.

"That is my wish," I cried, as the blade bit into my throat.

We have lived now for centuries within the green bottle and Zarifa was right, I had not understood its nature. Inside is an entire world, infinite and ever-changing. The smell of the salt air blows through that world and we dwell in a house that sometimes overlooks the ocean and some-times overlooks the desert sands.

Zarifa, my love, is as mutable, neither young nor old, neither soft nor hard. She knows the songs of blind Homer and the poet Virgil as well as the poems of the warlords of Ayyam Al-'Arab. She can sing in languages that are long dead.

And she loves me beyond my wishing, or so she says, and I must be-lieve it for she would not lie to me. She loves me though I have no great beauty, my body bearing a sailor's scars and a slave's scar and this curi-ous blood necklace where the scimitar left its mark. She loves me, she says, for my cynic's wit and my noble heart, that I would have given my wish to her.

So we live together in our ever-changing world. I read now in six tongues beside Greek and Arabic, and have learned to paint and sew. My paintings are in the Persian style, but I embroider like a Norman queen. We learn from the centuries, you see, and we taste the world anew each time the cork is drawn.

So there, my master, I have fulfilled your curious wish, speaking my story to you alone. It seems a queer waste of your one piece of luck, but *then most men waste their wishes. And if you are a poet and a story-teller, as you say, of the lineage of blind Homer and the rest, but one who has been blocked from telling more tales, then perhaps my history can speed you on your way again. I shall pick up one of your old books, my master, now that we have a day and a night in this new world. Do you have a favorite I should try—or should I just go to a bookseller and trust my luck? In the last few centuries it has been remarkably good, you see.*

A Ghost of an Affair

1.

Most ghost stories begin or end with a ghost. Not this one. This begins and ends with a love affair. That one of the partners was a ghost has little to do with things, except for a complication or two.

The heart need not be beating to entertain the idea of romance. To think otherwise is to misunderstand the nature of the universe.

To think otherwise is to miscalculate the odds of love.

2.

Andrea Crow did not look at all like her name, being fair-haired and soft voiced. But she had a scavenger's personality, that is she collected things with a fierce dedication. As a girl she had collected rocks and stones, denuding her parent's driveway of mica-shining pebbles. As an adolescent she had turned the rock-collection into an interest in gemstones. By college she was majoring in geology, minoring in jewelry making. (It was one of those schools so prevalent in the '80s where life-experience substituted for any real knowledge. Only a student bent on learning ever learned anything. But perhaps that is true even in Oxford, even in Harvard.)

Andrea's rockhound passion made her a sucker for young men carrying ropes and pitons and she learned to scramble up stone faces without thinking of the danger. For a while she even thought she might attempt the Himalayas. But a rock-climbing friend died in an avalanche there and so she decided going to gem shows was far safer. She was a scavenger but she wasn't stupid.

The friend who died in the avalanche was not the ghost in this story. That was a dead *girl* friend and Andrea was depressingly straight in her love life.

Andrea graduated from college and began a small jewelry business in Chappaqua with a healthy jump-start from her parents who died suddenly in a car crash going home from her graduation. They left a tidy sum and their house to Andrea who, after a suitable period of mourning, plunged into work, turning the garage into her workroom.

She sold her jewelry at crafts fairs and Renaissance Faires and to several of the large stores around the country who found her Middle Evils line especially charming. The silver and gold work was superb, of course. She had been well trained. But it was the boxing of the jewelry—in polished rosewood with gold or silver hinges—as well as the printed legends included in each piece—that made her work stand out.

Still, her business remained small until one Christmas Neiman Marcus ordered 5,000 adder stone rings in Celtic scrolled rosewood boxes. The rings, according to legend, "ensured prosperity, repelled evil spirits, and in 17th century Scotland were considered to keep a child free of the whooping cough." She finished that order so far in the black that she only had to go to one Renaissance Faire the following summer for business.

Well, to be honest, she would have gone anyway. She needed the rest after the Neiman Marcus push. Besides, she enjoyed the Faire. Many of her closest friends were there.

Well—all of her closest friends were there.

All three of them.

3.

Simon Morrison was the son and grandson and great grandson of Crail fisherfolk. He was born to the sea. But the sea was not to his liking. And as he had six brothers born ahead of him who could handle the fishing lines and nets, he saw no reason to stay in Crail for longer than was necessary.

So on the day of his majority, June 17, 1847, he kissed his mother sweetly and said farewell to his father's back, for he was not so big that his Da—a small man with a great hand—might not have whipped him for leaving.

Simon took the northwest road out of Crail and made his way by foot to the ferry that crossed the River Forth and so on into Edinburgh. And there he could have lost himself in the alehouses, as had many a lad before him.

But Simon was not just *any* lad. He was a lad with a passionate dream. And while it was not his father's and grandfather's and great grandfather's dream of herring by the hundredweight, it was a dream nonetheless.

His dream was to learn to work in silver and gold.

Now, how—you might well ask—could a boy raised in the East Neuk of Fife—in a little fishing village so ingrown a boy's cousin might be his uncle as well—how could such a boy know the first thing about silver and gold?

The answer is easier than you might suspect.

The laird and his wife had had a silver wedding anniversary and a collection was taken up for a special gift from the town. All the small people had given a bit of money they had put aside; the gentry added more. And there was soon enough to hire a silversmith from Edinburgh to make a fine silver center-piece in the shape of a stag rearing up, surrounded by eight hunting dogs. The dogs looked just like the laird's own pack, including a stiff-legged mastiff with a huge underslung jaw.

The centerpiece had been on display for days in the Crail town hall, near the mercat cross, before the gifting of it. Simon had gone to see it out of curiosity, along with his brothers.

It was the first time that art had ever touched his life.

Touched?

He had been bowled over, knocked about, nearly slain by the beauty of the thing.

After that, fishing meant nothing to him. He wanted to be an artisan. He did not know enough to call it art.

When he got to Edinburgh, a bustle of a place and bigger than twenty Crails laid end to end to end, Simon looked up that same silversmith and begged to become the man's apprentice.

The man would have said no. He had apprentices enough as it was. But some luck was with Simon, for the next day when Si-mon came around to ask again, two of the lowest apprentices were down with a pox of some kind and had to be sent away. And Simon—who'd been sick with that same pox in his child-hood and never again—got to fetch and carry for months on end until by the very virtue of his hard working, the smith offered him a place.

And that is how young Simon Morrison the fisherlad be-came not-so-young Simon Morrison the silversmith. He was well beyond thirty and not married. He worked so hard, he never had an eye for love, or so it was said by the other lads.

He only had an eye for art.

4.

Now in the great course of things, these two should never have met. Time itself was against them—that greatest divide—a hundred years to be exact.

Besides, Simon would never have gone to America. America was a land of cutthroats and brigands. He did not waste his heart thinking on it, though—in fact—he never wasted his heart on anything but his work.

And though Andrea had once dreamed of Katmandu and Nepal, she had never fancied Scotland with its "dudes in skirts," as her friend Heidi called them.

But love, though it may take many a circuitous route, somehow manages to get from one end of the map to another.

Always.

5.

Because of the adder rings—a great hit with the Neiman Marcus buyers—Andrea was sent to Scotland by Vogue magazine to pose before a ruin of a fourteenth century castle. The castle, called Dunottar, commanded a spit of land some two and a half hours drive along the coast from Edinburgh and had at one point been the hiding place for the Scottish crown jewels.

Windy and raw weather did not stop the Dunottar shoot; in fact it so speeded things up, the shoot finished early on a Thursday morning. Andrea then had three and a half days to explore the grey stone city of Edinburgh.

She loved the twisty streets and closes, with names like

Cowgate and Grassmarket and Lady Wynd, and the antique jewelry shop on a little lane called Thistle.

Edinburgh seemed to be a city of rain and rainbows. A single rainbow over the Greek revival temple on the hill, and a double over the great grey castle.

"If there is such a thing as magic . . ." Andrea found herself whispering aloud, "it's here in this city." For the first time she actually found herself believing in the possibility.

The first two days in Edinburgh went quickly, but she soon tired of tourists who spoke every language except English. She knew she needed some quiet, far away from the Royal Mile and its aggressively Celtic shoppes, and far from the Americanization of Princes Street, the main shopping road, where a Macdonalds (without the arches) sat right next to British franchises.

It was then that she discovered a hidden walk that wound around and under the city.

Leith Walk.

Leith had been the old port on the Firth and once a city in its own right, but was now a bustling part of Edinburgh. The old port area after years of decay was now being tarted up, and modernized flats with large *To Let* signs dotted the streets. At first Andrea kept mis-reading the signs, wondering why toilets were advertised everywhere. Then giggling over her mistake, she went aboard a floating ship restaurant for a quiet lunch alone.

She didn't mean to listen in, but she overheard an elderly English couple near her talking about Leith Walk, which sounded wonderfully off the beaten tourist path.

"Excuse me," she said, leaning over, "I couldn't help hearing you mention Leith Walk. It's not in my book." She pointed to the green Michelin Guide by her plate.

They told her how to find the walk which, they said, snaked under and over parts of Edinburgh along the Leith River.

"Though the locals call it the 'Water of Leith,'" the woman said. "And as you go along, you will often feel as if you had stumbled on to a lost path into faerie."

Andrea was struck by how earnestly she spoke.

"The Walk looks as if it ends up in Dean Village," the English woman added.

"An old grain milling center, that," interrupted her companion. "End of Bell's Brae. Off Queensferry. Solid bridge. Pretty, too." His bristly ginger moustache seemed to strain his words for they came out crisp and unadorned.

"But do not be fooled, my dear," the woman continued. "It becomes a mere trickle of a path. But it does go on."

"The path . . ." Andrea mused, remembering her Tolkein, "goes ever on . . ."

The English couple laughed and the man said something in a strange tongue.

"I beg your pardon," Andrea said. "I don't speak . . ." She wasn't in fact sure what language he had used.

"I beg *your* pardon," the man said. "Certain you'd know Elvish." His eyes twinkled at her and he no longer seemed so starchy. "I simply wished you a good journey and a safe return."

"Thank you," Andrea said.

She smiled at them as they stood, and went out, without—Andrea noticed—leaving any kind of a tip.

6.

Simon was not much of a drinker, certainly not as Scots go. He rarely went out with the lads.

He was a walker, though.

Hill walking when he could get out of the city bustle on holiday.

Town walking when he could not.

He always took his lunch with him and during a work day, he would spend that precious time walking, eating as he went.

Fond of hiking up Calton Hill or Arthur's Seat—both of them affording panoramic views of the city—Simon also liked strolling to the Royal Botanic Garden. There he'd dine amidst the great patches of carefully designed flower beds or, in winter, in the Tropical Palm House, enjoying the moist heat.

Occasionally he would take a sketch book and set off along the winding Water of Leith walk in the direction of St. Bernard's Well. He passed few people there, unlike his walks up Calton Hill or Arthur's Seat. And he enjoyed the solitude.

The little drawings he did as he sat by the river found their way into his silverwork—intricate twists of foliage, the splay of water over stone, the feathering on the wings of ravens and rooks.

He had begun such drawings as an apprentice, and continued them—with his master's approval—as a journeyman. He perfected them when he became a master silversmith himself.

In time he became famous for them.

In time.

7.

So you think you see the arc of the plot now. They will meet—Simon and Andrea—along the Leith Walk.

They will fall in love.

Marry.

And . . .

But you have forgotten that when Andrea takes her first steps along the Leith Walk, heading away from the old port towards Dean's Village and beyond, Simon is already dead some one hundred years earlier. There's not a bit of flesh on those old bones now.

It does present certain intractable problems.

For logic, yes.

Not for love.

8.

It was a lovely early spring afternoon and Simon was grateful to have a half day off. Having had an ugly argument with another of the journeymen over the amount of silver needed for a casting, he wanted some time to walk off his anger.

His anger was with himself more than anyone else, for the other journeyman had been right after all. Simon was not used to making such mistakes.

He was not used to making *any* mistakes.

The master valued Simon too much to argue over half a day. Besides, he knew that with Simon, nothing was ever really lost.

"Go on out, lad," he said. Though Simon was scarcely a lad anymore, the master still thought of him that way. "Walk about and think up some more of yer lovely designs."

Simon decided on following the Leith path, and he walked with a brisk stride that dis-invited even a nod from the few people he met along the way.

But by the time he got to St. Bernard's Well—that strange stone neo-Classical folly built by the Waterworks over an actual well whose waters were quite the vogue amongst the New Town gentry—the majority of his anger had passed and he sat down for a bit to sketch, his back against the stone wall.

There was a patch of uncurling ferns near his feet and he

loved the sight of the little plants as they unbent their necks. He got the patch down in seven quick lines and then, with three more lines, one fern became a horse's head.

Simon laughed at the conceit. Rather more fanciful than his usual work, but perhaps—he thought—perhaps it was time for *him* to uncurl as well. He was thirty-six years old and half his life gone by. What had happened to the dream that the boy who walked from Crail to Edinburgh had had?

He realized how dreadfully misplaced his anger had been that morning.

As he was thus musing, out of the clear slate of sky there came a crack of thunder.

"By God," Simon cried, and stood up quickly, preparing to run to the sanctuary of the folly. He was a son of fisherfolk, after all, and not about to believe the innocence of that blue sky.

As he turned . . .

9.

Andrea's walk along the Leith River had started quietly enough in bright sunshine. But the weather report on the television that morning had promised scattered sunshine and occasional rain.

"Or was it scattered rain and occasional sunshine?" she murmured. Each of her days in Scotland so far had begun with that same promise from the weather man. Each of those promises had been exactly fulfilled, Scottish weather being charmingly predictable.

The scattering began with a bit of spitting, not enough rain to be worried about only enough to be annoying.

Andrea had no idea where the next exit from the Leith Walk might be, and there was no way she was going to climb over the fence, go through that little woods, and then scale the stone wall she could almost make out, just to get away from a spatter. She'd been a mountain hiker too long to worry about such things.

Besides, she thought—jamming her pretty blue Scottish tam on her head and tucking her hair under it—in her khaki pants and Aran sweater she was more than ready for a wee bit of rain. In fact she positively welcomed it.

But the little rain suddenly turned into a downpour.

Luckily that was when she spotted the stone temple ahead. Racing for it, she got in the lee of the wall before the major flood opened up overhead.

Mounting the steps two at a time, she thought she was safe when—without warning—a bolt of lightning struck a little spire on the top of the temple's roof, traveled down a wire, and leaped over to the metal ornament on her tam.

She did not so much feel the shock as smell it, a kind of sharpness in the nose and on the tongue. Her skin prickled, the little hairs rising up on her arms. Then she sank into unconsciousness, falling over the side of the wall and onto the slippery grass below.

10.

A bolt from the blue, you are thinking.

How corny.

The sky *was* actually blue at the moment, except for patches of clouds scudding backwards, in an effort to escape time.

Andrea's eyelids fluttered open.

She sighed.

The first thing she saw was the face of a very concerned youngish man staring down at her.

The second thing she saw was that his eyes were the same bleached blue as the sky over them.

Then she noticed the ginger eyebrows and the cheekbones sharp enough to cut cheese with.

"Am I dead?" Andrea whispered. "Are you an angel?"

Corny yes.

But most lives are as filled with corn as a Kansas field.

Or—if you prefer—a cornfield in east Fife.

Different kinds of corn, of course.

Different kinds of lives.

11.

One minute Simon had been sitting quietly drawing. The next minute he heard the crack of thunder and after that a body came hurtling over the side of the stone wall and sprawled face up at his feet.

For a moment Simon thought it was a boy. The tam and the pants confused him. But once he'd looked carefully—at the face with its lambent skin, at the long black curls spilling out of the tam, at the soft swell of breast beneath the woolen jumper—he knew it was no boy.

Then the fallen girl's eyes opened. They were almost purple, enormous, lovely.

"Am I dead?" she asked. "Are you an angel?"

"Och, lass, I'm a silversmith. And how could ye have died from that wee jump?" he asked.

"I mean from the lightning," she said.

He glanced up, worried. After all—there *had* been thunder. But the grey clouds had sped away.

Glancing down, he said, "No lightning, lass. I think ye swooned and fell over the wall."

"I'm not the swooning type," she said.

"Then what type are ye?"

He meant nothing bad by the question, but she looked confused. Then she tried to sit up and seemed to be having difficulty doing it. So Simon put a hand to her back to help her up. And though he'd never put an arm around a woman before without being related to her, this seemed so natural that he did not give it another thought.

However, it was then that he realized she was not the *young* lass he'd taken her for. There were a few strands of silver in her hair, tangling through the curls. He imagined taking that silver and weaving it into a pattern on a bracelet.

As his master knew, nothing with Simon was ever lost.

12.

She saw his sketches, she pulled a small notebook from a back pocket of her trousers and showed him hers. They spoke of silver and gold and the intricacies of cloisonne. They talked of working with electrum and foil and plating. They compared the virtues of enamelling and embossing.

They did not speak of love.

It was too soon.

And soon it was too late.

Somewhere a minute or an hour or a day or a week later, they figured out the difference in time.

"You're an old man when I am born," she mused.

"I am dead when you are born," he said.

But time has a way of correcting itself. Of making sense of nonsense.

And one minute or an hour or a day or a week later, Andrea turned a corner of a street off Grassmarket—dressed now of course as a young woman should—and she went in one step from streetcars to Suburus.

"Simon!" she cried, turning back.

But Simon and his century were gone.

13.

Andrea returned home but she didn't feel at home. The sky over Chappaqua had a dirty, smudged look. The air reeked. She could not bear the billboards along the highway nor the myriad choices of toilet cleansers and bath soaps at the super market.

She shut off her tv and sold her fax. She went shopping for long skirts and shirtwaists in second hand shops.

She told her customers that she had a great deal of back work to do and gave them the names of several other jewelers they might patronize instead.

She said goodbye to her three friends.

"I'm thinking of moving to Scotland," she told them. She did not tell them where.

Or when.

Then she sold her parents' house, took the money in a banker's check, bought a ticket on Icelandic Air, and flew with a small suitcase of second hand clothes to Scotland.

The Royal Bank of Scotland was more than happy to open an account for her, and she rented a small flat in Leith.

Then she set to work. Not as a silversmith, not as a jewelry maker. She became a researcher, haunting the Edinburgh churches to see if she could find where Simon had been buried. To see if there was some mention of him in the town rolls.

Her search took her the better part of a year, but she had time.

The rest of my life if needed, she thought. Her parents' house had brought in a great deal of money. It was not money that worried her. It was the rest of Simon's life she was afraid of.

Once she'd been through every cemetery in the city she was at a loss, until she remembered that Simon had once spoken of being an East Neuk lad. On a whim she went by bus out to Crail, the little fishing village Simon had mentioned.

It was a pearl of a village with a mercat cross topped by a unicorn in the center of the upper town. The tolbooth was a tiered tower with a graceful belfry. When she went along the shop row, passing a bakery and a butcher's, she was stopped by a glass-fronted jewelry store. It sold both new pieces—rather simple and not terribly interesting—and antique ware. Glancing up at the sign over the lintel, she was stunned.

MORRISONS
JEWELRY SINCE 1878

Trembling, she went in.

14.

You've guessed it now.

How the story ends.

But you are wrong again.

Andrea does not find Simon—for he is long gone and no amount of standing about in electrical storms can bring her back again in time.

Who she finds is the great great grandson of Simon Morrison who is also named Simon.

And that Simon, on hearing the name Andrea Crow, immediately gives her a job as a jewelry maker in the shop because it has been a family legend—accompanied by a notarized document—that some time in the new century such a young woman would come. Black curls, violet eyes, and a master jeweler's skill.

In his early thirties, this Simon looks nothing like old Simon. He has a roundness to his face and a sunny disposition. He does not so much make jewelry as sell what others make.

After half a year, he proposes and Andrea accepts and they marry, though Andrea explains that some part of her will always belong to old Simon.

This young Simon understands. It is, after all, part of the family tradition. Scots are big on lost causes.

Andrea's designs become popular in Scotland and then England and then the Continent. Neiman Marcus rediscovers her work. She and Simon have three children.

And in time they fall in love.

In time.

Sister Emily's Lightship

I dwell in Possibility. The pen scratched over the page, making graceful ellipses. She liked the look of the black on white as much as the words themselves. The words sang in her head far sweeter than they sang on the page. Once down, captured like a bird in a cage, the tunes seemed pedestrian, mere common rote. Still, it was as close as she would come to that Eternity, that Paradise that her mind and heart promised. *I dwell in Possibility.*

She stood and stretched, then touched her temples where the poem still throbbed. She could feel it sitting there, beating its wings against her head like that captive bird. Oh, to let the bird out to sing for a moment in the room before she caged it again in the black bars of the page.

Smoothing down the skirt of her white dress, she sat at the writing table once more, took up the pen, dipped it into the ink jar, and added a second line. *A fairer House than* . . . than what? Had she lost the word between standing and sitting? Words were not birds after all, but slippery as fish.

Then, suddenly, she felt it beating in her head. *Prose! A*

fairer House than Prose—She let the black ink stretch across the page with the long dash that lent the last word that wonderful fall of tone. She preferred punctuating with the dash to the hard point, as brutal as a bullet. *I dwell in Possibility.*

She blotted the lines carefully before reading them aloud, her mouth forming each syllable perfectly as she had been taught so many years before at Miss Lyon's Mount Holyoke Female Seminary.

Cocking her head to one side, she considered the lines. *They will do,* she thought, as much praise as she ever allowed her own work, though she was generous to others. Then, straightening the paper and cleaning the nib of her pen, she tore up the false starts and deposited them in the basket.

She could, of course, write any time during the day if the lines came to mind. There was little enough that she had to do in the house. But she preferred night for her truest composition and perhaps that was why she was struggling so. *Then those homey tasks will take me on,* she told herself: supervising the gardening, baking Father's daily bread. Her poetry must never be put in the same category.

Standing, she smoothed down the white skirt again and tidied her hair—"like a chestnut bur," she'd once written imprudently to a friend. It was ever so much more faded now.

But pushing that thought aside, Emily went quickly out of the room as if leaving considerations of vanity behind. Besides the hothouse flowers, besides the bread, there was a cake to be made for tea. After Professor Seelye's lecture there would be guests and her tea cakes were expected.

The tea had been orderly, the cake a success, but Emily headed back upstairs soon after, for her eyes—always sensitive to the light—had begun to tear up. She felt a sick headache starting.

Rather than impose her ailments on her guests, she slipped away. They would understand.

Carlo padded up the stairs behind her, so quiet for such a large dog. But how slow he had become these last months. Emily knew that Death would stop for him soon enough. Newfoundlands were not a long-lived breed usually, and he had been her own shaggy ally for the past fifteen years.

Slowing her pace, despite the stabbing behind her eyes, Emily let the old dog catch up. He shoved his rough head under her hand and the touch salved them both.

He curled beside her bed and slept, as she did, in an afternoon made night and close by the window blinds.

It was night in truth when Emily awoke, her head now wonderfully clear. Even the dreadful sleet in her eyes was gone.

She rose and threw on a dressing gown. She owed Loo a letter, and Samuel and Mary Bowles. But still the night called to her. Others might hate the night, hate the cold of November, huddling around their stoves in overheated houses. But November seemed to her the very Norway of the year.

She threw open first the curtains, then the blinds, almost certain of a sight of actual fjords. But though the Gibraltar lights made the village look almost foreign, it was not—she decided—foreign enough.

"That I had the strength for travel," she said aloud. Carlo answered her with a quick drum roll of tail.

Taking that as the length of his sympathy, she nodded at him, lit the already ensconced candle, and sat once again at the writing table. She read over the morning's lines:

> *I dwell in Possibility—*
> *A fairer House than Prose—*

It no longer had the freshness she remembered, and she sighed.

At the sound, Carlo came over to her and laid his rough head in her lap, as if trying to lend comfort.

"No comfort to be had, old man," she said to him. "I can no longer tell if the trouble is my wretched eyes, sometimes easy and sometimes sad. Or the dis-order of my mind. Or the slant of light on the page. Or the words themselves. Or something else altogether. Oh, my dear dog . . ." She leaned over and buried her face in his fur but did not weep for she despised private grief that could not be turned into a poem. Still, the touch had a certain efficaciousness, and she stood and walked over to the window.

The Amherst night seemed to tremble in on itself. The street issued a false invitation, the maples standing sentinel between the house and the promise of road.

"Keeping me in?" she asked the dog, "or others out?" It was only her wretched eyes that forced her to stay at home so much and abed. Only her eyes, she was convinced. In fact she planned a trip into town at noon next when the very day would be laconic; if she could get some sleep and if the November light proved not too harsh.

She sat down again at the writing table and made a neat pile of the poems she was working on, then set them aside. Instead she would write a letter. To . . . to Elizabeth. "Dear Sister," she would start as always, even though their relationship was of the heart, not the blood. "I will tell her about the November light," she said to Carlo. "Though it is much the same in Springfield as here, I trust she will find my observations entertaining."

The pen scratched quickly across the page. *So much quicker,* she thought, *than when I am composing a poem.*

She was deep into the fourth paragraph, dashing "November

always seemed to me the Norway . . ." when a sharp knock on the wall shattered her peace, and a strange insistent whine seemed to fill the room.

And the light. *Oh—the light!* Brighter even than day.

"Carlo!" she called the dog to her, and he came, crawling, trembling. So large a dog and such a larger fright. She fell on him as a drowning person falls on a life preserver. The light made her eyes weep pitchers. Her head began to ache. The house rocked.

And then—as quickly as it had come—it was gone: noise, light, all, all gone.

Carlo shook her off as easily as bath water, and she collapsed to the floor, unable to rise.

Lavinia found her there on the floor in the morning, her dressing gown disordered and her hands over her eyes.

"Emily, my dear, my dear . . ." Lavinia cried, lifting her sister entirely by herself back onto the bed. "Is it the terror again?"

It was much worse than the night terrors, those unrational fears which had afflicted her for years. But Emily had not the strength to contradict. She lay on the bed hardly moving the entire day while Mother bathed her face and hands with aromatic spirits and Vinnie read to her. But she could not concentrate on what Vinnie read; neither the poetry of Mrs. Browning nor the prose of George Eliot soothed her. She whimpered and trembled, recalling vividly the fierceness of that midnight light. She feared she was, at last, going mad.

"Do not leave, do not leave," she begged first Vinnie, then Mother, then Austin, who had been called to the house in the early hours. Father alone had been left to his sleep. But they did go, to whisper together in the hall. She could not hear what they said but she could guess that they were discussing places to send her away. For a rest. For a cure. For——Ever——

She slept, waked, slept again. Once she asked for her writing tablet, but all she managed to write on it was the word light ten times in a column like some mad ledger. They took the tablet from her and refused to give it back.

The doctor came at nine, tall and saturnine, a new man from Northampton. Vinnie said later he looked more like an undertaker than a physician. He scolded Emily for rising at midnight and she was too exhausted to tell him that for her it was usual. Mother and Vinnie and Austin did not tell him for they did not know. No one knew that midnight was her favorite time of the clock. That often she walked in the garden at midnight and could distinguish, just by the smell, which flowers bloomed and bloomed well. That often she sat in the garden seat and gazed up at the great eight-sided cupola Father had built onto the house. His one moment of monumental playfulness. Or she sat at the solitary hour inside the cupola contemplating night through each of the windows in turn, gazing round at all the world that was hers.

"Stay in bed, Miss Dickinson," warned the doctor, his chapped hands delicately in hers. "Till we have you quite well again. Finish the tonic I am leaving with your mother for you. And then you must eschew the night and its vapors."

Vinnie imitated him quite cruelly after he left. "Oh, the vaypures, the vay-pures!" she cried, hand to her forehead. Unaccountably, Carlo howled along with her recitation.

Mother was—as usual—silently shocked at Vinnie's mimicry but made no remonstrances.

"He looks—and sounds—quite medieval," Austin commented laconically.

At that Emily began to laugh, a robust hilarity that brought tears to her poor eyes. Austin joined with her, a big stirring hurrah of a laugh.

"Oh, dear Emily," Vinnie cried. "Laugh on! It is what is best for you."

Best for what? Emily asked herself, but did not dare say it aloud. But she vowed she would never let the doctor touch her again.

Having slept all day meant that she was awake at midnight, still she did not venture out of the bed. She lay awake fearing to hear once more the horrid knock and feel the house shake and see the piercing white light. A line of poetry ran through her mind: *Me—come! My dazzled face.* But her mind was so befogged that she could not recall if it were her own line or if she had read it somewhere.

At the last nothing more happened and she must have fallen back to sleep some time after two. When she woke it was midmorning and there was a tray by her bed with tea and toast and some of her own strawberry preserves.

She knew she was well again when she realized Carlo was not in the room. He would never have left her side otherwise.

Getting out of the bed was simple. Standing without swaying was not. But she gathered up her dressing gown, made a swift toilette, then went downstairs carrying the tray. Some illnesses she knew, from her months with the eye doctors in Cambridgeport, are best treated like a bad boy at school. Quickly beaten, quicker trained.

If the family was surprised to see her, they knew better than to show it.

"Shall we have Susie and little Ned for tea?" she asked by way of greeting.

. . .

Sue came over promptly at four, as much to check up on Emily's progress as to have tea. Austin must have insisted. Heavily pregnant, she walked slowly while Ned, a rambunctious four-year-old, capered ahead.

"Dear critic," Emily said, answering the door herself. She kissed Sue on both cheeks and led her through into the hall. "And who is slower today, you with your royal front or me with my rambling mind."

"Nonsense!" Sue said. "You are indulging yourself in fancies. Neddie, stop jumping about. Your Aunt Emily is just out of a sickbed."

The boy stopped for a moment and then flung himself into Emily's skirts, crying, "Are you hurt? Where does it hurt? Shall I kiss it?"

Emily bent down and said, "Your *Uncle* Emily shall kiss you instead, for I am not hurt at all. We boys never cry at hurts." She kissed the top of his fair head, which sent him into paroxysms of laughter.

Sue made a *tch* sound with her tongue. "And once you said to me that if you saw a bullet hit a bird and he told you he wasn't shot, you might weep at his courtesy, but you would certainly doubt his word."

"Unfair! Unfair to quote me back at me!" Emily said, taking Sue's hands. "Am I not this moment the very pink of health?"

"That is not what Austin said, who saw you earlier today. And there is a white spot between your eyes as if you have lain with a pinched expression all night."

"And all morning, too. Come in here, Sue," Vinnie called from the sitting room. "And do not chastize her any more than I have already. It does no good you know."

They drank their tea and ate the crumbles of the cake from

the day before, though it mortified Emily that they had to do so. But she had had no time to prepare more for their small feast. Neddie had three pieces anyway, two of his own and one Emily gave him from her own plate because suddenly the cake was too sweet, the light too bright, the talk too brittle, and Emily tired past bearing it all.

She rose abruptly. Smiling, she said, "I am going back to bed."

"We have overworn you," Sue said quickly.

"And I you," Emily answered.

"I am not tired, Auntie," Ned said.

"You never are," Vinnie said fondly.

"I am in the evening," Ned conceded. "And sometimes in . . ."

But Emily heard no more. The stairs effectively muffled the rest of the conversation as she sought the sanctuary of her room.

I dwell in Possibility —

She sat at the desk and read the wavering line again. But what possibilities did she, indeed, dwell in? This house, this room, the garden, the lawn between her house and Austin's stately "Evergreens." They were all the possibilities she had. Even the trips to Cambridgeport for eye treatments had held no great promise. All her traveling—and what small journies they had proved—lay in the past. She was stuck, like a cork in an old bottle without promise of wine. Stuck here in the little town where she had been born.

She went over to the bed and flung herself down on her stomach and wept quietly into the pillow until the early November dark gathered around her.

It was an uncharacteristic and melodramatic scene, and when she sat up at last, her cheeks reddened and quite swollen, she forgave herself only a little.

"Possibly the doctor's tonic has a bite at the bottom," she

whispered to Carlo, who looked up at her with such a long face that she had to laugh, her cheeks tight with the salty tears. "Yes, you are right. I have the vay-pures." She stood and, without lighting a lamp, found the wash basin and bathed her face.

She was not hungry, either for food or company, and so she sat in the gathering gloom thinking about her life. Despite her outburst, she quite liked the tidiness of her cocoon. She doubted she had the capacity for wings or the ability for flight.

When it was totally dark, she went back to her bed and lay down, not to sleep but to wait till the rest of the household slept.

The grandfather clock on the landing struck eleven. She waited another fifteen minutes before rising. Grabbing a woolen shawl from the foot of the bed, she rose ghostlike and slipped from the room.

The house breathed silent sleep around her. Mother, Father, Vinnie, Cook had all gone down the corridors of rest, leaving not a pebble behind for her to follow.

She climbed the stairs up to the cupola for she had not the will nor might to brave November's garden. Still, she had to get away from the close surround of family and the cupola was as far as she could go.

She knew which risers creaked alarmingly and, without thinking, avoided them. But behind her Carlo trod on every one. The passage was not loud enough to waken the sleepers who had heard it all before without stirring, yet Emily still held her breath till they reached the top unremarked.

Putting her hand on the dog's head for a moment, to steady them both, she climbed up into the dome of the house. In the summer there was always a fly or two buzzing about the windows and she quite liked them, her "speck pianos." But in November the house was barren of flies. She would have to make all the buzz herself.

Sitting on the bench, she stared out of the windows at the glittering stars beyond the familiar elms. How could she have abjured this peace for possibilities unknown?

"Oh, Carlo," she whispered to the dog, "we must be careful what we say. No bird resumes its egg."

He grunted a response and settled down at her feet for the long watch.

"Like an old suitor," she said, looking down fondly at him. "We are, you know, too long engaged, too short wed. Or some such." She laughed. "I think the prognosis is that my madness is quite advanced."

When she looked up again, there was a flash of light in the far-off sky, a star falling to earth.

"Make a wish, Carlo," she said gaily. "I know I shall."

And then the top of the cupola burst open, a great gush of sound enveloped them, and she was pulled up into the light.

Am I dead? she thought at first. Then, *Am I rising to Heaven?* Then, *Shall I have to answer to God?* That would be the prime embarrassment, for she had always held out against the blandishments of her redeemed family, saying that she was religious without that great Eclipse, God. She always told them that life was itself mystery and consecration enough. *Oh, do not let it be a jealous God,* she thought. *I would have too much to explain away.*

Peculiarly this light did not hurt her eyes, which only served to convince her that she was, indeed, dead. And then she wondered if there would be actual angels as well, further insult to her heresy. *Perhaps they will have butterfly wings,* she thought. *I would like that.* She was amused, briefly, in her dying by these wild fancies.

And then she was no longer going upward, and there was once more a steady ground beneath her feet where Carlo growled but did not otherwise move. Walls, smooth and anonymous, curved away from her like the walls of a cave. *A hallway,* she thought, *but one without signature.*

A figure came toward her, but if *that* were an angel, all of Amherst's Congregational Church would come over faint! It wore no gown of alabaster satin, had no feathery wings. Rather it was a long, sleek, gray man with enormous adamantine eyes and a bulbed head rather like a leek's.

A leek—I am surely mad! she thought. All poetry fled her mind.

Carlo was now whining and trembling beyond measure. She bent to comfort him; that he should share her madness was past understanding.

"Do not be afraid," the gray man said. *No—the bulbed thing*—for she now saw it was not a man at all, though like a man it had arms and legs and a head. But the limbs were too long, the body too thin, the head too round, the eyes too large. And though it wore no discernible clothing, it did not seem naked.

"Do not be afraid," it repeated, its English curiously accented. It came down rather heavily on the word *be* for no reason that Emily could tell. Such accentuation did not change the message.

If not an angel, a demon—But this her unchurched mind credited even less.

She mustered her strength; she could when courage was called for. "Who—or what—are you?"

The bulb creature smiled. This did not improve its looks. "I am a traveler," it said.

"And where do you travel?" That she was frightened did not give her leave to forget all manners. And besides, curiosity had now succeeded fear.

"From a far . . ." The creature hesitated. She leaned into its answer. "From a far star."

There was a sudden rip in the fabric of her world.

"Can you show me?" It was not that she did not believe the stranger, but that she did. It was the very possibility that she had, all unknowing, hoped for, wept for.

"Show you?"

"The star."

"No."

The rip was repaired with clumsy hands. She would always see the darn.

"It is too far for sight."

"Oh."

"But I can show you your own star."

"And what do you want from me in exchange?" She knew enough of the world to know this.

For a moment the creature was silent. She feared she had embarrassed it. Or angered it. Then it gave again the grimace that was its smile. "Tell me what it is you do in this place."

She knew this was not an idle question. She chose her answer with care. "I tell the truth," she said. "But I tell it slant."

"Ah . . ." There was an odd light in the gray creature's eyes. "A poet."

She nodded. "I have some small talent."

"I, myself, make . . . poems. You will not have heard of me, but my name is . . ." And here it spoke a series of short, sharp syllables that to her ear were totally unrepeatable.

"Miss Emily Dickinson," she replied, holding out her hand.

The bulb creature took her hand in its and she did not flinch though its hand was far cooler than she expected. Not like something dead but rather like the back of a snake. There were but three long fingers on the hand.

The creature dropped her hand and gave a small bow, bending at its waist. "Tell me, Miss Emily Dickinson, one of your poems."

She folded her hands together and thought for a minute of the dozens of poems shoved into the drawer of her writing table, of the tens more in her bureau drawer. Which one should she recite—for she remembered them all? Which one would be appropriate payment for this gray starfarer?

And then she had it. Her voice—ever light—took on color as she said the poem:

> Some things that fly there be—
> Birds—Hours—the Bumblebee—
> Of these no Elegy.
>
> Some things that stay there be—
> Grief—Hills—Eternity—
> Nor this behooveth me.
>
> There are that resting, rise.
> Can I expound the skies?
> How still the Riddle lies!

When she was done, she did not drop her head modestly as Miss Lyons had taught, but rather stared straight into the starfarer's jeweled eyes.

It did not smile this time and she was glad of that. But it took forever to respond. Then at last it sighed. "I have no poem its equal. But Miss Emily Dickinson, I can expound the skies."

She did not know exactly what the creature meant.

"Give me your hand again."

And then she knew. "But I cannot leave my dog."

"I cannot vouchsafe the animal."

She misunderstood. "I can. He will not harm you."

"No. I mean more correctly, I do not know what such a trip will do to him."

"I cannot leave him behind."

The gray creature nodded its bulb head, and she unhesitatingly put her hand in its, following down the anonymous corridor and into an inner chamber that was something like a laboratory.

"Sit here," the starfarer said, and when she sat in the chair a webbing grew up out of the arms and bound her with filaments of surprising strength.

"Am I a prisoner?" She was not frightened, just curious.

"The lightship goes many miles quickly. The web is to keep you safe."

She thought how a horse starting too quickly to pull a carriage often knocks its passenger back against the seat, and understood. "And my dog?"

"Ah—now you see the problem."

"Can he sit here in the chair beside me?"

"The chair is not built for so much weight."

"Then he may be badly hurt. I cannot go."

The creature raised one of its long fingers. "I will put your dog in my sleeping chamber for as long as we travel." It took Carlo by the collar and led the unprotesting dog off to a side wall, which opened with the touch of a button, letting down a short bed that was tidily made. "Here," the creature commanded the dog and surprisingly Carlo—who ordinarily obeyed no one but Emily—leaped onto the bed. The starfarer pushed another button and the bed slid back into the wall, imprisoning the now-howling Carlo inside.

"I apologize for my shaggy ally," Emily said.

"There is no need." The gray creature bent over a panel of flashing lights, its six fingers flying between them. When it had finished, it leaned back into its own chair and the webbing held it fast.

"Now I will show you what your own planet looks like from the vantage of space. Do not be afraid, Miss Emily Dickinson."

She smiled. "I am not afraid."

"I did not think *so,*" the starfarer said in its peculiar English.

And then, with a great shaking, the lightship rose above Amherst, above Massachusetts, above the great masses of land and water and clouds and air and into the stars.

She lay on her bed remembering. Carlo, still moaning, had not seemed to recover quickly from the trip. But she had. All she could think about was the light, the dark, the stars. And the great green-blue globe—like one of Ned's marbles—that was her home.

What could she tell her family? That's she had flown high above them all and seen how small they were within the universe? They would say she had had a dream. *If only I could have returned, like Mother from her ramblings, a burdock on her shawl to show where she had been,* she thought.

And then she laughed at herself. Her poems would be her burdocks, clinging stubbornly to the minds of her readers. She sat up in the dark.

The light. The marble of earth. She would never be able to capture it whole. Only in pieces. But it was always best to make a start of it. *Begin,* as Cook often said, *as you mean to go on.*

She lit a small candle which was but a memento of that other light. And then she went over to the writing table. Her mind was a jumble of words, images.

I do not need to travel further than across this room ever again, she thought. *Or further than the confines of my house.* She had already dwelt in that greatest of possibilities for an hour in a ship made of light. The universe was hers, no matter that she lived only in one tiny world. She would write letters to that world in the form of her poems, even if the world did not fully understand or ever write back. Dipping the pen into the ink jar, she began the first lines of a lifetime of poems:

> *I lost a World — the other day.*
> *Has Anybody found?*
> *You'll know it by the Row of Stars*
> *Around its forehead bound.*

Afterword
The Writer and the Tale, or
How and When Inspiration Hits or Not

I have been known to reply to the question "Where do you get your ideas?" by saying "I don't know. The stories simply leak out of my fingertips." Where stories actually come from, though, is one of the great mysteries of the literary world.

How easy it would be if there were some central warehouse where ideas were stored, waiting to be claimed. A lost-and-found of usable motifs. A clearinghouse for plot ideas. A place where writers could send away for story starters.

But the truth is that even if such storage areas existed, what the ordinary visitor would find there would be only bits of rags and bone shanks and hanks of hair.

Writers are peculiar archeologists. We gather the backward and forward remnants of our own and others' histories, mining the final part of that word: his*tories.*

What we find there is always a surprise.

But there is a secret, a magical spell, that successful writers know—and I shall impart that to you now.

Ready?

The magic word is: BIC.

That's right.

BIC.

Butt In Chair.

There is no other single thing that is as helpful to a writer. William Faulkner understood this well when he said, "I write only when I'm inspired. Fortunately I'm inspired at nine o'clock every morning."

BIC.

However, for those who would like more precise answers as to where individual stories come from, here is what I remember—or think I remember—about how the stories in this book began.

A warning, though. I have a notorious bad memory. And I am, after all, a storyteller.

The Traveler and the Tale

There was an article in the *New York Times Book Review* section about Henri Pourrat, the great collector of French fairy tales.

That article started me thinking about how certain stories have, indeed, changed cultures. Or charged them. Or infused them. Folklorists would say that stories follow the culture, not precede it. But I am convinced that sometimes—as I say in this tale—"Only through stories can we really influence the history that is to come."

I sent the piece to Greg Bear for his influential anthology *New Legends*. He wanted it rewritten in a "straightforward space setting." I thought that he was wrong and sent it on to Terri Windling and Ellen Datlow for their *Ruby Slippers, Golden Tears* anthology. They thought I was right.

Obviously I did, too.

Snow in Summer

In a book about fairy tales that I have written with my daughter (*Mirror, Mirror,* Viking) I wrote: "The first time I remember reading the Grimms' 'Snow White' I was six years old . . . living in Manhattan. My mother had warned . . . both my brother and me not to open the door to strangers. In fact, she spelled out in some detail why not.

"So when Snow White—despite a similar warning from the dwarves—let the old witch woman in, I knew that she deserved what she got. With that peculiar moral certainty that six-year-olds (and some Republican congressmen and religious groups such as the Taliban) have, I was not at all surprised or horrified at what happened to Snow White. In fact, I believe I was somewhat miffed that she was rescued in the end."

That's why I began this story, an Appalachian version of the Snow White tale. Aided and abetted, I must add, by my husband and his relatives, all West Virginians. And by a book called *Salvation on Sand Mountain,* by Dennis Covington, which is all about snake-handling sects.

The story was first published in a Windling/Datlow anthology.

Speaking to the Wind

One of the three brand-new stories written for this anthology, this story includes an enormous amount of autobiography. Everything but the actual wind ride is true.

The Thirteenth Fey

Terry Windling was putting together an anthology about fairies. That was the outside impetus. The inside was my interest in redactions, or old (fairy/folk) stories told from a different point of view. Once you start a story in an outsider's voice, all sorts of strange and wonderful things can happen.

Granny Rumple

Another redaction, this story began with a discovery. I was working on a variety of fairy tales for a children's literature course I taught at Smith, and one of them was "Rumplestiltskin."

I was considering the moral center of the story. Something was horribly wrong. Here was a miller who lies, his daughter who is complicitous in the lie, a king only interested in the girl if she can produce gold. And the only upright character in the tale is sacrificed in the end.

So I looked more carefully at the little man, Rumplestiltskin, himself. He has an unpronounceable name, lives apart from the kingdom, changes money, and is thought to want the child for some unspeakable blood rites. *Thwack!* The holy salmon of inspiration hit me in the face. Of course. Rumplestiltskin is a medieval German story. This is an anti-Semitic tale. Little man, odd name, lives far away from the halls of power, is a moneychanger, and the old blood-rites canard.

I wrote an article about this idea and it was published in an academic book on Holocaust themes, edited by Dede Weil and Gary K. Wolfe. But the idea would not leave me and so, after a bit, I wrote this story. Windling and Datlow (again) to the rescue. It was published in one of their anthologies.

Blood Sister

This is actually a prequel to the novels *Sister Light, Sister Dark, White Jenna,* and *The One-Armed Queen.* (The first two were nominated for the Nebula.) Those novels and this story take place in a mythical kingdom called The Dales, which is—and is not—Great Britain. In The Dales, women have been brutalized, marginalized, and left out on hillsides as babies to die. Now they live together in communities known as Hames. In those books—as well as this story—I am looking at ways we tell hi*story*: through narrative, parable, balladry, folktale, and academic explanations. Like the old man and the elephant, we cobble together history and call it truth when it is actually just story. This was first published in an anthology called *Am I Blue: Coming Out from the Silence,* a book of stories that explored gay and lesbian adolescence.

Journey into the Dark

I woke up one morning with the four presents given to the young prince in my head. How could I refuse to go on? Later I found it was the perfect piece to submit to an anthology by Marty Greenberg and Richard Gilliam, called *The Book of Kings.*

The Sleep of Trees

I'm not sure when this one started, but it certainly received its impetus from my conviction that the Greek gods and a lot of artists have something in common: vanity, ego, a belief that what they do is more important than what anyone else does. I hope that's not the kind of artist I am. But for that, you'd have to ask my husband, children, grandchildren, and friends. This story was first published in 1980 in the *Magazine of Fantasy and Science Fiction,* and has had many reprints since.

The Uncorking of Uncle Finn

A part of a series of stories I'd planned around the family of fey in "The Thirteenth Fey," only this and "Dusty Loves" have been written so far. It was first published in the *Magazine of Fantasy and Science Fiction*.

Dusty Loves

A part of a series of stories I'd planned around the family of fey in "The Thirteenth Fey," only this and "The Uncorking of Uncle Finn" have been written so far. It was first published in the *Magazine of Fantasy and Science Fiction.*

The Gift of the Magicians, with Apologies to You Know Who

You Know Who is, of course, O. Henry, and the story is a Beauty and the Beast version of "The Gift of the Magi," where a poor husband and wife sacrifice for each other, and find they have given gifts that are, in some ways, no longer useful. She sells her hair for a watchfob; he sells his watch for special combs for her lovely long hair.

I couldn't resist the ending of this story. I couldn't.

My story was a long time coming, as I had gotten a *Complete O. Henry* for my thirteenth birthday and didn't write this until I was in my fifties.

The story was simultaneously published in the *Magazine of Fantasy and Science Fiction* and Marty Greenberg's *Christmas Bestiary*.

Sister Death

I was asked for a story by Barbara Hambley for an anthology she was planning on female vampires, called *Sisters of the Night*. I was still in Holocaust mode when she wrote to me. My Holocaust novel, *Briar Rose,* had come out three years earlier, and my short stories, "Granny Rumple" in '94 and "The Snatchers" in '93, were both stories on the Jewish/pogrom theme. So it was only natural that I thought about the great female demon—possibly a vampire—Lilith. I like the line "What are Jews that nations swat them like flies?"

Barbara placed the story last in the book, one of the two places of honor (the other, of course, being the first story).

The Singer and the Song

What can one do with a short-short story? Well, use it for fillers at a reading, of course.

I'd written this little piece and had been using it as filler for some time, and could think of nowhere to send it.

Then Robin Adnan Anders, the great drummer of the rock-and-reel band, Boiled in Lead, asked me to write a story for the liner notes of his latest solo CD, *Omaiyo.* (I'd written the song, "Robin's Complaint," with Robin for Lead's *Antler Dance* album. And—oh yes—lead singer and guitarist, Adam Stemple, is my son. It's good to know people in high places. Even better to be related to them!) I was not to be the only author on the CD. Robin had asked other friends, too, among them authors Steve

Brust, Emma Bull, and Adam's wife, Betsy. I sent Robin this story, which he duly printed.

Salvage

Occasionally I write real science fiction stories. Though in the end they always seem to be about poets or singers or dragons or some other fantasy-oriented critter. This one was published in *Asimov's*.

Lost Girls

Winner of the 1999 Nebula for best novelette, this story may possibly be the first children's story to win that honor. It came from my children's constant complaint, "It's not fair." (To be honest, they were all grown up and long past that whine when I wrote the story.) It also came from my conviction that Peter Pan and his boys might have been having a lot of fun, but not Wendy.

This story was first published in my own collection, *Twelve Impossible Things Before Breakfast,* and then in *Realms of Fantasy.*

I was at a children's literature conference in San Diego when the awards were announced. Calling home, I picked up messages from my machine, and discovered word of the Nebula. I couldn't find anyone to burble at for hours, so I finally told two relative strangers in a mall.

Interestingly enough, Pat Cadigan wrote a story on the same theme in the same year. The two stories were published months apart. Neither of us knew the other was working on such a piece. And they are absolutely and totally distinct and different from each other.

I do want to note that the book's editor, Michael Stearns, adores this story. So does my husband. But Bruce Coville, my best friend, finds it appalling. "Don't f**k with my childhood icons" is the gist of what he said to me. Or maybe something stronger.

Belle Bloody Merciless Dame

We have a house in St. Andrews, Scotland, where we spend long summers. Or as long as we can manage. I wrote this story there, overwhelmed by Celtic mists.

Words of Power

Don Gallo is an academic who has done a number of YA anthologies and he asked me for something for one of them, called *Visions*. I struggled for months and no story came. That summer I was teaching at the Centrum writer's conference in Port Townsend, Washington. (We were housed at Fort Worden State Park, which was used as the setting for Richard Gere's *An Officer and a Gentleman*.) Suddenly the story came pouring out. I had to put it aside to give lectures and to critique student work, of course, but otherwise I ate and slept and dreamt this story till it was done.

The story was reprinted in *The Year's Best Fantasy and Horror*.

Great Gray

The town in this story is my town, Hatfield, Massachusetts. And while I don't know anyone like the killer in this story, there is the Stillpoint Massage Center, as well as the barn-turned-into-a-house. Also, I actually witnessed the genuflecting scene at the end, where the birders "worship" the Great Gray owl with my son, Jason Stemple. (Sorry, Jason, for killing you off in this tale.)

However, what really started the story was a request from Ann Devereaux Jordan, who was at work on an anthology, *Fires of the Past*, stories about hometowns.

Under the Hill

One of the three new stories for this collection, "Under the Hill" began as an idea for a Marty Greenberg book, *Mob Magic*, which I never managed to finish in time. (Though my daughter, Heidi E. Y. Stemple, has a story in the anthology.) It took two years for me to figure out where this story was going. I call it Damon Runyon meets the elves.

Godmother Death

So Neil Gaiman asked me to contribute to a *Sandman* anthology and I wrote this story, which is based on a powerful folk tale that can be found in variants from Scandinavia to the Middle East. He accepted the story and sent the contract, which said that all rights to the story would belong to Marvel Comics till the heat death of the universe, as they held the copyright on the *Sandman* characters in their iron fists.

I pointed out to Neil that Death as a lady was not an idea original to the *Sandman* mythos, citing numerous folk stories: a Peter Beagle story, "Come, Lady Death," and my own story, "The Boy Who Sang for Death," all of which vastly predated the Marvel comic. Poor Neil, he agreed with me, but could not fight that particular fight. So I told Neil to tell Marvel where to put their contract.

Of course, I was much more polite than that. I am *always* polite. Then I yanked the story, which gave me the perfect thing to submit to another anthology, *Black Swan, White Raven,* when the opportunity presented itself.

Creationism: An Illustrated Lecture in Two Parts

There were two wars raging in the book world when I wrote this particular piece. One was the Salman Rushdie battle in which an Iranian mullah put a fatwah (a sentence of death) on author Rushdie because he had published a novel thought to be blasphemous. The other were the ongoing Creationist stories, where the No-Nothings—who believe God created Heaven and Earth in exactly seven days exactly so many years ago—were trying (and in some cases succeeding) to remove science books about the Big Bang Theory and dinosaurs, etc., from school libraries. This was my only *Pulphouse* story. They folded soon after.

Allerleirauh

Editor Terri Windling was working on a dynamite anthology, *The Armless Maiden,* a book yoking child abuse and fairy tales. She was already going to reprint a story of mine and a new poem ("The Face in the Cloth" and "The Mirror Speaks") when this story came tumbling out of me. It's based on a Brothers Grimm Cinderella variant, one in the incest strand, and while I wanted this to have a happy ending, the story insisted otherwise. When I read it before publication at the Centrum writer's conference, a woman came up to me and begged for a copy of the story to give to her daughter, a survivor of childhood incest. Of course I immediately Xeroxed it for her. I only hope that in some small way it gave her daugter a voice.

Sun/Flight

This is one of three pieces I've done on the Daedelus/Icarus myth. The other two are *Wings,* a picture book with illustrations by Dennis Nolan, and a short poem published in *Parabola Magazine:*

Icarus

Death did not come black and cringing.
Wingless
In the dawn,

But banking upward toward the sun,
He burst full nova
And was gone.

I also won something called the "Daedelus Award" in 1986, for a body of fantasy short fiction. I have never heard again from the group that issued the award.

Dick W. and His Pussy; or, Tess and Her Adequate Dick

Surprising? Not really, if you know me. I have a somewhat raucous sense of humor, though I rarely write that stuff down. Still, when a friend told me about an anthology called *Dick for a*

Day, a feminist volume, I decided to chance this fairy tale redaction of "Dick Whittington and His Cat." The one time I read it out loud was at a party in Chicago thrown by my dear friends, professors Dede Weil and Gary Wolfe. Author Joe Haldeman laughed so hard, he fell off the piano bench. I got a standing O (sorry about that) from novelist Philip José Farmer.

Become a Warrior

Marty Greenberg asked me to submit something to a volume of warrior stories, which was lucky since I'd already started this one. It took a couple of twists I wasn't ready for and which I am quite fond of. Especially that last line.

The story was reprinted in *The Year's Best Fantasy and Horror.*

Memoirs of a Bottled Djinn

Author Susan Shwartz and I were at some convention or other discussing short fiction, and I came up with the idea of modern stories from the Arabian Nights tradition. But I was so mired in other projects, I told her, "You do it!" She did, sold it to Avon as *Arabesques* (great title!), and bought this story from me. I call it my homage to my husband because it's about a sexy middle-aged man.

A Ghost of an Affair

This is the third new story for this book, all three of which were written in Scotland. But this is the only one with any Scottish flavor. Our Scottish house is only a few miles from Crail, where half the story is set, and a few more miles from Edinburgh, where the story ends. Our best friends in St. Andrews are the Morrisons, so I borrowed their name.

I'd started the story years earlier hoping to send it to a ghost story anthology. But—as happens rather often to me—idea and plot didn't come together until much later. When it finally worked, I was able to finish the tale in under a week.

I like romance as much as the next person. But sometimes good marriages are compromises. As this story shows.

Sister Emily's Lightship

This story won the 1998 Nebula for short fiction and has already been widely reprinted.

One cannot live in my part of the Connecticut Valley, twenty minutes from Amherst, and be unaware of Emily Dickinson. Her presence and her poetry are everywhere. The very robins sing her name. ("The Robin's my criterion for tune," she wrote.)

Years ago I was reading some of her poetry, which was set down in a gorgeous book about her life, with paintings by the precise and particularizing Nancy Ekholm Burkert. At that very moment, reading the poem about "a band of stars" which ends the story, I got the idea for Emily and her meeting with an alien. (I always called the story idea "Emily meets the Martians," but the Red Planet sort of went by the wayside. Literally, as you shall soon see.)

The idea sat around, about one and a half pages worth of typescript, for nearly ten years. I knew it was a good idea, but I never quite got around to it, though I used a lot of Emily's poetry in other ways—in speeches, in articles, and in some fiction as well.

And then we bought a house in Scotland. Named Wayside. Nice segue!

In Scotland I found I was writing a lot about America. And Americans. About alienation, if not aliens. Suddenly I began working on the story of Emily D and her Martian/alien visitor for real.

This sudden immersion in the story was complicated by the fact that the holdings at St. Andrews University did not include a whole lot of Emily D scholarship. In fact, the latest critical biography they had was over twenty years old! I had the housesitter ship my own books over to me. (The most expensive way to do research!) I was especially interested in the feminist critics, as well as the new research about Emily's long battle with eye problems. I was tickled to discover that she called herself "Uncle Emily" to her nephew Ned. Polly Longsworth, an old friend of mine and a Dickinson biographer of note, had been the first to discover Emily's complicity in her brother Austin's long affair with neighbor Mable Loomis Todd, but more work had been done since Polly's groundbreaking book and I wanted to read it all! So I read—and wrote—and read some more.

And then editors Patrick and Teresa Nielsen Hayden came for a visit, on their way to a convention.

I thrust the draft of the story at Patrick. For two days he said not a word. It was agonizing. I do not normally force my attentions on unwilling m/e/n editors. At last it was close to the end of their visit and Patrick had just come down the stairs into the living room.

I squeaked, "What do you think of my story, Patrick?" He gave me a stricken look and raced back up the stairs.

What did that mean? Had I embarrassed him? Had I given mortal offense? Was my career at an end? I hadn't a clue.

Seconds later, Patrick raced back down, thrust the manuscript at me, and said, "I want it for my anthology, *Starlight*. But it needs revision in three places."

The three places were so slight—a word in one place, a phrase in another, and the deletion of my afterwords/historical explanation. I just nodded and gratefully handed over my ten-year-gestated child to its new pa.

P.S. Patrick bounced my next story—sent by mail for *Starlight 2*. Then he bought a story I handed him for *Starlight 3*, when the Nielsen Haydens visited Scotland once again. Is there a lesson to be learned here?